BY DEMONS
BE DRIVEN

GRIMLUK, DEMON HUNTER VOL 4

ASHE ARMSTRONG

First Edition, October 2021

ISBN-13: 978-0-9963409-8-4

DEDICATION

To everyone who struggled to make it through the pandemic. You're not alone.

CONTENTS

ACKNOWLEDGMENTS

Huge thanks to everyone who pulled together to help me meet my Kickstarter goal. There are a couple of you in particular who went above and beyond. It was a win that I needed.

Special thanks to my new editor for being pretty freakin rad and very enthusiastic about working on this book with me. It meant a lot.

To Benet for being hyped since day one and being a very inspiring DM.

CHAPTER 1

It was the Witching Hour. The malevolent force he was hunting had only been active during these hours, when magic was at its most potent and mortals most susceptible to its effects. He kept no watch, but Grimluk knew it was time. He could feel it in the chill of the air, cold even for an early autumn night. He'd been waiting outside the little shack, underneath a tree, meditating; honing his focus.

According to his client, Kazu, the thing had been masquerading as a protective spirit known as a baku. Baku were rare on the continent of Ornesea. Most of them existed in the far east, in countries Grimluk only knew from a few of the books he'd studied as an apprentice, but when families migrated, sometimes the spirits followed them. Baku were relatively benevolent, usually aiding children with curing non-demonic nightmares. A prayer was needed, and always with caution. Calling a baku was a last resort for the parents of the suffering child. If the nightmare didn't satisfy the spirit, it could turn on the child and eat more than the nightmare, devouring hopes and dreams as well. That's why it had taken so long for his client to realize what was happening. It had devoured not just his child's nightmare, but kept going, feasting on her dreams and then her hopes, nearly leaving only a shell. They thought that was the end of it then, that the child would sleep once more, and they could begin the recovery process.

But it kept returning, night after night, eventually feeding on Grimluk's client. Father and daughter were left drained and miserable the creature fed on them. Beyond the nightmares, beyond the dreams, beyond their hopes, to the very essence of their lives, taking small bites out of their souls. Once the pair died, the demon would be free to feast on their souls in full. After speaking to the child, Hoshi, Grimluk could see that if she didn't get sleep soon, she would likely die. The poor thing had a deathly pallor to her and was so still and quiet, she seemed dead already.

Grimluk had found telltale signs of a spiritual presence: ectoplasm, mostly, as well as a dark miasma that hung in the air of the little shack no matter how much light was let in. He'd suspected the demon had been the cause of the nightmares, subtly creating the need for a baku, and Hoshi's story confirmed that. The nightmares had begun—merely bad dreams at first—before descending into full blown terrors. The ritual prayer may have even called a baku forth, but if the demon was strong enough, it would have consumed the spirit.

In the end, it didn't matter. A dark presence had answered the prayer. Dreameater demons were vicious. The nightmares they created were for torture, for pain. They instilled fear—not to feed off of it like fear demons, but to make the effects of the dreams worse, silently tormenting their victims.

The creature was back and likely to finish off Hoshi. Grimluk watched the yard silently, his mind serene from meditating. The thing moved unseen to the shack, the only sign of its presence being the blue ghost fire coming to life and dying with each step. The fires grew and flickered brightly in front of the door to the shack, turned black, and disappeared. Grimluk stood and went to the door, silent as a predator, and laid out a dark blanket on the threshold. The blanket was embroidered with a pentacle and five sigils in silver thread; a demon trap. If it got past him, the trap would catch it, rendering it unable to escape until he killed or released it.

With the trap placed, Grimluk waited another moment. The worst part about hunting dreameaters was needing to wait until it was feeding before you could attack it. He pressed his ear against the door and when he heard the whispered cries of the child, he slipped in.

The shack was but a single room, a simple wood structure with a tin-covered roof. In one corner was a cast-iron stove, a counter, and a small table. In the other was a meager but large bed. And standing against the bed, translucent and glowing an ethereal light, was the dreameater. Its body was flabby and pale, the light it cast dimming and flaring from what could be referred to as its heart. Its thick legs ended in rough claws, while its spine was covered in bony protrusions that undulated from its head to its tail and back again. Already, the walls around the bed were covered in a sheen of ectoplasm brought on by the demon's influence. Grimluk drew his revolver and aimed at the thing's almost elvenoid head, where its ears drooped and flapped while the trunk sticking out of its face was jammed into the little girl's temple. A second trunk reached out from the first for Kazu.

Hoshi cried out again, as softly as a cooing dove.

Dreamer and dreameater both screamed when he fired the gun. The bullet ripped through the creature's trunk, severing it. The demon fell away in a thrashing madness before righting itself and racing past Grimluk, almost too fast to react to. When it passed the door and hit the trap, it screamed again, the sound something like a child's impression of a dying horse and a squealing hog all at once. He opened the door wide and fired one last time. The screaming didn't stop so much as disappeared. The air cleared of the sound like it had never happened.

Green ichor spilled out from the trunk and the hole in its head in waves, smoking and stinking of brimstone. He waved the smell away as he holstered his gun and knelt down, pulling a massive knife from behind his back as he did. The knife pierced flesh like that of a rotting carcass: too soft and wholly unpleasant. The knife slid through it like water, passing cleanly into the faint, sputtering glow of the thing's heart. A flick of the blade shook loose the blood, slinging a bit of the green ichor onto the corpse.

Kazu, dark-haired and eyed, stepped carefully outside as Grimluk stood. The man's eyes were deathly purple, baggy, rimmed red and watery.

"It's dead, sai," Grimluk said.

"That is it?" he asked, his accent a bit stiff as he eyed the corpse at Grimluk's feet with disgust. "The demon is dead and will not bother us anymore?"

Grimluk nodded at the man. "Dead. I'll dispose of the body in a moment. Your little girl pass out when it died?"

A sob choked the man as he collapsed. "Gods,

yes. Right back to sleep and nearly me with her." Another sob fled the man's throat, taking a nervous laugh with it. "I will mark your bounty and then I beg you leave us be, hunter. I pray to never see you again."

Grimluk sighed. A common response and an understandable one, given the man's predicament. "Happy to oblige," he said gently, pulling the bounty from his pocket.

The man took the paper with a trembling hand. "Two gluts. Will she be okay?"

"Reckon she'll want to sleep a lot for a while. Just let her. Be gentle."

"Orc says to be gentle. That's my daughter in there, sai. Now take this and leave." He made his mark on the bounty and slapped it onto Grimluk's chest.

Grimluk took it as the man's hand slid away. Kazu dragged both hands down his face as he went back inside. After a moment, Grimluk knelt next to the demon's corpse. As before, the knife passed swiftly through the flesh as he removed the head. More green, goopy blood spilled out. Next, he plucked a thin, folding knife with a clipped point and a honed edge out from a pocket inside his coat. Quietly, Grimluk set about carving an expulsion circle, sometimes known as an exorcism circle. It was similar to the demon trap in design, but the circle had openings between the points of the star, essentially doing the opposite of what the trap did. Once finished, the body convulsed violently before sucking into itself with a dull pop. The only sign of its remains were a little puddle of ectoplasm and the head, which felt like thick jelly to the touch.

He gave one last glance at the little shack before heading back to town.

Tosawa's peacekeeper office was easy enough to find. The town was small in population, but spread out among a crossroads and several outer streets. Despite the hour, the door was still open. He passed through a bit of lingering pipe smoke as he entered. Most of the town had appeared to be human, with a smattering of elves and dwarves, and now he found a pair of diminutive halflings. The one nearest the door tapped their pipe thoughtfully upon seeing Grimluk, clearly the source of the smoke. The other halfling was sitting behind a desk only a few feet away. They both looked up at Grimluk with bright eyes and bushy heads of dark, curly hair, possible relatives. They also both wore what amounted to the peace-keeper uniform: vests over work shirts, with denim trousers, their oversized, hairy feet still visible, an old habit most halflings still tended toward.

"How can we help ya, sai?" the one with the pipe asked.

"Here to claim a bounty."

"Say true? Which un?" the other halfling asked.

"Demon at the Kazu fella's place," Grimluk answered, setting the demon's head on the desk in front of him and pulling out the bounty notice. "Here's proof of the kill and he made his mark on the notice."

The halfling with the pipe started at the sight of the head and began coughing up smoke. "Gods, man, warn a lady, first, won't ya?"

"Beg your pardon, sai."

"Let's get on with it," the one behind the desk

said, pulling out a ledger and a metal box. "Name and guild association."

"Grimluk, Hunter's Hollow, New Gilead."

"Very good. He made his mark and we have proof. Two gluts to ya and then head next door and let the magi-tell operators know the bounty's claimed." She opened the box and pulled out two rectangular pieces of paper. "Anything else?"

"What's this?" Grimluk asked, taking the paper.

"Governor's council put out a new policy last year," the halfling at the desk began. "I s'pose it ain't reached New Gilead yet. Paper money is to replace gluts. Eventually bilts, too."

"That right?" Grimluk replied, inspecting the new currency. The paper felt more like cloth, with similar markings to the coins and a gold sheen to it. Each edge was marked with a 1, decorated with flowery antiquated elven-style flourishes, and various official-looking markings and numbers.

With a shrug, he folded the bills and placed them in the coin pouch hidden inside his coat. "Much obliged."

"Sai…what do we do with this?" They pointed to the ruined head, dribbling its viscous green blood.

He sighed. "You know, we been reportin' to you peacekeepers for as long as I can remember and almost every time, one of you asks that question. Fertilizer. Or have your witch or magician dunk it in war water. Probably don't give it to a wizard. Ain't met one yet that didn't try to 'harness its power'. Damned idjits. And maybe write this down in case it needs doin' again."

"Very well," the halfling said in a miserable tone.

"Fine, now get on next door," the pipe-smoking halfling replied. The tone made it difficult to tell if she was hostile or just disinterested. Either way, Grimluk did as he was instructed.

The magi-tell office was fairly empty, save for the clerks and operators. Humans sat at desks behind the clerk's counter, one hand on crystal orbs and the other scribbling down messages. The crystals were a part of a communication system, known by most as magi-tell, that allowed for nearly instantaneous messages to be sent out, albeit in small bursts due to the energy and focus required to use the orbs. It allowed for notice boards in any town that had an office and an easy supply of work for a variety of jobs, including demon hunting.

"Welcome, sai," one of the clerks began, before looking up from his stack of papers.

Grimluk approached, watching the friendliness drain from the man's face. "Demon bounty at the Kazu home has been claimed. Reckon the board needs an update."

"Kazu, yes, I see," the clerk responded flatly. "Chidi, Kazu bounty's been claimed. Send out an update soon as you're able."

"I'll do it momentarily, sai."

With a nod, Grimluk walked to the wall-length bounty board behind him. Four job columns greeted him. The Guarding column was all but empty. Labor was fairly full with listings for the autumn harvests that were getting under way now. His eyes passed to the Hunting column. Not quite as sparse as Guarding, but pretty close. A copy of the job he'd just finished still hung there, joined by several others. The first read "Imp Infestation" at the top. This was probably the most common job a demon hunter could take. He'd killed scores of imps over the last ten years and expected he would keep doing so until he retired or died on the job.

The three other notices mentioned "rye aunts" and "field maidens," two names for what amounted to the same thing. There were many names for harvest demons. Notices about these things always started cropping up around the peak of summer and lasted until the first snows fell. The demons manifested in the fields of farms, moving through corn stalks, wheat, anything that grew tall. Children were usually their targets—hurting them, turning them into strange beasts or merely controlling their minds. Quite dangerous.

The last notice spoke about "brain drinkers." As Grimluk recalled, those were fairly nasty beasts to deal with as well. The things were actually similar to dreameaters, but less subtle and far more aggressive. If not killed immediately, a brain-drinker would leave people as nothing but blank slates at best or shuddering husks at worst. The former could be made to serve the demon, while the latter would be little more than an empty vessel, which led to new issues entirely.

As he thought over the jobs, a faded yellow notice finally caught his eye on the Other column. It was the only listing, done up festively. Curious, he read it.

DUNVICH FOUNDERS FESTIVAL
TO HONOR THE FORMATION OF OUR SMALL TOWN
WE CALL OUT TO ALL WITH A BRAVE HEART

COME JOIN FOR FOOD, HISTORY, AND GOOD FORTUNE

He grunted and returned to the bounties. The brain drinkers were probably the most dangerous, but the harvest demons were a problem as well. "Where do the roads go from here?" Grimluk asked the clerks. "How far are these places?"

"Oh, Main Street heads east a few days and then forks north and east on yet. Second Street heads north and south, but them's mostly for the farmers. None of our farmers have the demons in their crops. Brain drinkers was just claimed 'fore you arrived. Them other farms is on east. You'll want to avoid the north, sai. The wizard's town is no place for anyone these days. Don't even think the farmers have crops anymore."

Before Grimluk could thank the clerk, the other clerk spoke up. "Listen to Mitchell, there, sai. Dunvich ain't been a town worth seein' for long years now. Prospered once, but most likely cursed now."

"Yar," came a third voice, whose owner had remained unseen, until the dwarf stepped out of an office in the back. "Founded by a right, proper wizard. Their folks traded with us for a time, but after the Sunderin', e'rythin' seemt to dry up out there. They have that festival every year to honor the wizard, with promises of prizes for brave folk. Fools wander up that way sometimes, figure they'll win some treasure and make somethin' of themselves. Some come back, others don't."

"People see stuff out that way. Kids like to head out there sometimes, see who's bravest, who can get closest to the town," the first clerk, Mitchell, added with a dismissive grunt. "Few ever make it. Say the road there spooks 'em too badly."

"My grandpap once wandered up that way, for the festival, he said, and got chased off by somethin' what looked like a giant bird," the second clerk, Chidi, followed up.

The dwarf nodded solemnly before adding, "That were after the Sunderin'. We sent a hunter out there after that. Never came back. Sent a couple more since then, but they says ain't nothin' there but people dealin' with trolls and, what were it? Gas pockets."

Stories like this were common in Grimluk's travels. Some of them were the truth, others exaggerations that grew to overshadow the truth. Rarely were they outright lies, especially after the Sundering fifty years prior. The Sundering, supposedly caused by greedy dwarves hunting treasure in the middle of the continent, had ruined those same lands, turning them into what was now known as the Wastelands. With the Sundering came an increase in demonic activity and new cults had started springing up with it. They never lasted long. One run in with a hunter and they scattered. Grimluk was always more suspicious if there weren't stories like this. He listened to the three of them ramble on about rumors and hearsay. Everything from various demons to dragons, and even an old tale of a giant moving through the trees.

"Much obliged for the directions, friends," he finally said, interrupting the conversation. "I'll head east then." They merely nodded politely, falling back into a discussion of their neighbors as he exited. East then. If he happened upon something that needed killing along the way, he'd take care of it. Otherwise, he'd try to find his way to one of the farms and put down some harvest demons. Come morning, he'd be on the road once more.

The area grew hillier as he traveled over the next four days. A dense forest filled the area, creating the semblance of a tunnel along the road. Limbs reached overhead and leaves filtered the light from the sun, creating vast shadows as leaves turned and fell. As he neared the fork the clerk had mentioned, and saw the signpost, the air grew still and almost quiet. All birdsong had ceased except a strange, repetitive song trilling up and down before pausing. The song grew louder and more dissonant the closer he got to the signpost as other birds joined in the song. Some sang in time with each other while others kept their own pace, but the melody was the same from all of them. Grimluk found his hand on the butt of his gun as he realized something was watching him. The songs changed as another voice joined them. As the trilling song echoed among the trees, a long, low whistle began underneath it all. When he stopped at the signpost, the strange birdsong and the whistling ceased, leaving only the sound of a sudden breeze.

The post had three signs on it. One pointed back the way he'd come with "TOSAWA" on it, while the one below that pointed east with a list of three more towns. Above them all was a faded sign that read "DUNVICH," pointing north. Another long, low, warbling whistle filled the air as he looked at the sign and the road north.

Trying to ascertain where the sound was coming from, Grimluk looked around at the trees. He turned a full circle, hand still at the ready to slap iron if needed. He saw nothing and the whistle died away. His throat rumbled.

Dryad. Maybe a leshy, he thought. Dryads, spirits of the forest, rarely interacted with travelers, but some of them liked to play pranks. A leshy, on the other hand, was a more territorial forest spirit and had a nasty habit of leading travelers off the paths and roads forged by mortal use. Grimluk knew better than to leave the road unless he had to, and even then, the leshy would have to attack him directly. Hunters used a blood magic enchantment on their boots that kept them from becoming lost. He'd recently renewed that enchantment, too.

With a shrug, Grimluk started heading east again. The leshy or the dryad had probably scared off the clerk's grandpap, or else he'd been drunk. Maybe both.

He managed two steps before the creature came screaming down at him from above. A piercing shriek exploded in the air just before a set of massive talons wrapped around Grimluk's shoulders, slicing into his skin with ferocity.

He looked up to see the bird creature he'd been told about. It was tall as a middling human, with a wingspan that seemed double or triple that. The feathers were a dirty white and gold, and the head was that of a human with full, black eyes, and a thin, black beak where its nose and mouth should have been. Long, blonde hair mingled with feathers, waving in the breeze as it tried to carry Grimluk away.

It managed to get him off the ground by about ten feet from pure speed and strength before Grimluk jammed the barrel of his revolver into its thigh and fired. The bullet ripped through one thigh and into the other, causing the thing to drop him. It screamed in pain, the sound mingling a human and an owl.

Grimluk hit the ground in a roll and came up with his gun trained on the beast, but the demon was moving too fast despite its size and heading north in a hurry. The owl-woman was a harpy, also known as a lechuza, an alkonost, and a number of other names from all over Arkod. It was a type of demon knight, servants of demons who gave them great power; power that grew as the demon implanted within them corrupted the knight's soul. Harpies were typically practitioners of magic who decided they wanted more power and made deals with demons. Most of them had been town magicians in life. Some wronged, some fed up with serving the community good, others just spiteful and cruel to begin with. Like almost all demon knights, they were dangerous. Grimluk followed.

CHAPTER 2

For another week Grimluk traveled the road to Dunvich, passing boarded up waystations and fighting the harpy on and off. The demon knight would strike while he tried to rest or eat, pushing him slowly toward exhaustion. He gave as good as he got, however, and after five days of skirmishes, the harpy was growing slower. She lacked the kind of demonic power required to shrug off bullets from his gun. The runes along the barrel meant they could hurt demons, and hurt her they did. More powerful demons could fight past the wounds up to a point, possibly even healing them, but even then, his weapon caused pain the demons couldn't ignore. He'd tried to use the demon trap blanket to dissuade the attacks, but he could never predict which direction she'd come from and she always saw him before he saw her.

Despite being tired and hungry, he pushed on. When she attacked on the sixth day, Grimluk managed to shoot her right shoulder as she dove for him again with murderous intent. The bullet struck and she went careening past him, shrieking the whole way. She nearly crashed as she attempted to right herself, but avoided a disastrous fate, kicking off the ground and high into the air. As Grimluk chased after his prey, she dove back down and hurried away, farther than he'd seen her go in the days prior. She tended to disappear among the trees where he couldn't see, most likely to lick her wounds before circling back and trying again. This time, she aimed for the horizon. He did his best to keep watch for her while he ran but eventually, the speck in the distance dropped somewhere and he saw no further sign of the demon knight.

Grimluk rested undisturbed that night, though he slept lightly, just in case.

Sometime during the afternoon the next day, he happened upon another waystation. Far from boarded up and abandoned, the lanterns were lit; little flames flickering in the distance, aided by the clouds overhead. He'd still seen no sign of the demon knight, and now here was an active waystation on an abandoned road. Either she'd fled further on or this was a trap. He expected the harpy to shriek from the sky, screaming for vengeance at any moment. What Grimluk didn't expect were the voices shouting as he approached. Nor the gunshot as he happened upon an apparent robbery.

Carefully, trying to avoid making the porch boards creak, he crept up to a window and peered in. A pair of outlaws stood, guns drawn and aimed at the workers behind the counter, barking orders. One of the outlaws was an elf, their dirty blond hair tied back, brown hat sitting comfortably to allow the pointed tips of their ears room, and a red paisley bandanna resting over their face. The dwarf, stocky even for a stocky people, wore no hat, and the blue bandanna did little to hide the bushy red beard beneath. They waved their gun with each order, clearly angry about something.

One of the workers—a middle-aged human woman by the looks of it, with mousy hair, a dark complexion, and bloody clothes—held her shoulder and said something about the lack of money. The dwarf nearly pistol-whipped the woman but the elf managed to calm them.

Finally, the dwarf demanded they hand over whatever they did have. The woman, grimacing in pain, began piling things into a bag obediently, albeit slowly. Grimluk let out a sigh and stepped back. The situation felt entirely off. A harpy had led him here, but instead he found thieves.

"Hurry up, gods-damn you!" shouted the dwarf.

Whatever was going on, he would help. An ambush would work. There was enough room between the door and window that he could hide between them. The interior wasn't especially large, with the counter on his left if he entered. As the door opened toward him, he could slam it into one of the outlaws. Or, if it opened to the inside, he could shove his way through. Either way, it would end quickly. Grimluk waited for the elf to look away again and slid toward the door. The hinges pointed toward him and the plan fell into place in his mind.

It didn't hurt that he cut an imposing figure, either. An orc dressed all in black and covered in the patina of a nomad was a sight few wanted as a surprise.

"Gimme that!" the dwarf barked, causing the woman to yelp. Heavy boots started his way. The door slammed open and he slammed it closed again, knocking the elf into the doorframe. With surprising grace, Grimluk spun to the other side of the door, taking hold of the elf's shoulder in one meaty, green hand. He gave a quick but sharp pinch to their collar, digging his fingers into the nerves beneath in a move designed to incapacitate the victim quickly and painlessly. The elf went slack in his hand and he let them drop to the boards with a thud as their partner joined the fray. The dwarf hesitated just a moment, their eyes on the fallen elf, before screaming with fury. Grimluk took that hesitation and used it for all it was worth, planting a boot square in the dwarf's face as he started to scream.

"Fuck!" the dwarf cried out as they crashed into the re-opened door.

Grimluk didn't wait for them to regain their senses, kicking the dwarf's gun away before pinching their neck as well.

"Everyone alright in there?" he called. He grabbed the bag from the dwarf and headed inside with it. "It's all right, you're safe now."

Another dwarf, gray-haired and pale-skinned wearing buckskin, stepped from behind the counter with a double-barreled shotgun pointed at Grimluk's chest.

"The fooks you want, orc?" the dwarf practically growled in a thick accent. "You's with them? Come to finish off ol' Bjorn, eh? You got the drops on me once, but not agains."

A sigh escaped Grimluk's lips. "No, sai, I'm not with them. I caught them on their way out, got your goods right here." He shook the bag.

"Not with them?" Bjorn muttered, looking from the bag to Grimluk's face. "Why should I's believe an orc, eh?"

Gently, Grimluk set the bag down on the floor and took a slow, deliberate step back. "Reckon the choice is yours, but I should warn you. That scatter-gun'll just piss me off."

"For fuck's sake, Bjorn, put it away," came a shaky voice behind the counter. "Stop wavin' your cock about and help me, ya old fool!" Slowly, the human woman limped out from behind the counter. "If the orc were here to end ya, you'd be ended. Bet my life on it."

Bjorn seemed to consider her words. "Alright, fine then. Damned fool spits down two barrels any-how." With that, the dwarf lowered the gun and retrieved the bag. With a grunt, Bjorn set it on the counter and began checking it over.

"Beg a pardon, stranger," the woman started, her skin pale and clammy. "We d-don't get many v-v-visi-tors this f-far out anymore. And h-he's not seen any... any—"

Grimluk cut her off with a quick hush and helped lower her to the floor against the end of the counter. "I know a thing or two about wounds. Let me take a look at this?"

She nodded her consent, so he peeled the shoul-der of her shirt and brassiere away. The wound had been a lucky shot. It had avoided bone, mercifully only tearing up muscle, and hadn't exited.

Quick as he could, Grimluk set his bag down and dug through it to find a rolled up leather pouch. In it were the tools he occasionally used to remove bullets from his own body, alongside some bandages and a green, foul-smelling salve he applied to the wounds, which healed them fairly quickly and reduced scarring to nearly nothing.

"I'm going to pull the bullet out, sai. It's likely to hurt. Do you want somethin' to bite or do you reckon you can handle it?"

"Bjorn...leather," she said, turning toward the dwarf, who was now watching the proceedings.

"Fook's sake, Maeve," the old goat complained but found a few scraps of leather, holding them to her mouth. She bit down fiercely and nodded to Grimluk.

He took up the little claw device from the pouch and inserted it into the bullet wound. She squirmed and moaned through the leather, but never cried out. It only took a moment to grab the slug and extract it. Once free, Maeve sagged, breathing hard.

"I'm going to put this salve into the wound," he said before she could spit out the leather. "It'll hurt quite a bit at first, but by tomorrow, this will be a bad memory and a faded scar."

She nodded once more before he jammed some of the viscous liquid into the wound. This time, she nearly screamed. He wouldn't have blamed her. The first time he'd used the stuff as a child, it had hurt worse than the claw-wound it'd been used on. That was when he learned not to underestimate imps.

After smearing the salve all over the wound, he cut a length of bandage, folded it into a square, and pressed it down firmly, where it adhered like glue. "Try to leave it alone until this time tomorrow, if you can help it. The bandage'll stick on its own."

The leather fell out of Maeve's mouth. "Appreciate it, stranger."

Grimluk nodded before looking back toward the slumped bodies as he rolled up his kit. "Those two'll be out cold for a good while. Heard tell that this road don't see many travelers these days. All the other waystations were boarded up, why not you?" Suspicion nagged at him, though he tried to contain it. This woman having a similar wound to the harpy was egging on the paranoia from the past week. The thieves had fallen quickly, mundanely enough, but that didn't mean everything was as it seemed.

"We don't have much these days, stranger. Truth told, we'll be boarding up soon, too. Coaches don't come this way no more. Folks go to Dunvich only but once a year, if that. Reckon you're headed there for the festival, ain't ya?"

"Fah!" shouted Bjorn. "Fookin' festivals. Town's a joke. Shoulds be closed up, too."

Grimluk's throat rumbled. "Heard somethin' about a festival. If Dunvich has a bounty board, I reckon I'll find some way to make a bilt or two. You at least got a water pump I can refill my skins with?"

"A pump we gots, orc," Bjorn replied a touch more amiably this time.

"Mind if I make use of it before I head out again?"

"Fah. What does I care? You'll be the last. Once you leave, I'm boardin' this bastard up and headin' home."

Grimluk nodded. "Fair enough, friend. Obliged all the same."

"Aye, it's over the corner theres."

Grimluk knelt next to the pump and unstrapped his waterskins from his bag. He hated to waste water this way but there was no basin he could see so he just held them under the flow and pumped steadily until each skin was full again.

"So, how far is Dunvich?" he asked when he finished.

"About another league," Maeve replied. "If you'd like, you can toss your bedroll here for the night and set off tomorrow. We don't have no beds, but plenty of space."

"I think that'd be just fine," Grimluk replied. "I'll bring in the guns from them two outside. You got any way to deal with 'em or should I wake 'em up and send 'em on?"

"Oughts to fookin' kill 'em," Bjorn replied.

"Ignore him," Maeve replied. "Obvious we ain't got any peacekeepers out here, so unless you wanna escort 'em to Dunvich, I s'pose you can send 'em on."

Grimluk nodded and stepped back outside. The pair hadn't stirred an inch. The elf was snoring softly as he bent down and grabbed their guns. To be doubly sure, he patted them both down for knives. The dwarf had a long knife and the elf a skinning knife and a folding knife.

"Sais?" he called.

"Yes?" Maeve replied.

"Reckon I'd feel better taking these two on to the peacekeepers. You have a spare sack I could put their weapons in? Maybe some lengths of rope, too? I can pay."

"Lotta rope in the stalls out back. Help yourself. Might be a sack or two as well."

"I'll look and see, then."

The stalls turned out to be a livery of sorts,

which were in a surprisingly shabby state. Despite the late afternoon sun being at his back, the structure was quite dark. His instincts perked up as he took in that strangling darkness. The light should have illuminated the interior beyond the door, but instead, it was choked off just barely past the threshold. Either a wizard was practicing spells within or there was something else entirely.

Something demonic.

If that was the case, it could also mean the waystation was a trap. Maybe the woman, Maeve, was the harpy. Or maybe they were just regular folk. Maybe they didn't even realize what was going on. There weren't any horses and Bjorn had said he was shutting the station down. There were plenty of times he'd taken small jobs to clear imps and similar demons from barns and cellars, so it wouldn't be too unbelievable that the last two workers of a waystation had no idea their horse stalls were infested. He could clean it out and then approach the topic gently. Hopefully, Maeve wasn't the harpy.

If they were just common folk without any clue as to demons in the area, it was unlikely they could even pay for the job. They were clearly on hard times as it was. If it wasn't a trick, he could write this job off as a freebie. He didn't even have to tell them what he'd done. He'd just have to see how bad it was.

Grimluk pulled his bag up and hastily pulled out a small bottle. The dark glass contained an alchemical oil designed to burn away ectoplasmic manifestations and constructs. Ectoplasm was mostly cold and sticky, but spirits and some demons used it or left it behind when they interacted with the physical world. He'd had several bottles of oil for a job he did a few months back involving a nasty beast that had built a nest using blood. With careful use, he'd managed to kill the demon and ended up with one bottle left over. Now seemed like a good time to use it.

He stepped close to the open doors, peering inside. Though Grimluk strained, he couldn't hear anything over the fading call of the cicadas. He stepped inside to the very edge of the darkness and looked around. To his left, he could just make out part of the stalls. To his right, a small table and more stalls. Beyond both was a wall of inky, unending darkness. Once more, he strained his hearing, turning his head to catch any sign of the thing that had done this.

Faint whispering.

Without looking at the bottle, Grimluk pulled on the wick to draw it out. He let his eyes close as he focused on trying to discern where the whispers were coming from. It was moments like this that made him wish the orcs had been blessed with sensitive ears like the elves. He let out a sigh when his efforts failed.

"Spark-a-dark," he muttered, "what's my desire? Bless this camp with fire." The hasty version of the campfire spell did its job. Sparks and a minuscule flame flickered from Grimluk's fingertips, setting the wick alight.

With the oil ready, he hurled the bottle into the darkness, aiming upwards and to the left. The bottle disappeared into the sticky shadows, seemingly swallowed up, and he hoped he'd aimed right. The unmistakable sound of glass shattering followed.

Then, white flames and a muted cry of pain.

Grimluk reached into his long, black coat with both hands and pulled his knife from its sheath, along with a hatchet. Like the gun, these weapons had also been designed to fight demons. The blades were made of a mix of steel, silver, and some other metals, all ritually forged. The knife was etched with the Elder Sign, while the hatchet had the killing runes. The ancient sigil of the Elder Sign held power over demons, including repelling and warding them when used in conjunction with other bits of arcana Grimluk had never bothered to learn much about.

He waited calmly as the purging fire consumed thick, goopy strands of darkness, now revealed to be a web of sorts. As each strand burned, more and more of the unnatural darkness receded, revealing the barn's contents. There were buckets, horse blankets, and various coils of rope, along with a few lanterns, pitchforks, and shovels. And something skittering farther into the shadows.

"By the power of my mortal will," Grimluk practically growled, keeping his voice low, "I call you, demon! Step forth from the shadows! Step forth to your doom, o foe of life!"

The thing hissed, retreating farther and farther into the dying shadows, always just out of sight as it flitted to and fro. The white flames burned hard, though, and soon the demon could hide no longer as Grimluk stepped into the barn, heavy boots thumping on the wood.

A monstrous creature the size of a dog moaned woefully as it skittered across the back wall, trying to keep to the shadows. Its arachnid body was hairless and black as pitch, like it was made of shadow even in the light of the purging fire. Its legs were like a cricket's, facing the wrong way, which it used to propel itself in sudden leaps while it moaned and whispered in some strange language.

Grimluk let out a growl. "I said come forth, demon."

As the last of the webbing died in the flames, the demon stopped and looked at Grimluk, not with the eight eyes of a spider, but with an upside-down elvenoid face of bone white. Its eye sockets were filled with tiny, black shapes that reminded Grimluk of a wasp's nest and its mouth was an unmoving oval filled with an eldritch light.

Grimluk could feel the thing's efforts to get into his mind, pressing against it with unseen weight. It would never succeed. The tattoo on the crown of his skull guaranteed that, keeping his mind sealed from psychic attacks, demonic or otherwise.

The demon leapt again, higher this time. "Free me, mortal," it cooed in a raspy voice. "I know so many secrets. Secrets that could be yours. Even about you. I could—"

With a grunt, Grimluk hurled the hatchet at the demon, making his reply plain. The demon's words faded away as it collapsed to the barn floor, thrashing in silent agony. Grimluk stepped forward to finish the job.

"I may be forbidden from your mind, mortal," it rasped, the light in its mouth fading slightly, "but I see your heart. Violence infests you. You will be lost in a hunter's nightmare."

Kneeling, Grimluk plunged the massive knife through the approximate location of the thing's neck, ending the abomination and its words for good.

Milky fluid spilled out the corpse in waves, smoking and stinking of brimstone. He waved the smell away as he retrieved the hatchet and moved away to inspect the corners and crevices for any webbing or eggs the flames might have missed. Once Grimluk was satisfied, he knelt beside the demon corpse and removed its strange head, which felt like hollow bone, with his knife. He gave it a shake, slinging the dribbling blood onto the corpse before wiping it down on a horse blanket. Then he found some rope and headed back outside.

With the demon dead and the barn cleansed, Grimluk made quick work of tying up the would-be thieves. He took his time, concentrating on making the bindings tight and thorough enough that the pair would find escape nearly impossible. He'd made an effort to learn a few knot tricks for just such occasions. Once finished, he dragged them inside and propped them against one of the walls.

"I see ya found the rope," Maeve remarked, now out of the floor and sitting in a chair. She was very pale but seemed stable.

"I did," Grimluk replied. "Awful dark in that barn, though."

"Were the big doors closed again? Sometimes Bjorn forgets to open 'em. Sorry 'bout that, sai."

A rumble filled Grimluk's throat. Maybe they hadn't known. "Not a problem. It was just a small demon," he replied, setting the skull on the counter.

"Gods!" came Maeve upon seeing the skull. "You killed it?"

"Reckon so."

"Bjorn! The stranger found a demon out in the barn!"

"A fookin' demon?" came the old dwarf, appearing from a side room. "Good thing there's weren't no horses."

Grimluk grunted in affirmation at that and watched their faces. Bjorn was eying him pretty hard in between looking at the skull. Maeve was staring at the head, one hand over her mouth, a few winces of pain the only other emotion he could see beyond surprise.

"S'pose you'll be wantin' a reward, yeah?" came Bjorn. "Ain't gots nothin' for ya."

"Reckon not," Grimluk said with a nod. "Wasn't about to ask."

"A fookin' saint of an orc. Fah!"

"Either of you got a garden, you can crush this up and spread the dust around. Demon bones make surprisingly good fertilizer. Otherwise, I'll dispose of it."

"Do what ya want, orc, I gots to take a shit," Bjorn replied as he headed for the outhouse.

"Don't mind him," Maeve offered wearily. "He's still mad that one there tricked him. He hadn't seen another dwarf in some time. Got used against him."

"Understandable," Grimluk replied as he pulled out a little brass tube filled with chalk. He drew the expulsion circle on the skull and watched as it cracked and twisted before disappearing in a flash of light.

"So you saw that thing through the dark, then? Orcs really can see in the dark?" she asked, a hint of trepidation in her voice.

"Might be some can see in the dark better than others, but this orc is not one of them. I knew what to look for."

She nodded at that, seemingly pleased with the

answer. Occasionally, he still ran into such questions. A fair amount of people still viewed orcs as dimwitted brutes, good for little more than physical labor, whatever that labor might be. Some had strange views on orcish biology: redundant organs; able to see in the dark like cats and elves; obligate carnivores; venom in their tusks. One time, he'd even met someone who swore orcs had acidic drool that could burn wood and tarnish steel.

They were a strong and enduring people, though. Much like the dwarves. But, like anyone else of any other race, some had different abilities and talents. Grimluk could withstand bullets—several, in fact—and blades. The wounds he didn't bandage up right away—with a helpful coating of salve, from Mint, the elven healer of his guild—scarred like large pockmarks. Even Mint couldn't quite say why it was. Grimluk thought maybe it was just the product of his own magical potential. Magic coursed through all people in endless directions. Some people had incredible potential that they tapped into easily. Others had to study and develop through intense training. Some folks had their potential manifest in other ways. Local magicians, witches, and alchemists worked through more intimate methods, usually keeping people healthy or farmland fertile. Witches were especially adept at dealing with matters of reproduction; ending pregnancies, preventing them. They could even help change your body into one you were happier in.

Until the previous year, he'd had a necklace of the slugs he'd pulled off his skin. Despite the leather cord running through them, it was quite apparent what they were. Occasionally, he'd found it useful for intimidation. For people who were getting in the way of a job or just proving to be nuisances.

Thankfully, Bjorn and Maeve were not nuisances, even if the woman might think some strange things about Grimluk's people. The thieves, on the other hand, would be nuisances. And they'd be nuisances for the next league of travel. But that was okay. Grimluk really did not want to leave the waystation at the mercy of two outlaws after he left, especially considering the dwarf showed quite the temper. No, he'd get them to the peacekeepers in Dunvich and maybe see what this festival was all about.

CHAPTER 3

The morning air was crisp with a hint of the approaching winter. The sun shone brightly, with the overcast clouds having cleared away during the night. By all accounts, it was a lovely fall morning. Except for the pair of cursing outlaws that insisted on spoiling it all. Grimluk and the others did their best to ignore them as he prepared for the journey. It was only a league to Dunvich. He could make that in less than a day on his own, but he doubted the outlaws would be so accommodating. He'd had to knock them out again in the middle of the night.

All things considered, it was probably the best rest the thieves would ever have. Something about the manipulation of those nerves left the victim feeling refreshed, which meant that the pair were feeling more than up to the task of hindering his every step. Skins full and an extra bag of jerky and hardtack in his bag, he gathered the elf and the dwarf up, said his goodbyes to Maeve and Bjorn, and got moving.

The first few hours were the most difficult. He'd had to pull his gun on them to get them going again once they realized they weren't getting out of their binds. He'd never kill them. He'd never taken another mortal's life and he certainly wasn't about to start with two ornery outlaws.

They didn't need to know that, though.

The pair spent some time whispering to each other, in between bouts of curses and malicious comments. Grimluk could ignore those. They didn't really bother him. Around noon, another round started up again and he just shook his head.

"The two of you are about as surly as a hungry troll," Grimluk remarked. "And just as loud."

"Better'n an orc," the elf spat.

The dwarf added to it with a string of expletives Grimluk found impressive in their creativity. Maybe they should have been a poet instead of a thief. When he stopped responding to them, they eventually grew quiet, glancing at each other again, and then at him, eyes full of contempt.

"Reckon you two are tryin' to figure out how best to take me down and get runnin'."

The looks on their faces told him he was right. The dwarf, angrier still for having been found out, charged Grimluk. He simply yanked the rope lead hard and the dwarf stumbled and fell. The elf leapt, attempting to kick Grimluk in the face but he was ready for it, blocking the attack by throwing his forearm into the incoming leg. The force pushed the elf away and Grimluk stepped on the back of the dwarf's neck.

"I was hopin' to let you make this journey on your own two feet, with some dignity," Grimluk began, "but carryin' you makes my life easier. So, you have two choices. Continue on peacefully, under your own power. Or if you'd like to keep playin' fools, I put you back to sleep and carry you there like babes."

"Fuck you, you rot-suckin' bastard," came the dwarf.

"Yar, ain't no goblin gonna take me in," followed the elf.

A growl escaped Grimluk's throat at the utterance of that word. Goblin. "Friend, you just forfeited your choice."

With a yank of the rope, the elf came stumbling toward Grimluk. Elves were capable of great agility, however, and they recovered quickly and attempted to attack Grimluk again. They managed to land a single blow on Grimluk's chest before he got his hands on their shoulder again and squeezed. Hard. The elf's eyes fluttered and they crumpled into Grimluk's waiting arms. A grunt and moment's effort later and the elf was laying across one of his shoulders.

The dwarf was trying to get to their feet again, too blinded by rage to do a good job of it. Grimluk reached down and yanked them up by their scruff. "Your turn, friend. What's your choice?"

"I'll fuckin' kill ya! I'll tear yer throat out!"

"So be it." The dwarf collapsed into Grimluk's leg.

He let out a long sigh as he started walking again. Even though he'd move faster now, he worried maybe the peacekeepers would try to arrest him, too. He also hoped the harpy would steer clear now. He'd felt something watching them for an hour or so. Grimluk figured it was either the harpy overhead or in the trees. Maybe even an actual leshy or dryad, like he'd suspected at the crossroads. Might be something else entirely, but he wouldn't know unless it showed itself.

That was always something a wanderer needed to remember. On top of thieves and killers, there were leshies, of course, but also griffins, feral trolls, all manner of territorial and trickster spirits, various beasts who'd escaped from wizards' towers, and a variety of other creatures, both malicious and benign. In the darkest of woods, long abandoned by even the native Orneseans, there were the spiders, who occasionally wandered from their webs and holes when food was scarce. That didn't even touch the nameless things that wandered the Wastelands back west and the dark places of the world. Each provided their own perils but were rarely something a healthy demon hunter couldn't handle. The things in the Wastes weren't usually inclined toward waiting or stalking. A few did wait, though, watching silently and barely seen.

Grimluk wasn't in the Wastes, though. If the thing following him was a leshy, it would eventually try to get him lost but it would fail. The enchantment on a demon hunter's boots also kept them pointed in the direction of whatever their goal was. He was no different. His goal was Dunvich and Dunvich he would find. Mostly, he didn't much feel like having to protect the outlaws as he protected himself. Whatever it was, it was keeping its distance.

At least the weather felt good. This time of year was good for traveling. Grimluk wanted to enjoy it, especially after a week of harpy hunting and the two jokers on his shoulders.

That enjoyment would not last. The closer Grimluk got to Dunvich, the stranger the air felt. Likewise, the road began to diminish, clearly unused for some time. Packed dirt grew thinner, replaced by grass that would eventually reclaim the road entirely. He'd seen various tribes burn the land sometimes, controlling the spread as a means of cultivating the land and keeping it healthy. The area around him now seemed like it hadn't been touched in a long, long time. The trees seemed choked by the thick weeds and brush. The grass growing on the road was likewise tall.

And still he felt something watching him.

When Grimluk could see Dunvich in the distance, something massive and bipedal moved away from the road, apparently not caring if it was seen. At the same time, a raptor's cry rang out in the distance. It was likely the thing had been watching him for some time, but he couldn't tell if it was the thing he'd felt at first or if it had joined in at some point. He could only speculate either way.

Might be the thing was sizing him up. Might be the people of Dunvich needed his help. Granted, it'd be for a price, but on the road, bullets and food still cost him. He knew more than a few demon hunters who were shrewd when it came to earning a few gluts. And it was always gluts. Even for imps, bilts weren't always enough. Grimluk would occasionally let the price dip but hunting was still his job and plenty of people gave him reasons to keep the minimum price of two gluts where it was.

So he pressed on, ready to dump the load on his shoulders. What he found when he arrived was about what he'd expected from what the clerks had told him. The town seemed very much like its best days were long past. Dunvich was a worn-down place that looked as if a good storm could flatten it. The nearest building—a house as best he could tell—told the story like a corpse after a battle. Porch wood sagged, stained from age and water, with patches of black here or there across the walls. The roof had once been fully shingled but now had a patchwork of tin covered in rust. Several of the window panes had been busted out and never replaced. And the lantern at the door, an ancient thing holding a nub of a candle, was likewise busted. It was truly amazing that ivy hadn't claimed the building back. From what he could see, the only structure that looked sturdy was the temple looking down on the town from a hill maybe a half a mile or so away. Grimluk had seen ghost towns in better shape than Dunvich. Unlike the ghost towns, though, Dunvich wasn't just a town of echoes. The people were very much alive, bustling to and fro with carts and crates or baskets held out in front.

The yellow banner above him read, "Welcome Outsiders" in blocky, faded white letters, and a strange symbol of curved lines around a spiral on either side. He moved toward the nearest person. "Afternoon, sai," Grimluk said, doing his best to touch the brim of his hat.

"Oh my," the human woman gasped as she realized what he was and what he was carrying.

"Pardon, friend, could you point me to the peacekeepers' office?"

"Oh, uh, yes. Yes, it's down that-a-way," she replied, pointing as she did, her initial shock fading into a smile.

He looked where she pointed. Instead of one main street, it was split into two. It looked like businesses were on the right, along with a few houses with the rest of the homes on the left where they were now.

She continued, "Either side is fine. You'll see it between the streets. Are ya here for the festival, sai?"

"Obliged," he said with a nod. "Haven't rightly decided yet. Need to drop these two off and then I reckon I'll do so."

"Don't get many orcs out this way. You a bounty hunter, sai?"

"When the need arises," Grimluk replied with what he hoped was seen as a playful grin.

"Well, I do say," she muttered, a soft smile on her face. "If them two you're carryin' are bounties, you ought to stick around for the festival! You'll fit right in. I'll let ya get on with it. Hope to see ya again, sai."

Grimluk bowed his head and continued on. He couldn't remember the last time he'd been greeted so warmly. And with two people on his shoulders no less. His nerves were still a little high after the trip but she'd seemed genuine. Maybe this Dunvich was less rundown and more sleepy. At least, he hoped so. There was still a demon knight somewhere.

Like the woman, the peacekeepers surprised him, too. All humans and not one of them even insinuated he was actually the one at fault. If they had, they were so subtle about it, he couldn't pick up on it. As it turned out, the elf and dwarf were wanted, with a reward of five gluts each.

As Grimluk collected the bounty, still coins and not the new paper money, the sheriff of the peacekeepers approached him. She was stocky, with deeply bronzed skin, dark eyes and hair, and carried the familiar sights of a peacekeeper's shield badge on her vest and revolver on her hip. She moved with the confidence of someone accustomed to being in charge.

"Sheriff Ziskind. Kelila Ziskind," she said, extending a hand. "Friend, I tell ya what, if I didn't know better, I'd say yer timin' musta been the Fates at work."

Grimluk shook the woman's calloused hand. She gripped tightly and squeezed. He returned the gesture as best he could without hurting her. It wouldn't take much effort to crush her hand. "Grimluk. Reckon so?" he replied.

"I'd set my watch on it, if the damned thing still worked."

"The festival?" Grimluk inquired.

"The festival," she said with a nod.

"It's a good thing your watch don't work. 'Fraid I don't know much on the details, though they've been hinted at a time or two."

"Collectin' that bounty and you say ya don't know the details? You joshin' me, partner?"

"All true. Thought maybe I'd take a gander after hearin' about it back in Tosawa. Then I happened upon those two at the last waystation. Folks didn't say much other than it was a festival."

The sheriff let out a whistle. "Well, shit. Seems it really was the Fates then, huh? Figure I oughta explain it then. If you're interested."

"I find myself a might curious. If it'll interrupt anything, though, just point me to the bounty board and I'll be on my way."

Sheriff Ziskind dismissed his concerns with a wave of her hand. "This is the whole point of the festival. Come on, I'll walk ya to the hotel and explain." The sheriff led him back outside, speaking as she did. "See, ya showed up havin' committed a deed of bravery and that's what the festival is about. Been a while since we had more than one or two people show up. The railroads are pullin' people away from these ol' roads as they build 'em. The Fates must be pleased with us. Countin' you, we have five outsiders this year. Elder Whateley ought to be ecstatic about that."

"This festival honors the brave then?" Grimluk inquired.

"Brave and selfless. I won't spoil the whole story, but the short of it is after the Whateleys, long days past, helped our town, we decided to honor them. Bein' the noble family they is, they turned it around as a chance to honor others who might've just helped out like they did. Ya prove yer worth through a trial at the end of the festival, kinda like ya did catchin' them two assholes, and ya get honor and glory. Make sense?"

Grimluk's throat rumbled as he thought on it. Even if honor and glory were on his list of priorities, what could such a town have to offer anyone? "Reckon so."

The sheriff nodded, leading him down a new street that went just far enough to be considered a street. "Some show up with bounties or some such, also like you, hopin' maybe that'll win 'em the prize. It's only for the festival though. Either way, we have the outsiders stay over here at the Restin' Rooster. Raimi's a good man, gives free room and board through the festival, if ya have the stones for the danger."

As she led him inside the Resting Rooster, a wave of incense washed over Grimluk. Conflicting scents each vied for his attention, overwhelming his nose all together. It wrinkled—at least as much as an orc nose could—and he pushed out a sharp breath through his nostrils, hoping to force some of the smell out. He never had liked incense and perfumes and age wasn't changing that.

Sheriff Ziskind didn't seem to notice as she spoke with the person at the hotel desk. She introduced Grimluk as a new outsider, explained that she had given him the basic rundown of things, and then did something else that surprised him: she asked if they had any beds comfortable enough for an orc.

The man behind the desk, his skin so brown it bordered on black, stroked his beard and nodded his wrapped head as he listened to the question. "Ah, yes, my friend," he began, his accent thick and unfamiliar. "We will take care of you. I have just the room for you. Very comfortable. One of my best."

"Much obliged," Grimluk offered as the man took a key from the board behind him and headed around the desk. "To you, as well, Sheriff."

"I'm glad you're stayin'," she replied as she began to leave. "Raimi'll treat ya right. Enjoy the room and feel free to look around once you're settled."

"I think I will."

"Come, we go now," Raimi urged.

With a brisk pace, the pair headed to the second floor, to room 19 in the front corner. The room was filled with large, plush-looking furniture. The fabric was all faded, clearly worn a bit thin, and the wallpaper was a simple two-tone in subtle shades of white, peeling in a few discrete areas. The highback chair near the window had long lost its sheen, with fraying threads popping out here and there. The wood pieces were dark but the varnish was faded and splotchy in parts. The bed's blankets, like the chair, were fraying but still usable. The bed itself was large but he recognized immediately that it wasn't long enough for him. It fit in with the rest of what he'd seen of the town so far but seemed comfortable all the same.

As he looked over the room, his gaze returned to the man, who was looking at him expectantly. "It's a good room, friend. Appreciate the hospitality."

Raimi gave him a beaming smile. "Only the best to honor the bravery of the Whateleys, sai! Settle in, please."

With that, his host handed over the key and left Grimluk alone. Dusk was setting in, so he decided he'd do the same. Come tomorrow, Grimluk would explore some. For now, he'd enjoy the room as much as he could. Maybe the supper included with his room would be a good one. Maybe he'd stop worrying about the harpy for a while. Maybe he wouldn't have to worry about finding it until he was leaving again. Maybe the feeling of unease that was creeping in on him would stop.

Maybe.

The smell let Elder Whateley know his grandson had returned. The boy had a unique odor that was unmistakable in its power, no matter how they tried to wash him. At some point, they'd just accepted it for what it was: a sign of the boy's parentage.

Elder sat at his desk in the main room of his

family's house, staring at the shrine to one of his gods. The desk was old and plain, serviceable for his uses. Candles sat on either side of several clay and stone figures. Elder was staring at the middle one, a thing somewhat on the abstract side. For all intents and purposes, it was a mound of orbs. That was the simplest expression of Yog Sothoth's true form. The one most easily expressed so an inferior mortal mind could grasp it.

He turned to regard his grandson as the boy's heavy steps clomped across the floor behind him. Wilbur towered over everyone and it meant he had to slump over when not in his own room upstairs. "What news, m'boy?"

"He is coming, Grandfather," Wilbur replied.

"And?"

"She goaded him on the road. He survived to the waystation. K'llyx is no more."

Steepling his calloused fingers, Elder asked, "Who was more injured?"

"She was."

A smile tugged Elder's cheeks. That was good news indeed. He turned back toward the shrine, looking at one of the other clay figures. This one looked like a chimera, of sorts. There were soft details of a vulpine body, a head with an exposed skull and saber-toothed teeth, with six eyes, and a tail that wrapped around the base. His personal god. And his master.

"Well done, Wilbur. I must make contact. Make sure no one disturbs me in the temple."

"Yes, Grandfather." Heavy footsteps receded, followed by the spring on the screen door.

Elder Whateley removed a stiletto dagger from

his desk drawer. The blade was black like obsidian but did not shine. It almost seemed to swallow the light, increasing the darkness of the blade. With a grunt, Elder stood and made his way down the hallway and into the temple next door. The heavy, ironwood door slid open with a gesture and Elder made his way to the back, behind the pulpit where he tended his pack. There wasn't a statue here, it wasn't needed. In place of a statue was a mirror frame with no mirror. Old stains ran on the inside of the frame, but where the mirror should have been was a patch of blackness in the center. Elder faced the hole, arms raised.

"O god and master of the forests," he uttered, beginning prayer in the language of the gods. "Thou who rejoicest in the baying of dogs and spilt blood." At the invocation of blood, Elder pricked his small finger with careful practice.

"Who wanderest in the midst of bodies amongst the hunted, who longeth for blood and bringest terror to mortals. Rundyyk, king of beasts, look favorably on your servant now!" With each line of the prayer, he pricked another finger until only one was left. "And with the pricking of my thumb, I beseech thee: Come!"

The final word hung in the air, an unnatural echo that was soon swallowed by whispers of its kind. The blood that welled up from his thumb trickled up into the air, pulling more from the other wounds with it. The mirror frame shook as the blood moved into a flowing circle within it. The blackness in the frame pulsed and grew outward once, then again a moment later, before a snout pressed through it a final time. As the mirror back ripped open, the blood ring spread out along either side, flowing with a hissing power. Two massive, clawed hands rested upon the blood's edge as the head shifted through, shadow clinging to its form while soft red light spilled through the tear between worlds.

Elder bowed at the waist, willing his back to give his god the respect it was due. "Master."

"Priest," came the bone-deep voice. "What news do you bring?"

"My lord, the festival is near. We have quite a bountiful feast for you this year."

Lips peeled back, revealing the perfect, razor-sharp teeth that lay behind. "Go on."

"There shall be five, once the latest arrives. He may be there by now."

A long growl shook the temple. "Five mortal souls. Is even one of them a worthy prey?"

"At least one of the four already here is, perhaps another as well. One is a charlatan but mayhaps he'll prove us wrong. They pale in comparison to the one who approaches." Elder looked up at his god's shadowed face. "An orc, m'lord. A hunter."

Another growl shook the temple, this one pleased. The lips peeled back once more, revealing his god's awe-inspiring array of teeth again. "It has been so long since I have hunted one of their kind."

"Wilbur looked in on him. Seems he scared off your knight and kilt Rom's youngin'. Still in fine shape. A prey most worthy, I'd wager."

Rundyyk reached one of its claws out, palm up, clenching its digits. "Come," it commanded, wrenching the claw back. Crackling energy followed the movement while the word floated unnaturally in the air. More energy burst into being in the center of the room, arcs slashing wildly as it built up.

A blinding flash made Elder look away. No matter how many times it happened, he was never ready for that light. A thump and soft grunt called his attention back, though. The knight was there now, from wherever she'd been. She wore her human guise. Mousy brown hair, dark complexion, her clothes bloody from a shoulder wound. She was kneeling in supplication to their master, head bowed for a long moment before she looked up.

"Master," was all she said, in a breathless voice.

"Tell me of the orc."

"Had I been fighting him instead of leading him, the battle might have gone either way. He is well-trained. Quick. Maybe even clever. I do not think he suspected me at the waystation as he took the time to heal the wound he dealt. He is powerful, Master. He will bring you glory."

"Seal the town, priest. The hunt begins. And you, keep watch above. You are to leave the orc be unless he gives you a reason to attack. If that happens, kill him if you can. If he kills you, all the better. Your eternal rewards await."

"Yes, my master!"

"Lord, are the stars right? Is our true work to finally begin?" Elder inquired eagerly.

"I feel them moving. Soon," uttered Rundyyk, receding back into the tear before it closed. "The return draws nigh, priest." The stink of brimstone wafted in its wake as the portal sealed. The harpy took her true form once more and left almost as quickly as she arrived, exiting through the window in the steeple.

Elder nodded as he moved toward the door back to the house. "It has begun."

CHAPTER 4

The dreams woke him in the middle of the night of past jobs but different, as dreams tended to make things. These were...almost pleasant. Grimluk found the demons quickly and destroyed them with equal speed and precision. But there was an underlying feeling to it all that made him anxious. He rose, silently, and stood at the window, looking out on the town. He could see it all. Clouds were thick but not thick enough to bar moonlight completely. The moon would be full soon, he noted. He also noted several disparate people holding lanterns, each at a different point in town and heading northwest. Most likely peacekeepers making nightly patrols. Light from the temple caught his eye as well when flames flickered to life at its front. More townsfolk trickled out of their homes or in from the footpaths that connected to the main road, all heading toward the temple. Either one of the human gods liked night worship or something else was going on. The need to piss beckoned, however, so he filed what he'd seen away for morning and found his chamber pot.

When he woke the next morning, it was to a cloud-filled sky that threatened rain. That never bothered him. The canvas of his duster was waxed, protecting him from the rain and snow. Similarly, his hat was made of beaver felt of the highest quality. The elk-skin bag he carried was treated as well, and designed to keep water out. If rain found him, he'd only give pause if a storm opened up.

After breakfast, Grimluk decided to explore Dunvich. He started by wandering the main street. With the festival preparations underway, he ended up in the town square. He watched as townsfolk worked on building a stage of sorts. Put up banners and bows on the streetlamps. The banners all had the swirling symbol he'd seen coming into town. As he walked and watched, a man approached him, waving him down as he did.

"Stranger, a moment, if you would." The man was somewhere near middle-aged, with dark hair and eyes, and the tanned skin of someone accustomed to working under the glare of the sun.

"Sai," Grimluk responded with a nod.

The man offered his hand. "Seth Cooper."

"Grimluk," he replied with a gentle squeeze.

"The sheriff tells me you're the newest outsider to join us. Are you plannin' on stayin'? Takin' part in the festival?"

"Leanin' that way, friend. Sheriff Ziskind only gave me the barest of details. Don't s'pose you could give me some more?"

Seth hesitated. "I surely would like to, ya see, but it's tradition to retell the story of what happened at the opening ceremony. I could not rightly rob you of the experience, sai. I would simply ask for patience and encourage you to stay on."

He seemed a sincere fellow. Grimluk looked

around again before rubbing at his chin in thought. He was mighty curious. And he still needed to look for signs of the harpy. He also realized that he needed a shave. Coarse stubble pricked at his fingertips. He followed the stubble up to the side of his head and felt the low growth of his hair.

"Reckon that makes sense. I'll see it through, provided you point me to the barber," he said with a tusky grin. "Seems I've let myself get a little wild these past few weeks."

Seth let out a laugh. "Fair 'nuff, sai. Head back the way you came, take a left, and go on down a ways. You'll see the pole."

"Appreciate it," Grimluk said as he headed that way.

The barber's pole was faded, long past its prime. The roof sagged gently but held up. The screen door had holes in it and the spring was rusty but likewise still functional as he pulled it open and stepped inside. An old, pale-skinned human man covered in liver spots greeted him by way of a grunt as he turned to face Grimluk. He still had a headful of hair, pure white and coiffed neatly, but his eyebrows had fled, possibly to his ears and nose as white fluff poked out from them noticeably. His eyes were a faded brown that still had a fierceness to them as they took in the sight of the orc in his doorway.

Grimluk recognized the look. The man was trying to decide whether to turn him away.

"An orc, is it?" came the man's voice, surprisingly powerful for his size.

"Last I checked," Grimluk offered. He didn't bother trying to push friendliness into his voice. The barber would serve him or turn him away.

"Hmph. Yeh come fur the festival, aye?"

"Came for other reasons but stayin' for the festival. Was hopin' I might get a trim."

The barber approached. "Hat off, sai."

Grimluk doffed his hat and ran a hand through the strip of hair running down the center of his skull. It was a touch on the fuzzy side, as was the rest of his head, which normally remained bare or near to it. "Shave, too, if you would."

The barber nodded. "Sit," he commanded, motioning to the chair. "Hair's twen'y fi' pence, shave's ten."

Grimluk hung his bag and coat on the nearby rack, along with his hat. He took a moment to gather the man's pay and a five pence extra, and took a seat where the old man instructed him, reaching over to drop the coins into the pay jar. The chair was small; the leather old and pliant. It wasn't the most uncomfortable he'd ever been, so that was something.

"Reckon ya'd like to keep yer look," the barber asked as he wrapped a sheet around Grimluk, adjusting it as needed.

"I would. Take the strip down a little. Everything else can go."

Without another word, the barber ran his fingers through Grimluk's hair and across his scalp. The smell of talc and soap found their way into his nostrils. The old barber set to work, scissors snipping their path, taking away the fuzziness from the majority of Grimluk's head.

Grimluk let his eyelids droop and let the man work. The snipping went quickly and then the barber went to the wash basin and began to work the shaving soap into a thick lather with his brush. Satisfied, the barber applied the lather all over Grimluk's face and skull and then stepped away to the wash basin again.

He returned once more with a hot towel, which he wrapped around Grimluk's face. The world fell away under the towel and Grimluk let out a contented sigh.

"Not too hot, then, sai?" the barber asked.

Grimluk grunted approvingly. A new sound came to his ear then. A sound he knew well: a blade against leather. When the towel came off, the old man looked over Grimluk's face, nodded, and reapplied shaving soap.

The straight razor touched his head first. The old barber's hands shook at first but once he set to work, they were as steady and sure as could be. The blade followed the strip of hair down in steps, rasping as it took the hair around the strip away. One stroke, two, three, and a fourth, each spaced by a fresh stropping, following the hair's edge to the point it ended at the nape of his neck. As the barber worked, Grimluk watched in the dusty, faded mirror as three new faces stepped inside. Two humans and a halfling.

One of the humans—both men, by the looks of them—had a peacekeeper shield badge pinned to his shirt. The other wore buckskin and a raccoon-skin cap. The halfling, on the other hand, might have been the dandiest dude that Grimluk had ever seen. The dude's outfit practically assaulted his eyes with its colors and patterns. Pink shirt, blue waistcoat, drooping green bow tie, and black and white checkered trousers, with various matching shades and other hints of color sparkled across the outfit through accessories and buttons. The overcoat was a floral-patterned purple and it was all topped off by a very fine black bowler hat.

"Be with you in a moment, sais," the barber said as he set to work on the other side of Grimluk's head.

As before, the old man's work was quick and sure-handed. When he moved to Grimluk's face, however, the pace changed. The barber worked as wonderfully as he had until he got around Grimluk's mouth. For a moment, he seemed rather perplexed on how to shave around tusks. That was why Grimluk rarely got a shave from anyone but an orc. The old man surprised him, however, as he decided to use the tusks for leverage by resting his hand on them when needed. It was a bit of a strange sensation but it got the job done.

"One thing more, sais, and then I'll help you," the barber informed the trio.

"Nothin' for me, Mortimer," the peacekeeper said. "Was just showin' these two over. Reckon it's a day for outsiders in your shop, eh?"

The barber grunted as he worked some oils face, rubbing stiffly, though not unpleasantly, across Grimluk's scalp and face. Once finished, Grimluk felt better than he had in a long while. He rose, nodding to the barber. "Sai."

The halfling dude sauntered over, removing his coat and hat and handing them to Grimluk. "Be a jewel and hang those up, friend," he very politely demanded as he climbed into the barber's chair. Grimluk sighed, rolling his eyes, and went ahead and hung them up on the lower racks before retrieving his own things and stepping outside.

The crisp fall air raked over his freshly shaved scalp as he ran a hand down the strip of hair before putting his hat on. The shave had been fine work, as had the trim. He stood on the buckboard porch, taking in the sleepy little town. The festival preparations would probably be finished by the evening if he had to guess. That gave him plenty of time to look around. The nagging feeling that there was something off had reached its peak and Grimluk was sure—or as sure as he could be—of what that feeling was now.

Hospitality was certainly common among the peoples of Ornesea, but in a town full of humans, not one of them looked at him with disgust, and only a moment's worry. Not one said a careless word about orcs. He'd been treated with respect, even friendliness, by everyone he'd encountered. And he'd had one of the finest shaves of his life.

Maybe it was cynical of him, but he was a demon hunter and had encountered similar circumstances before, in study and on his own. Orcs should be treated with respect and dignity like anyone else, but the sad truth of the world was that his people were as likely to receive those things as they were to receive scorn and fear. Individuals might extend those courtesies but a whole town? That was a rarity. On top of that was the welcoming of outsiders, the harpy, the thing on the road, as well as the demon at the waystation, and the midnight congregation. Grimluk still needed some solid proof, and hoped he was wrong but he doubted it.

He stepped off the porch and slipped away, behind the barbershop and up the hill behind it. If the road here was any indication, he'd find something in the woods. He'd need to keep his wits as sharp as the barber's blade in case the harpy or the lumbering thing made their presence felt again. By his reckoning, there was a cult in Dunvich.

Dunvich felt alive and bustling thanks to the preparations for the festival. That changed as Grimluk moved away from the town. The farther he went through the trees toward the hills that surrounded the area, the quieter it got. No birds. Not even a breeze to rustle the branches overhead. Just a stillness and quietness that felt very much unnatural. And it was made all the worse by the droning of cicada song. For whatever reason, cicadas wouldn't stop unless a demon was crushing them under its limbs. At best, the song faded into the background. At worst, the song twisted into something heralding the demonic activities.

Grimluk wasn't entirely sure which this was.

Fall was rolling in slowly this year and there was still a touch of green to the trees. With leaves not yet covering the ground, Grimluk was able to move fairly quietly. Even still, he would stop and listen, survey his surroundings carefully, and take note of anything. He pushed his senses as hard as he could but nothing came to him. He could still hear Dunvich below, so he pushed farther into the woods, into the foothills.

After a few hours, Grimluk stumbled upon a strange path. There were tracks leading away from Dunvich but they weren't elvenoid. Weren't a troll's tracks either, of that he was sure. He knelt to inspect them closer.

"Roots?" he muttered, gently plucking the remnants of a tree root from the hole. He checked the next hole and found the same thing. It was like something had been planted and then dug up with each hole. Tufts of grass speckled the holes. They'd been here a good while. All the same, they marched ahead. He followed the path, coat open and ready to loose his revolver if need be.

The holes widened as they went. With each new hole, more root remnants remained behind, dried out and more like husks. The screech of a bird echoed from the sky as Grimluk caught the scent of rotting vegetation. And the sight of a black boughed tree.

The tree was centered in a clearing among a larger grove. The holes lead right up to it. It was a squat thing compared to the trees surrounding it but still stood several feet taller than Grimluk. It was, however, only a little wider than he was.

He stopped at the edge of the clearing, watching for any signs of life. The cicadas grew louder as he waited, keeping behind one of the larger trees as he looked around. A rush of thoughts filled his mind. What would he find out here? Other people? A farm perhaps? Was this a trap? He doubted that last thought. The town was a trap, that much was obvious now. Why would any outsider come this way when the town was going out of its way to accommodate, even pamper them? No, this wasn't a trap. It could still present danger, however.

The cicada song ebbed once more as he stepped into the clearing. Approaching the tree, he heard something like crying as the leaves of the black tree swayed softly. While the crying was obvious, it was still unlike anything he'd heard from another mortal, or even a ghost. The feelings tangled within those noises were clear, however. Despair mingled with agony in those strange sounds.

He pressed toward the black tree, its bark was covered in what looked like tar. The rotting smell grew stronger and he could see now that the tree bore fruit. Apples the color of the deepest arterial blood hung from the branches. The crying stopped when he approached, followed by a low moan that sounded like a tree bending in a storm.

A voice spoke in a language he had never heard. Or maybe he had but had never realized what it was. He felt the anger in the words clearly, though. Grimluk walked toward the source of the voice, to the side of the tree facing directly away from Dunvich. A face was set into the black bark.

"Shit," he mumbled as realization dawned on him. "I mean no ill will, spirit of the trees."

The face slowly regarded him. It was slender, pitted, weeping tears of the tar-like substance. It let out a moan as it looked at him.

"W-hhh-" it began, before stopping. Its eyes rolled in their sockets for a moment before settling on him once more. "Wh-whoooooooo…arrrrrrrre…yooouuu?"

Grimluk looked at the weeping face and took in the black bough once more. "A friend, I hope. By my reckoning, you are a dryad. Am I correct?"

"Dryyyyy…aaaaad. Yyyyyyyesssss," the face said.

"What has happened to you?"

"Wuh…wwwwwizaaaard. Trrrrrrrapped." One of the apples shook. "Ffffffffruit."

"Is the wizard still around?" Grimluk asked gingerly. The dryad was suffering badly but the information could be important.

"Nnnnnnno," the dryad replied. One of the lower branches moved toward him. "Fuh-ffff-freeeeeee...me..."

Grimluk opened his mouth to answer but the dryad's hazy eyes flicked up and went wide. The screech of the harpy followed. Instinct threw him forward and away from the razor sharp talons. The harpy rushed past, fury in her cries, and circled around for another attack.

"Blasphemer!" the harpy cried. "You shall die!"

Grimluk was ready for her, though. He moved slowly, like he'd hurt himself avoiding her attack while he slipped the demon trap blanket out of its loop on his bag. He'd clearly found something he wasn't supposed to. If she'd only been meant to lead him to Dunvich, she would not rest until he was dead now.

She was fast but he'd been counting on it. Still, he barely turned in time. The knight's eyes registered what was happening as he unfurled the blanket, tried to change direction. Her momentum was too great to alter and it brought pain as she slammed into Grimluk's chest like a cannonball at point blank range. The magic of the trap pinned the harpy to it while Grimluk let it go. She fell to the earth like a stone, piercing shrieks stabbing his ears as she thrashed around like a hornet in a glass jar.

Stumbling back, Grimluk rested against the dryad for a moment, gripping his ribs. If he'd been anyone other than an orc, his rib cage would have shattered. His breath was labored as he growled, "Be still! I will it!"

Demon traps allowed the trapper some measure of control over the entity within. She'd fight against his will the whole time but unless she was ancient, she'd never win that battle. The harpy went rigid at the command but maintained a glare that would have frightened any sane person. Demon hunters weren't quite sane, though, some more so than others—Grimluk included. It was part of the training. You learned to fight chaos and hatred incarnate which meant immersing yourself in blood, guts, psychic torture, and abject cruelty. And sometimes the things you encountered were difficult to even comprehend. He'd encountered another such thing just before the start of the year.

"Reckon you and I need to have words," he growled at the harpy.

She shrieked through gritted teeth. "I'll kill you once I'm free."

Carefully, Grimluk tucked the corners of the blanket back until the demon trap was mostly clear. He drew his knife, jammed it into the dirt, and began drawing a triangle around the trap, amplifying its power and creating a Great Circle.

"Now then, why did you lead me here? Were you the woman at the waystation?" he asked the harpy.

The surprise in her eyes was unmistakable but it was quickly swallowed by rage once more. The question lingered though as the harpy refused to answer. Grimluk walked around the trap slowly. The harpy kept her eyes locked on him at all times.

"What demon does the cult serve?" he continued.

That got a response. The demon knight shook violently, trying to break free of his will. She'd never get free of the trap, especially now, but she could still make noise. If there were any other knights, or other demons, she could bring them here with some effort.

A weary sigh rolled out of Grimluk. "Will you not answer me?"

"Never," she hissed.

He hated this part of fighting a knight. The final decision. "Maeve, wasn't it? How much of you is left in there? Can you give up your demon and embrace your mortality again?"

He'd asked that question a few dozen times since he'd become a full-fledged demon hunter. At first, it'd been a hopeful question. Demon knights made a choice. This also meant they couldn't be exorcised without incredible risk. They could, however, make a new choice right up until their soul had been completely devoured. That point of no return depended on the things they'd done, what they'd allowed of the demon inside. Still, they could choose redemption, if they wanted it. Only one knight had ever turned away when Grimluk had offered the choice. Every other time, they'd chosen the demon. Eventually, he'd begun dreading asking.

It was a choice an orc understood, even if the circumstances were only vaguely similar. Once upon a time, orcs were the enemies of every living person alive. Orckind had been enslaved by dark magic, giving them no choice. They were weapons until the moment they'd been freed and the Great War ended. Then, it was a fight to prove they weren't evil, that they could do good, that they weren't unthinking, unfeeling engines of destruction. So Grimluk had to keep asking the question, to offer the knights a chance at redemption.

Maeve stared at him for a long moment, predatory eyes piercing into him, looking for a chance to strike. The strange birdsong began again as Grimluk and his adversary held each other's gaze. Gently, she started laughing. It built up until she couldn't contain it anymore and she doubled over, croaking with laughter. "I am power. I am fury incarnate, orc. I am me and I've made my choice."

The years of hunting settled onto his shoulders as Grimluk's hand slid to his revolver. Ten long years. "So be it." His gun slid free and delivered the consequences of the question. Of her...of its choice. Two shots, to the head and heart, ended the demon knight's existence. The corpse flew out of the circle and landed in the grass with a heavy thud. Feathers fluttered in the air, as did a spray of blood. The bird song, which had grown louder with the knight's laughter, reached a fever pitch. The frenzied birds burst from the treetops, taking to the sky and left silence in their wake.

His arm dropped with the weight of the gun. After a long moment, he moved.

The dryad's branches shivered, trying to reach for Grimluk as he approached again. White tears flowed from its eyes. "Freeeeeee...meeeeeee," it asked once more.

Grimluk let out a heavy sigh. "'Fraid I'm no wizard. I wouldn't know how to end your curse." The whole tree seemed to deflate at that. It was an ancient, weary sound full of creaks and groans. When the dryad spoke again, it felt like a slap in the face.

"Deathhhhhh," it said as simply as it could.

Dryads were mostly benevolent. Occasionally

mischievous, but they and their kin were the hearts of many forests. Properly respected dryads could mean the difference between building a homestead that could survive four months of winter or being starved to death. Even the logging companies had to make deals with them. Killing one was not something you did without consequences.

"You're sure?" The question weighed heavily on his tongue. A request not to be taken lightly.

In response to his question, the dryad moaned again and shook itself once. Grimluk sighed and retrieved his hatchet. The job would take too long with the hand axe, but the dryad had suffered for who knew how long. It was time to end it.

Grimluk looked at the hatchet for a moment. With a grunt of effort, he swung. The blade of the axe sunk into the tree with a wet shunk. The dryad moaned in pain. He swung again, using his considerable strength to tear through the trunk as quickly as he could. Each strike sounded more like he was hitting a troll's fat hide, and the deeper he struck, the more of the tar-like substance flowed. He could hear the dryad crying again but he recognized the notes of relief at the coming end of its suffering.

Normally, you could only kill a dryad by finding its heart tree and felling it. Whether this was its heart tree or just its prison, Grimluk couldn't say, but the dryad seemed sure he could kill it. Given how corrupted the thing looked, he was inclined to agree. Whatever the wizard did, this was the heart tree now.

Each swing felt heavier than the last one. He reminded himself he was saving the spirit from a miserable, painful existence, likely a slave for some unknown purpose. It was the right thing to do, merciful even.

It had to be.

After half an hour, he'd gotten through enough of the trunk that a hard kick sent the tree tumbling over with a heavy crash. He stepped over to the fallen trunk and found the dryad's face. He knelt down and bowed his head to it.

"Spirit of the Forest," he began, softly, "I set you free. May your seed find new life elsewhere."

"Sssseeeeeeed…" it moaned. "Pppppro-teeeect…" A creaking, choking sound came from the dryad's mouth, shaking its felled form. Its cheeks puffed out, as much as they could and, with one final shuddering effort, it pushed out a huge seed from its mouth that rolled into the grass. As all the color faded from the tree, it spoke one last time.

"Thhhaaaank…yoooouuu…"

The black thing ceased to move, now nothing more than an ashen trunk. Grimluk touched the brim of his hat and bowed his head in a moment of silence.

Gingerly, he picked up the seed. He'd never seen or even heard of such a thing happening. He inspected it carefully in the palm of his hand. It fit there, looking like a vaguely heart-shaped acorn. He turned it over, grateful that the seed seemed free of the corruption that had covered the tree. The dryad—or its offspring, he wasn't entirely sure—would get a fresh start.

He started to slip the seed into his bag before thinking better of that idea. He needed to store it in something or else it might be crushed. He would not fail the dryad in its final request.

He unrolled his medical pouch. The soft leather was padded, protecting his field dressing tools, bandages, and the small bottles of salve. He plucked one of the bottles from its slot. The greenish gel was nearly used up, so he dropped the seed into the bottle with a soft plunk.

As he looked at the seed some more, curiosity struck him. The salve, when applied early enough, could close up his wounds enough that scars never formed. Without the stuff, his body would be covered in bullet holes, claw, and blade marks. What could the stuff do for other living things? Would the salve purge any unseen taint in the seed? It was an interesting thought. He knew it protected from infections, so maybe it could help. In any case, it would keep the seed safe until he could find a new place to plant it.

For now, he had a cult to find and stop. He looked at the fallen tree and the demon knight one last time and let out a growl. It was time to get back to work.

CHAPTER 5

It was an hours-long trek back to Dunvich and Grim-luk's mind was whirling with thoughts. Thus far, he'd only run into the one demon knight, along with the lumbering thing that had watched him and disappeared in the woods just outside of town. The dryad had been cursed to an unknown purpose, and everyone in town was too nice. And, if he had to guess, he'd say the festival was to gather sacrifices.

The worst thing is that it all felt so obvious. Grimluk wasn't sure if that was his training, his experience, or cynicism creeping in. Cults favored lonely places where they could move without being harassed by peacekeepers or hunters. Dunvich, by all accounts, was such a place. Without more information, all he could do was make guesses.

When Grimluk arrived back in Dunvich, the afternoon sun hung low in the sky, casting a glorious blaze. He slipped out of the woods near the town's entrance and followed the same path he had the day before. One of the locals greeted him. She was carrying a crate of something or other and stopped to ask what he was up to. He told the partial truth. He'd gone for a walk. He added that the area around Dunvich was quite lovely and the woman, whose eyes were uncomfortably focused on him the entire time, seemed pleased by that response. She wished him a good evening and continued on wherever she'd been headed to begin with.

He decided to wander the town some, trying as much as he could to make it look like he was doing nothing more than sightseeing, to observe the festival preparations, the people, the buildings. He didn't have much light left. The sky's blaze was dimming, already lessened by the trees and buildings.

When he could, Grimluk peered into the dark holes and crevices of the buildings. If he couldn't get close to check something out, he looked from beneath the brim of his hat. He had charcoal-colored eyes that could almost disappear with enough shadow to obscure them and dusk was always the best time for that trick. He looked the people over as well, wondering if he'd catch sight of anything else Abyssal or whether the cult was more organized than that. With a demon knight, and what seemed to be a whole town to themselves, he suspected they were organized. The people all smiled and waved to him as he walked. He politely nodded back to each of them even as he measured them up and inspected them.

The buildings showed him more of the decay that filled Dunvich, but he got a better look at a patch of the blackness he'd pegged as mold. Whatever it was was vein-like and shiny, pulsing gently like a dying worm. Some houses had more of it than others, but the more he looked, the more he noticed. Carefully, and as quickly as he could, he sliced some of it with his big knife. It withered and faded to ash on contact, confirming his suspicions that it was demonic in nature.

As far as he could gather, the people were regular humans. Which made sense. Not everyone in towns where cults had infested were even aware of what was going on. Sometimes, the cult was small. On the other hand, sometimes the cult's influence spread like a plague, touching every adult. Those that had families went on to corrupt them as well. Including their children, who might not even understand what they were doing.

Though some were. Sometimes people were born with a wrongness in them that manifested even at a young age. Even wonderful parents could not set that wrongness right, if something worse got to the child first. Grimluk had seen such children before. Thankfully, they were a rarity. But the last one had been the worst he'd seen. The job had been a strange one and he'd ignored his instincts. It had cost the little Wastelands town dearly. In his shame and uncertainty, he'd left too early, allowing the boy, Nicholas Quinn, to escape after having bound himself to a fear demon. He'd even sacrificed his mother, Cassie, to the thing. His father, Peter, had fallen to the fire of an undead dragon, itself accidentally summoned by Nicholas's apparent ally, the mayor of the town.

Grimluk had left Greenreach Bluffs with the boy's sister, Gwen, adopting her as his own sibling. The poor girl had had a prophetic spirit imprisoned inside her, courtesy of her brother, used as a means to spread fear through the town. Orcs knew the power of belonging and saw family as more than blood, but more than that, he knew the people would still fear her and, with no one to look after her, it seemed the best idea he had. As they'd traveled together, he'd grown more and more attached to her.

After all that, and everything that followed, Gwen had, at the age of seven, decided to train to become a demon hunter. Because, like him, she felt guilt over her brother. He'd hated the idea of her living this life. It wasn't his choice to make, though, despite how hard he pushed against it at first, and he hoped her training was going well.

He let out a long sigh. "Reckon I should write home," he muttered as he walked, eyes still vigilant. Gwen would turn nine in the coming winter. Grimluk resolved to be there for her birthday. He'd missed the last one tending to an imp infestation. He'd also missed the anniversary of her adoption into his family.

He shook his head, hearing his cenka chiding him, his dakka calling him a big green ass. The smile that caused was bittersweet.

As he neared the edge of town, the array of colors that was the dandy dude's clothing caught Grimluk's attention. The halfling dude came sauntering toward him, furry feet slapping the ground with confident movements. He couldn't help but notice that those furry feet had been trimmed neat as you please. To his recollection, this was the first time he'd ever seen a halfling trim the hair on their feet. The hair on their knuckles was more common, especially among cooks. The little fellow was a dandy indeed.

"Oh, hello again," the halfling offered. "Shouldn't you be back at the barbershop? It took, what was his name? Mortimer? It took Mortimer hours to get me and that other fellow taken care of."

Grimluk eyed the dude. "Pardon, friend, I'm not sure I follow."

"You are the barber's assistant, are you not? Must be new, too. Didn't see you last year."

"What part of me looks like a barber's assistant?" Grimluk replied, crossing his arms.

"Well, I just mean...that is to say, you're an orc. I just assumed..."

A sneer threatened to curl Grimluk's lip. "You assumed...?" he asked.

The dude coughed uncomfortably. "I just mean to say, orcs tend toward odd jobs. Perhaps he wanted you to look presentable for work, which is why he was—" the dude looked Grimluk up and down, "—working on you when I got there."

Grimluk let out a weary sigh. This was still better than being called a goblin, but that was not a difficult feat to achieve. "Look, dude, don't rightly know what it's like where you come from, but if you plan on heading any farther west, you best rid yourself of such notions. You'll live longer."

That seemed to catch the dude off guard. Their chestnut eyes went wide and they visibly gulped.

"Apologies, sai!" they began, hands up in a placating gesture as they moved cautiously around Grimluk. "I–I meant not a thing by it. You understand. M–my mistake."

"I do understand. And I'd be much obliged if you'd do better in the future. If not for our sakes, then for your own."

"Too right, sai, too right. Sometimes my mouth gets the better of me. Ornes–hum City just has its own way of doin' things, sai. You understand."

Grimluk eyed the dude for a moment, studying their face for any hint of insincerity. Grimluk wasn't immune to lies but he was usually pretty capable at spotting them. He sensed none from the dude and nodded his head. "Reckon I do, though I've never yet been that far east. As of this moment, this is the farthest east I've been in my travels."

"Is that right?" the dude asked, a note of curiosity in their voice.

"It is," Grimluk replied.

"What brought you all this way?" the dude asked. Before Grimluk could answer, the dude snapped. "Of course. If you are not the barber's assistant, or some such, then you're a fellow outsider, am I correct, sai?"

"You are."

The dude let out a sigh of their own this time. "I am sorry, friend. I have truly been an addle-brained fool this day. I s'pose it would be right to make amends. I'd like to invite you to join a poker game with myself and the other outsiders this evening. Provided you play, of course."

Grimluk thought on the offer a moment. It had been a while since he'd played a good round of poker. "Reckon that'd be mighty fine."

"Excellent!" the dude said with a smile. "I believe we're starting around seven this evening, after supper."

"At the hotel?"

"Exactly there. They have a fine parlor they've set up for us."

Grimluk nodded. "I'll be there."

"I'm glad for it," the dude said with a flourished bow. "I'll let the others know. Don't you worry. I'm sure they'll be eager to swap stories, too, so be ready!"

A simple grunt was all the response Grimluk

offered. The dude started to turn away. "Oh, manners. What is wrong with me today? The name's Dex. Dex Lovemead."

"Grimluk."

"Very nice to meet you, despite my boorish behavior, sai. Until tonight!"

As Grimluk watched Dex head back into Dunvich, a light grin pulled at his lips. "Gonna feel a little bad takin' the dude's money now."

Dex introduced Grimluk to the other outsiders at supper that night. The human in the buckskin was Kruger Szép, who looked Grimluk over with blue eyes as he gave a single, hardy pump of Grimluk's hand. He seemed of middling height for a human, solidly and broadly built with a barrel chest. Given the handshake, Grimluk felt certain the man's work required a fair bit of strength and, by his dress, guessed lumberjack or trapper. His beard was still bushy, but Grimluk could see where the barber had worked to clean it up. The smell of beard oil was hard to miss.

Next was a human woman by the name of Imogen Mulloy. She was on the taller side for a human woman, wearing her mouse-brown hair short and shaggy. It reminded Grimluk of his cenka, who kept hir hair in a similar cut. Imogen's eyes were a simple brown that held in them a sharpness he found unsurprising, given the ragged scar on her lip. She wore clothes not dissimilar to a peacekeeper's uniform, browns and reds with touches of black and white, but her vest and boots were of a higher quality. Imogen was direct, almost curt, in her greeting and attempted to crush Grimluk's hand when she shook it. He liked her immediately. She reminded him of a ranger he'd met near the start of the new year in a town called Downingville. Manyara had shown immense bravery and heart in his fight against a demonic creature he'd never heard the like of. He was sure Imogen was made of the same stuff.

After that was a pair of elf twins, Klovekethrin and Besskulethrin, who also answered to Silvers and Bess. The pair stood shorter than Imogen. Klovekethrin's eyes looked like bars of silver in moonlight, which explained the nickname. Bess's eyes had the color sapphires-in-sunlight. The combination of their black hair and eye colors made them incredibly striking, even among a people known for such things. They wore dark clothes that hugged their bodies almost snugly, yet revealed nothing of any curves or features underneath. The colors were deep and rich and seemed nicer than travelers would need. In unison, they offered their hands to Grimluk and offered him their salutations. He shook them in turn.

The group moved to take their seats at a table in the dining room where some of the hotel staff were setting various dishes. The room's wallpaper was similar to the stuff in his room at first glance, but had a slightly different pattern and color. Like his room, it was faded and peeling in places. The parlor itself was spacious enough to house them all comfortably, as well as several other tables. A series of windows covered the wall. All the windows had a common layer of dust to them. At the back of the room was a large swinging door that led somewhere else Grimluk couldn't see. Likely the kitchen.

"Well, now that we've all met," Dex said, climbing up into their own chair, "shall we introduce ourselves proper?"

"What did you have in mind?" the twins asked together as they each prepared a plate.

Kruger snorted. "Mean no offense, but I wish y'all wouldn't do that."

"Why?" the twins replied.

"It's damned unsettlin'."

The twins looked at each for a moment. "We do so humbly apologize, sai, and shall attempt to unsettle you no longer."

Grimluk shook his head, holding back a grin as the twins continued on, now clearly trying to get a rise out of the man.

"Gods-damned weirdos," Kruger rumbled. "Sorry I fuckin' asked."

"Anyways, sais," Dex interjected, "I thought we could chronicle what we do and what brought us here."

"Sounds fine by me," Imogen offered. "I would like to know who I'm competing with." At hearing her speak more, Grimluk realized why she sounded curt. The scar made her careful with enunciations.

"Reckon so," he offered, readying his own plate with salted beef, an ear of corn, rolls, and a pile of greens.

"What the orc said," came Kruger.

"Very well," Silvers said amiably.

"I'll be happy to go first, unless anyone would care to volunteer," Dex offered. When no one said anything, they began. "I must confess, this is my third year attempting to win the prize. When I came two years prior, I had done little of note. I thought perhaps the challenges would be simple games but alas, I was mistaken." They sighed.

"The challenges proved too much for me and I retired, eager to train myself for the following year. Poetry may keep me going in life but it does little to prepare the body. Still, it has given me interesting new perspectives. The collection the experience brought me was published shortly before I returned last year. I might've won, too, had a brutish thug not hurled me into a tree." At that, Dex turned to Grimluk. "I would politely request you not abuse your, no doubt, prodigious strength in such a way, sai."

Grimluk shrugged and nodded, digging into his food. Two attempts prior. Either Dex had the best luck on the planet to walk into a cult den and survive or they were just that worthless to them. Though Grimluk wondered, what if the dude was a part of it all now? Or was the cult even that much of a threat?

He stabbed some of the beef as he thought and cut off a piece. Salty and chewy in just the right ways and the cook had added more seasoning before serving. His father, Urgroz, would approve of such methods. The man was an amazing chef in his own right and kept everyone in Hunter's Hollow fed right.

Paranoia about the cult and Dex could wait, though. The conversations could provide some extra information to help him put the pieces together. When his turn to speak arrived, Grimluk decided he would leave out being a demon hunter. A sensible precaution, given he had no clue who was allied with the cult and he now had suspicions about Dex.

Dex finished up speaking about themselves by talking about the poetry collections they'd published, talking up two of their more popular poems, and looking dejected when no one recognized them. "Who's next, then?" they asked. "Imogen? Twins?"

Imogen, taking a deep pull from her cup, spoke up in her clipped and curt tone. "I was a peacekeeper. Come from Ensmuth. Fishin' town farther east. Got tired of all the strange shit."

"Strange shit?" Grimluk asked.

"Folks don't look right, act weird. Opposite of here. Local temple always gave me the creeps. Wasn't allowed in. Never pushed it."

"Hm. Never heard of a temple keepin' folks out," Grimluk commented.

"Fuck 'em," Kruger offered. "Pro'ly some local ancestor trollshit."

Imogen shrugged. "Didn't matter much. Worst part, was a fishin' town, sure, but everywhere smelled like fish. Rotten fish. Everywhere."

"Sounds atrocious," Dex offered, wrinkling their nose in disgust.

Imogen shrugged again, taking a bite of beef. "Moved on after one of the locals did this." She pointed at the scar. "Figured I could find other work. Bounties. Riding shotgun. Courier routes. Made some gluts recently on an outlaw bounty. Heard about the festival, thought I'd try my hand."

Kruger spoke up next, through a mouthful of food. "Trapper by trade," he began. "Spend most days down in the Territories, come to Westlynth and New Gilead when work calls. Happened to be in the area and heard about the festival, though folks made this place out to be a lot worse than it was. Buncha hog-wash, though. Figured, the festival seemed like a thing to try. Reckon if I can carry a hunnerd pounds a furs, fight off thieves and swindlers, I can handle a little danger."

He downed the rest of his beer. "Shit, had a whole posse set on me once. Kilt three, broke the rest. The orc knows how it is. Don't ya? Folks set on ya on the road and you do what ya gotta."

Grimluk finished what was in his cup, letting out a sound of satisfaction. "Reckon not," he replied as he refilled.

"Trollshit. You ain't gonna sit there and tell me that. I've known some orcs in my time, seen what some folks tried to do to them."

With a nod, Grimluk answered. "Folks try and go home reflectin' on their efforts."

Kruger looked on, confused. "You tellin' me you ain't never kilt no one?"

"Reckon so."

Kruger studied Grimluk's face for a long moment. Then he started laughing. "Fuck. Gods-damned orcs got the best poker faces. Had me goin' there. Watch your bilts around this one."

There was a certain level of satisfaction Grimluk took at people who didn't believe he'd never taken a mortal life before. It flew against the expectations of his people. On occasion, it meant people underesti-mated him, thinking him too soft. Those were always the people who expected the worst of him. The ones who had been the cruelest and expected the same from everyone else.

Too often, those were the people who found their way to demons.

The twins spoke up next, alternating their story

fluidly between each other. "We work as psychopomps. We've always felt closer to the spirit world. They rarely deceive as mortals do. Their conflicts are easier to end. Elemental spirits have simple needs."

"No wonder yer so creepy," Kruger said with a snort.

The twins looked at him blankly before speaking together. "Yes, that is why we are so creepy."

At that, he wrinkled his face in disgust, grumbling as he hunkered back down over his food.

"Spirit callers," Grimluk mused. "My sister has that gift."

"Does she respect them?" the left twin asked.

"Reckon so. Made friends with a little pack of tricksters. Got them addicted to cookies."

Both of the twins smiled at that, with more warmth than they'd shown up until then. "She sounds lovely," Bess offered.

"She is," Grimluk confirmed. He couldn't help but smile as well, especially remembering the half-seen little spirits gorging themselves on sweets while Gwen giggled at them. The girl had a way of getting to your heart.

"Please send her our greetings when you see her next," Silvers said before continuing, Bess nibbling at their food. "We heard of the festival after helping some spirits find a better home than the family they lived with. Though the spirits tried to help them, the family remained ungrateful and insisted they were mere pests. We found a more appreciative family. The first family informed us of Dunvich as way of thanks instead of the gluts they owed us."

Everyone but Dex shook their heads at that, tsking as they did.

"We called a poltergeist upon them in return and headed this way."

Everyone stopped to stare at the twins for a long moment. Then Kruger spoke up. "The fuck's a poultrygeist?"

The twins turned slowly toward him and the look on his face said he was having regrets at asking. "They are angry. And they are not quiet about it."

"Sorry I fuckin' asked. Gods, yer creepy little fuckers."

After a few minutes of silence, save for chewing and swallowing, the table looked at Grimluk expectantly. He shrugged. "Bounty hunter. Was lookin' for my next job, found it by chance, it led me here. Festival was mentioned, but didn't know much about it 'til I got here. Sheriff explained it so I thought I'd stay."

"You really know how to tell a story, orc," Kruger muttered.

Grimluk shrugged again. "Reckon it's better to keep things simple when I'm able."

Silence fell over the table as everyone took to their dinners with vigor. Once everyone was satisfied, Dex suggested it was time to begin the poker game. The outsiders moved to the gaming parlor, a room a little bigger than the dining room they'd come from, and took to the first felt table they found. The felt was a faded blue, worn and frayed in places. The chairs were sturdy enough still, though Grimluk could feel his gently sag as he sat. The chair wouldn't permit his regular use but that wasn't exactly a problem.

When everyone was comfortable, Kruger grabbed the deck. "Reckon I'll get things started," he said, cutting the cards several times. "We'll keep things simple. Five-Card Draw, only jokers wilds, two pennies to get ya started, and build the pot through ten rounds. Everyone in?" When everyone affirmed, he nodded and began dealing out to his right. The twins opted a single hand, playing together to the surprise of no one. Once the cards were dealt, everyone picked up their hand and threw down two pence.

Grimluk held the ace of hearts, the six of diamonds, the ten of clubs, the nine of spades, and the five of spades. Potentially a good hand, if he could draw successfully. Ultimately, it wouldn't matter, though. He was more concerned with any information he could glean or gather.

"Discard as you like and draw on your own," Kruger offered as he slapped down two cards and drew their replacements. "And don't be shy," he continued, raising by five.

Imogen discarded once and drew, meeting the raise silently. The twins folded.

Grimluk laid down the nine and the ten and drew the ace of diamonds and the four of hearts. A pair at the very least. He met the raise as well before asking, "Anyone know what the challenges are to be?"

Dex frowned and folded, laying their cards down. "They were different each time. The first year I tried, there was only a scavenger hunt of sorts, with a couple of items. I found one but had it stolen from me. Last year, it was all physical challenges, hence getting tossed into that tree. No details have been shared for this year yet. They usually keep them pretty quiet, in my experience."

"A scavenger hunt? Sounds like some shit for

kids and dandies," Kruger retorted. "Lay 'em down." He spread his hand out. The king of hearts, a black joker, and three of a kind with threes greeted the table. Imogen laid down four queens. Grimluk nodded, laying down his pair of aces. Imogen smiled and gathered up the cards to shuffle and deal.

"This is a silly game," the twins said in unison.

"Ain't so creepy when yer losin'," Kruger replied, producing a cigar. He bit off the cap and spit it into a nearby spitoon before lifting his hand, whispering an incantation, and lighting the cigar. Thick smoke puffed out across the table like fog off a lake.

"Same rules," Imogen said as she dealt.

As Grimluk played, the others bantered about the game. They seemed unconcerned with discussing the festival. At one point, he asked Dex what the story about the festival was but the halfling said it would be rude to spoil the tradition of learning about it.

Eventually, a new question struck Grimluk. "Dex."

"Yes?"

"Anyone else ever come back to try again?"

"With me? One person, last year. I would think the others felt it was too much of a hassle. Several of them were hurt last year, as well. But as for me, well, art is hungry for inspiration, is it not?"

"Reckon so."

After ten rounds, and a ten glut pot, Grimluk and Imogen ended up splitting the winnings. Kruger seemed shocked that he'd been beat in the ninth round after winning four in a row. Imogen nodded to Grimluk.

"A fine play, sai," she said, as they counted their coins and bills.

"Reckon so," Grimluk replied, nodding back. He picked up two of the bills, marked for one glut each, and held them up. "Still not sure how I feel about paper money."

"It'll replace glut coins at least once the banks get them all pushed out everywhere," Dex offered. "Especially popular in the capitals, it seems. I believe even Varnerton has been making the change as well, and they're always so behind the times."

Grimluk grunted and filled his wallet. "Reckon coins'll be good everywhere else for a while yet."

"Most likely," Dex agreed, "but it's still legal currency and should be honored no matter the location."

"Maybe. Don't reckon anyone in the Borderlands would care. Paper can burn up and fly away. Metal's a bit harder to lose when a demon wind comes out of the Wastes."

Everyone looked up at him at once, expressions of surprise on their faces. "You've been that far west?" Imogen asked.

"A time or two," Grimluk said as he stood.

"The stories I've heard," Kruger muttered. "I ain't afraid of no one but I ain't stupid enough to head that far out."

"Reckon you'll live longer then," Grimluk offered, slipping his bag back over his shoulder. "Even the Borderlands get strange. Not like out here." Which was partially true. Demon hunters had work all over this side of the continent, but it wasn't just demons that caused trouble near the Wastelands. Whatever actually happened when the dwarves sent their expedition out west and caused the Sundering had agitated every spirit in the area, as well as set loose a new horde of demons and unleashed monsters no one had ever heard of. Near the northwest edge of New Gilead, Grimluk had had to fight off giant worms from a small town. He'd heard rumors of the things farther south as well.

There were other things out there, too. Great, lumbering things no one could ever quite make out. Sometimes the Wastes even mutated animals into hideous nightmares that might as well have been demons. Sometimes they were.

Now he found himself in an area where a dryad had begged for death, a demon knight had kept watch, and something else entirely might be wandering the woods. If he kept pulling threads, he'd find the source of it all and put an end to it.

The five other outsiders looked askance at Grimluk. "What?"

"Is it really as bad as I've heard?" Dex asked.

"Sometimes. Folks both brave and foolish have made homes along the border. Some in the Wastes. Peacekeepers work a little differently out there but whether folks volunteer or not, most of the time, they get on just fine. Half of the towns named Border Rest are decent places. The other half not so much."

"How many Border Rests are there?" Imogen inquired.

Grimluk muttered as he thought it over. "Ten, last I saw."

"Why so many?" Kruger followed.

"Easy enough name," Grimluk replied with a shrug. "Sometimes folks just name a town out of convenience."

"Indeed," the twins replied.

Without much else to say, Grimluk moved on out of the parlor and started for his room. The others remained behind a moment and he knew they'd whisper about him a little. It'd probably buy him a little privacy, at the least. At least, he hoped it would.

CHAPTER 6

The corpse was incomplete. Lantern light revealed the truth of that matter as Elder Whateley stood over the fallen demon knight. Wilbur loomed silently next to him. The demonic aspects of the knight had begun rotting when she'd died and now, almost nothing was left but a nearly headless skeleton alongside some flesh, bits of muscle, and the organs.

"Gather up what bits of her inside will hold up, m'boy. No sense in lettin' her go to waste."

"Yes, Grandfather," Wilbur replied dutifully, pulling the huge jar that hung from his shoulder forward.

Elder turned from one corpse to the next, casting his lantern light on the fallen tree that was once a dryad. His dryad. The orc was proving troublesome already. Rundyyk had told Maeve not to attack unless the orc gave her a reason. Finding the dryad was a good reason. It would be a setback for sure. He knelt next to the dryad's face and jammed his calloused fingers into its mouth, cracking wood as he did so. With no seed in its mouth, he jammed his hand in farther, searching deeper.

Still nothing. "Well, shit."

"What troubles you, priest?" came a third voice.

"It seems the orc may have absconded with the heartseed. We'll need to get it back before we can make any more apples after this."

"I can do this," came the voice. "It should prove no issue to slip into his room as he sleeps. Were enough gathered for the festival?"

"There were enough for several pies," Elder replied, turning to what amounted to his second knight. The thing was not actually a demon, nor a mortal, but it had sworn service to Rundyyk. "How do the others compare to, what did you say his name was? Grimluk?"

The unseen voice huffed. "The fur trader is a boor. I'd have thought Grimluk would've been the same but he is surprisingly quiet. The twins and the peacekeeper could prove valuable, however. Their sensitivity to spirits and magic could make them powerful sacrifices. If the woman were converted, she could become a knight, though another sacrifice would be just as apt."

Elder nodded at that. "Even the boors serve their purpose. Get on back and get the seed, then."

"Very well, priest."

He was not particularly hard of hearing but the thing moved in near silence all the same. More than anything, Elder knew it had left by the lack of presence more than any sound. He struggled back to his feet as Wilbur approached.

"A lung, liver, kidneys," he reported, the jar now filled. "The bullet destroyed the heart and second lung."

"Thank you, m'boy. We'll make use of them yet." He looked back at the tree. "Damn shame. Still, once we have the seed, we can raise a new dryad. One loyal to our master."

"Yes, Grandfather. Will I get to play soon?"

"I'd reckon so. Patience, m'boy. Good things come to those who wait."

"Yes, Grandfather."

"Well, let's get me back home. My bones are none too pleased at coming all the way out here."

It didn't take long to work the spell. The portal slipped open as Elder uttered the final word, splitting the dirt and filling the clearing with eldritch light. Portals were necessary but made his joints ache fiercely. Always had, too.

The pair entered their home once more and the portal disappeared behind them.

A mighty need to piss woke Grimluk up. His eyes opened blearily as the realization filled his brain. As luck would have it, that same need meant he saw the halfling dandy as they slipped across his room from his very locked door. He remained still and quiet, watching to see what Dex planned on doing. The dandy stopped at the table Grimluk had set his bag on and began very quietly opening it.

The halfling had moved incredibly silently, even for bare feet on carpet. Grimluk looked down and noticed that the large, hairy feet were gone, replaced by two, small appendages he couldn't quite identify in the dark.

He'd been right. Dex was a part of this. That

didn't explain what they were doing digging through his bag, though. Grimluk reached over and turned up the lamp with one hand and reached under his pillow for his knife with the other.

"Need some help, friend?" he asked as the light grew.

Dex froze in place. The silence engulfed the room for a moment that seemed to stretch for too long before Dex was suddenly in Grimluk's face. Steel pressed into his neck as he lay there, looking into the dandy's now animal-like eyes. He didn't bother trying to inspect the knife.

"You just sit there nice and easy and you'll be back asleep in a moment," Dex said softly as they placed their free hand on his cheek. They locked eyes with Grimluk and began chanting in a language he'd never heard.

He got the gist of the words soon, though. He could feel a vague sense of drowsiness trying to over-take him. The tattoo on the crown of his head kept the spell from working properly. It was a kind of mind seal. Its primary purpose was to keep demons out of a hunter's head, but had the added benefit of keeping psychics and spellwork out, as well. Dex was trying to put him to sleep. Probably meant to tamper with his memories, too, something far too dangerous. Last Grimluk heard, it was also very illegal to do so.

When it became obvious the spell wasn't work-ing, Dex sighed and clenched their teeth. "Forgive me, Master. I do this for the greater good."

The knife slid across Grimluk's throat smoothly, drawing a thin line of blood. It stung about as much as a really bad knick while shaving, though a knick that stretched the length of his throat. He sighed and grabbed Dex by the throat as he rolled up to a sitting position. The halfling's eyes went wide as their knife fell to the carpet with a dull thump.

"How?" they croaked.

"Just the way it is. Now, friend, I reckon you should tell me just exactly what you want. And maybe just what you are." He looked down at Dex's feet. They looked something like the hooves of a young doe. "Those ain't the feet of a halfling." Grimluk moved his thumb, checking for a pulse. It was incredibly weak. With the fear on the halfling's face, their heart should have been pounding like a rabbit's, but there it was, steady thumps several seconds apart, more like someone passing on.

Dex's fingers dug into Grimluk's wrist with sudden ferocity. "I'll be your death," they said, their voice turning to a bassy growl.

The shift in strength surprised Grimluk, but he held fast. He slid his knife all the way out from under the pillow as Dex's mouth began splitting open to reveal rows of jagged teeth. The blade slid out with barely a whisper. This time, it was Grimluk's turn to hold a blade against flesh. The massive blade reflected in the lamplight like a dark rainbow as he pressed the flat of it, where the Elder Sign was etched, into Dex's forehead using the force of it to drive whatever the thing really was to the floor.

The dude grunted in pain as wisps of smoke began billowing from where the blade touched their forehead. Grimluk pulled it away. He expected to see the Elder Sign burned into Dex's forehead. Instead, the skin was now red and irritated everywhere the blade had touched.

"Hm. Now, friend, what are you and what do you want from me?" Dex tried to thrash away from Grimluk's grip by way of answer. He pressed the blade into their forehead again. "Answers. Now. You a demon?"

Dex gave a pitiful little moan as the blade seared flesh once more. Very slowly, the thing masquerading as a halfling began turning pale and translucent. When he pulled the blade away again, the skin there was bright red like a burn, slivers of smoke rising away from the area.

Jagged convulsions and spasms racked the small body. "N–not a demon," it choked out. While the flesh had changed, so had the rest of its face. The eyes were losing their lids, stretching out into perfect silvery orbs with white slit pupils. Still, the Elder Sign left no mark on the skin, which meant that something else about the blade was doing this. Whatever Dex was, it really wasn't a demon.

As he thought that over, the thing finished changing. All that was left of its form was a nearly transparent creature with twig limbs. The heart in its chest flashed periodically in the same rhythm Grimluk had felt before. The body remained small, though it grew beyond the size of a halfling, becoming more equal to a very tall dwarf or a short human.

"That's one question mostly answered," Grimluk whispered, readjusting his weight. "Now, I reckon you're a servant of whatever demon the cult here serves. That doesn't explain why you were diggin' around my bag."

"K–k–kill me," it wheezed. "I w–will never...never be–betray my master."

"Tell me or I put the blade to you again."

The thing's silver eyes went huge at that but still, it only repeated itself. He could feel how weak it had become under the touch of his knife. It was the only reason the thing managed to surprise him when it swung a suddenly club-like arm at his head. Mostly, it just pissed Grimluk off and he pressed the knife down into the thing's bulbous head once more.

The club arm shrank back down as the thing's hand gripped his forearms, furiously pulling and pushing. The shapeshifting thing tried to get into his mind again. He could feel it pressing against him, managing to press vague notions of letting it escape. It muttered in its strange language again as it did so, desperate now. As it struggled to keep from speaking anymore, Dex bucked, throwing its hands up in a flash to push the knife up and away from its forehead.

Grimluk expected attempts to get free but he didn't expect it when Dex brought the blade back down through its own face. Milky white blood began pouring out from the massive wound as Grimluk's weight pressed the knife cleanly through the thing's head. He was shocked to find it felt very similar to cutting through a demon. There was no resistance. The blood bubbled and hissed, burning against the blade. With a growl, Grimluk pulled back and finished the job. With a grunt, he drove the knife into the thing's firefly heart. A spurt of the pale blood shot out of the wound but the death blow was true.

As Grimluk stood from the corpse, it began to dessicate. Here and there, green flames burned up the blood until the body dried up completely. Despite all that, the corpse changed yet again, turning to a sort of jelly that looked a lot like ectoplasm, but more viscous and opaque, leaving a stain behind on the carpet.

Grimluk sat on the edge of his bed and looked at the stain.

"Well, shit." He found a towel to wipe his blade clean with. His throat rumbled as he thought. He still didn't know what Dex had been after or if anyone else would follow up, but he suspected it had to do with the seed. He had to figure out how he wanted to handle things now. With whatever Dex was now gone, the cult would notice. It might put them on the defensive. Even worse, Dex being a shapeshifter meant that there could be other shapeshifters as well. Maybe even the other outsiders. He'd need to test them if he could. Sleep first. And maybe a couple of quick traps.

Only the twins were awake when Grimluk arrived for breakfast. They offered him a unified good morning as they filled their plates. Breakfast was a pile of biscuits and sausage gravy that set his mouth to watering immediately. The twins were slow to gather their food and he found them joining him at the table after he sat down. The pair said nothing, simply smiling as they ate. He appreciated the company—as much as he could after last night—and the quiet, but still remained vigilant. With Dex having been a shapeshifter, it was easy to mistrust. Shifters always presented that issue, it seemed. If it wasn't for the fact that he had banished the thing, he'd be worried about the return of the shapeshifting creature he'd fought just before the new year.

That would be a trial all its own with a cult involved. But it was gone. No, now he had the cult and gods knew what else. Just what on Arkod had Dex been? What was the point of trapping the dryad?

Were the other so-called outsiders actually outsiders or were they like Dex? He pondered all of it while he ate in silence.

Kruger and Imogen didn't show up for breakfast until mid morning and by then everything was cold. Kruger looked like he'd spent the night drinking. Imogen looked marginally better, apparently with enough wherewithal to seek out the coffee pot. She held her cup up reverently, taking in a deep whiff before downing the thing in one go.

Kruger watched this all happen, a slack-jawed look on his face, before he blurted out, "Coffee!" His own cup was filled and gone just as quickly as Imogen's. Unlike Imogen, whose second cup she sipped at slowly, Kruger downed his second, and third, in the same fashion. Finally, with a plate of cold food, he plopped down at the table.

"Dex take his loss hard?" Kruger asked. "Little bastard's been up first thing the last three mornings."

"Haven't seen him since last night," Grimluk answered with a shrug. Which was true.

"Maybe he's preening," Imogen offered, sipping her coffee.

Kruger snorted. "My Lily White Arse, a poem."

"Do go on," the twins said in unison.

"Don't start," Kruger said, shoveling a chunk of biscuit into his mouth. "It's too fuckin' early for that shit."

"It is after ten," they replied one after the other.

"And I spent last night celebratin' my fuckin' loss, so it's too early."

Grimluk tipped back his mug and finished it off. "Reckon the festival will start soon?"

"This afternoon," Silvers responded with a nod. "If I'm not mistaken."

He nodded. "Wonder how things'll go."

The sound of boots drew everyone's attention toward the foyer. Sheriff Ziskind walked into the dining room as if on cue, a smile on her face. "Mornin', y'all. Things'll be startin' in a few hours. Thought it might be time to give ya the details, as the guests of honor."

"Shouldn't Dex be here for that?" Grimluk asked.

The sheriff paused, looking around at the table. "Where's he gotten off to?"

"No one's seen him since last night," Silvers offered.

"I'll see if I can find him. He's already familiar with all of this. We like to uphold tradition around here but this is his third year. I'm sure he's just down at the tent watchin'."

The table gave a collective shrug before Sheriff Ziskind continued. Grimluk wondered if they already knew Dex was dead or not. It seemed likely the sheriff knew what it had been and didn't seem worried at the absence. They either didn't know or it didn't entirely matter.

"Tonight is the feast, but before that, y'all'll learn about the history of Dunvich and the event this festival celebrates." She stopped and beamed for a moment. "It's still such an honor to do this every year and I just want to take a moment to tell y'all how special it feels to have all of y'all here this year. We haven't had this many folks show up since...Oh, I can't even remember. This year is really somethin' special, I tell ya what."

"So we get a history lesson and then you feed us?" Kruger asked.

"Basically," the sheriff responded. "Everyone's cookin' up a storm by now. If anyone has any requests, make 'em quick and I'll see what I can do."

"Beef liver if anyone has it," Grimluk said. "Raw is fine, but a few seconds on a hot griddle works, too." Imogen wrinkled her nose at that but said nothing about his choice of food.

Sheriff Ziskind nodded, her face placid. "Easy enough, I'd wager."

"Strawberry pie," the twins said eagerly.

"Long as there's meat and liquor, I'm happy," Kruger followed. Imogen agreed with him with a few simple nods.

"You'll be plenty pleased." Sheriff Ziskind smiled again. "If there ain't any questions, I'll leave y'all to yer afternoon." When no one spoke up, she nodded. "Until then!"

With that, she turned and headed into the hotel proper. Grimluk could hear her talking to Raimi about which room Dex was staying in. He pretended to look into his cup as he frowned. The sheriff was assuredly a member of the cult. It was rare that peacekeepers weren't infiltrated. Sometimes it was just deputies, other times, sheriffs, and still other times, the whole damn lot of them. That's how it'd been the previous summer in a little town called Perfection. All except one deputy. But there, the peacekeepers had been the cult, under a tyrant judge.

Grimluk worried Sheriff Ziskind might start snooping once she figured out Dex was dead. The stain that was Dex had faded quite a bit but you could still see it if you looked. Then again, it wasn't entirely shaped like a person. For now, though, she had no cause to suspect any of them. He doubted his disappearance would entirely remain a mystery by the evening.

On the other hand, the likelihood of the outsiders being intended as some sort of sacrifice or converts could sway her mind there. Taking the long view, what would one creature, mortal, demon, or otherwise, meant as a plant among potential sacrifices, matter if the potentials were ready for what was to come? Grimluk stood and went to refill his mug. Instead of returning to his seat, he stood at the nearest window, looking out upon the sleepy, decaying little town.

I'll have to be careful, he thought. Shapeshifters and wizards. Demons'll show their ugly fuckin' heads soon, too. His throat rumbled as he mulled things over. The possibility of fighting an entire town rolled across his mind. He could do it if he had to, but the amount of unknown factors would make the ensuing fight that much harder. He couldn't immediately know what was human and what wasn't. Right now, the thieves he'd brought in, the twins, and himself were the only members of another race, which was something. He hoped.

At the very least, he wouldn't have to worry if anyone got his gun off him. It was bound to him with blood magic, enchanted to never hurt him. Anyone that tried to fire it at him would find the gun dry-firing. If anyone tried to club him with it, it'd feel no worse than a pillow.

His knife, on the other hand, would be his only

means of fighting off anything that wasn't human, should this possible fight take place. And a knife being waved around could easily harm mortals. He needed to be prepared and he needed to be careful.

With a quick gulp, Grimluk finished what was in his mug before slipping his coat and bag on and heading outside. It was time to look around some more.

Chapter 7

The townsfolk moved about, heedless of Grimluk as they carried tables and banners. He slipped silently across main street and, when he was sure no one was looking, disappeared behind the two shops at his back. He searched the walls for any signs or sigils. When nothing appeared, he headed away from the town proper and into the woods around it. This side, like the other, where he'd found the dryad, was well grown. Once he was into the tree line, he was certain he'd be fairly obscured still. Ultimately, he would make for the temple, but there might be other clues around the hill.

After walking some ways back, he turned and kept Dunvich to his right as best he could, with the temple's steeple being visible through the treeline. The woods were silent, save for the crunch of leaves under his feet. The land surrounding Dunvich was a blaze of red, yellow, and orange as the trees shed their leaves for winter. The sky grew more overcast as he walked. He was unsure of what, exactly, he was searching for since he had no specifics. Though cults rarely shared marks, there were certain constants he could recognize. Grimluk had dealt with cults only a handful of times, but basic wards and circles were hard to miss.

As he pushed deeper into the woods, a strange smell came to him, something he was unable to place. Grimluk looked around to find a source but saw nothing. No strange flowers, rotting trees, or decaying animals. His throat rumbled as he continued, the smell seemingly following him or just covering the area. Eventually, the sound of running water met him. He turned toward it and came across a burbling creek several feet across. It ran clear, hiding its true depths. Whether it could reach his waist or merely his ankles, he couldn't tell. Not wanting to get soaked either way, Grimluk simply leaped across with a grunt.

He followed the creek for some ways. The smell grew stronger as he did. He didn't follow it long before he discovered what appeared to be a long abandoned path. He only recognized it as such due to the width of it and the worn nature of the dirt by the creek. The path was nearly completely overgrown, save where the dirt had been packed too hard from use to support growth without help. Following the path, he found a clearing and something that surprised him. There in the clearing, under the gaze of the Dunvich temple, sat three longhouses, created from the trees themselves. To Grimluk's eye, each building seemed to be hundreds of trunks in the unmistakable shape of a building, connecting into a canopy above, like some sort of immensely fat, hollow tree.

He made his way toward the longhouse closest to him. Grimluk had no idea just how long they'd been here, undisturbed, but there was a stillness in the air that said years, maybe even decades. A blanket hung in the doorway under the entrance canopy, ripped to shreds and full of moth holes, loose threads waving gently in the breeze. He slipped inside and looked around. It was dim but, thanks to the light from openings in the ceiling, he could see well enough. There were structures inside that ran the length of the building, some formed in the same way as the longhouses—twisted and shaped from the natural world—while other parts were worked and formed with tools as needed. Ladders ran along the structures, handmade and movable. He spied bed rolls scattered about the first and second levels, denoting this as the bunk house. The structures served as something like bunk beds, with the first platform raised off the ground, and two more above that. Several fire pits were laid in the middle of the path. Most of the bed rolls were shredded or in piles and there was a layer of dust and decay to everything in sight.

The bizarre smell was even stronger here, and the strange birdsong had started up again, albeit faintly. Something about the smell finally slid into place in his mind. Brimstone. Whatever it was smelled of the Abyss, but it was more than that, too. There was the smell of brimstone, yes, but also of muddy animal and something unpleasantly tangy. The separate smells mixed together in such a way that it was nearly overpowering. Whatever it was, he was sure it wasn't good. There could be another knight watching him. He unsheathed his knife as a precaution, and as a tool to inspect the area.

He bent down near one of the bedrolls and looked it over. It was more of a pallet than a roll. Grimluk used his knife to lift the blanket up and shake some of the dirt away, sprinkling it on the furs below. The pattern was not one he'd seen before, but had some of the hallmark designs that so many of the tribes shared in their craftwork: soft, geometric shapes and a scattering of stripes of differing thicknesses in reds, blacks, whites, and yellows. Once the dust cleared and settled, he set the blanket back down. The discolorations became obvious in the light. He scraped away some of the brown. More dust came with the blade but the rest remained, having settled deep into the material. It was stained.

He looked around at the platform and planks above, and noticed more of the discolorations, albeit less clearly. He got closer and followed the edge of the discoloration. He stepped back to get a full view of what he was looking at and his brows furrowed when the pattern became apparent. It looked like someone had thrown a bucket of paint or sap or some other dark substance. He made his way down the path. Some of the blankets, and especially the furs, had the same heavy discoloration, along with the bunk platforms. He climbed one of the ladders to get a look at the top, testing its strength before he did so.

He found a small pile of bones in the vague shape of a hand half-covered by one of the blankets and he realized what those brown spots were: blood, long dried. Looking around, Grimluk spotted more bones. He'd taken the ones below for parts of the platforms or missed them all together. He had no idea just how long it took a body to break down naturally, but between the state of the fabrics and furs, he figured it was safe to assume it had been decades at the very least. Another worrying thought followed: had the citizens of Dunvich murdered the tribe?

Grimluk was fairly certain that if he inspected the other two longhouses, he'd find more bones and more bloodstains, along with the remnants of whatever supplies the tribe had had. Whether demon or mortal was responsible, it had been incredibly brutal. As he looked around with his new realization, Grimluk spotted ribs poking out of the dirt near one of the pits. There were a couple of dirty skulls, holes punched in them, staring at him from several corners. He was amazed there weren't ghosts all around him. If he was right about just how bad this had been, that kind of attack had the potential to create them out of most of the population. He wasn't sure if it should worry him more that there weren't any spiritual echoes.

Then again, maybe he was reading too much into it. Maybe this had happened before the town had been made. Maybe there had been ghosts but they'd been freed by spirit callers. Maybe.

"But if the cult did this," he muttered, "just how gods-damn long have they been here?" There were a lot of maybes and unknowns right now. Too many for his liking.

He decided to search the other longhouses, more to confirm his suspicions, while the birdsong continued softly. Bloodstains, tatters, smashed jars and ruination met him, with scattered bones throughout. As he stood outside again, the hairs on the back of his neck raised. Something was watching him.

He slipped casually back into a longhouse. The feeling of being watched got worse but it didn't feel like eyes. It felt like there was a presence but…distant, almost like he was in the middle of a far away storm. He waited. The longhouse shifted and creaked. And the walls started bleeding. Everywhere he'd recognized blood splatter turned red, as if it was fresh from the vein once more. The blood glistened in the gray light of the afternoon.

Both the smell and the presence faded away after a moment that felt longer than it had any right to. The glistening blood faded, as well, returning to the faint, brown stains. A gust of wind howled through the longhouse as Grimluk left. He turned to look toward the temple staring down at him. He headed for the hill.

It wasn't that much farther from the campsite, nor was the hill particularly big. The climb was more difficult from his need to keep quiet and out of sight. The trees thinned near the top but they were still big enough to hide his bulk. The temple was similar to several he'd seen in his travels, painted black, right down to the door handles. Next to it appeared to be an old, faded-white house. Like the rest of Dunvich, the architecture of both was very human in its style, with slightly more grandeur given to the temple. The temple was different from the rest of Dunvich, however, in that it was well-maintained. Not a speck of paint was flaking. The house, meanwhile, was chipped and peeling. The roof sagged. The porch leading up to the second floor via a ramp also sagged.

He watched for about ten minutes to make sure no one was around before he darted toward one of the windows of the church. Despite his size, he moved stealthily when the situation called for it. The windows were just low enough he could get a look inside. Pews were lined in two columns facing a pulpit with a large frame of some kind behind it. Atop the frame was a blackened elk skull with the biggest spread of antlers he'd ever seen. Grimluk didn't really keep up with any of the gods but even still, the skull seemed a strange sight.

He moved back around to the corner and watched for signs of life once more, noting the absence of the birdsong. Wood creaked loudly, alerting him to movement. Coming down the ramp of the house, with an obvious limp, was a person that, from a glance, was taller than Grimluk by a few feet. They looked like a human man but the features were almost goatish, with a long face and large ears that seemed halfling in their shape, round with soft points. They wore a beard that curtained their chin but from the side, Grimluk could see there was little chin to speak of. Their clothes consisted of trousers, a shirt, a vest, and heavy boots, all on the verge of tattered and threadbare. Their hair was wild and shaggy, skin tan and veiny, with several veins prominent around the eyes. They stopped in front of the door to the house.

"Grandfather," the giant said, their voice bassy and resonant in a way that felt wholly strange even to Grimluk's orcish ears. "Are you soon to be ready? It will be time to start shortly."

"Almost, m'boy," came the reply from behind the screen door. "Almost. We must pray first. Join me."

"Yes, Grandfather," the giant said, stooping through the doorway.

"Shit," Grimluk muttered. As quickly and quietly as he could, he slipped away, retracing his path. Once he was back down the hill, he started running. He'd let time get away from him.

As he neared town again, he slowed, moving more deliberately but swiftly. He cut around toward the road and slipped out of the woods, making his way back into town. Grimluk saw very few townsfolk as he headed back to the hotel. Most likely, they were handling the final preparations down in the tent.

He reached the Resting Rooster quickly. Sheriff Ziskind called after him as he began to open the hotel door. "Was just comin' to get the lot of ya. You didn't spoil any surprises, did ya?"

Grimluk turned, holding the door open. "Reckon not. Just went for a walk. Legs get restless if I sit too long."

She gave a laugh as she entered the hotel. "Had a cousin like that. Ended up wandering into a monster's nest because of it. Hopefully you tend to have better luck."

"Mostly," Grimluk replied with a nod.

A chuckle escaped her at that. The two of them continued on to find the other outsiders. The twins were in the sitting room, reading. Silvers had a copy of a J.H. Tobin's Practical Guide and Compendium of Spirits and Manifestations, something Grimluk was passingly familiar with. It contained information on the many types of spirits, along with speculations on the nature of ghosts and other such topics. He was pretty sure that Vatris, the loremaster back in Hunter's Hollow, had a copy. Bess was reading a beat up penny dreadful with a redheaded elf on the cover.

"We'll be starting soon," the sheriff informed them. "Are you both prepared?"

Setting aside their books, the twins looked up and nodded their heads. Sheriff Ziskind smiled and walked off to find Kruger and Imogen. Grimluk opted to stay behind, a twinge of curiosity overcoming him.

"Would you mind if I take a look at that for a moment?" he asked, moving toward Silvers.

They seemed to think it over for a moment before handing it over. "Please be gentle."

He took it gingerly and flipped through. The first section appeared to be all about the various types of elemental spirits, with different grades based on their temperament and power. He flipped through some more, passing through dozens of spirits until one caught his eye. Mylings. He'd dealt with some last summer. They were like ghosts, but tainted by demonic influence, literal pieces of the souls of those who'd been sacrificed unwillingly to a demon. One of them had even managed to change into a spirit of vengeance.

He held the book out, open for Silvers to see. "You see many of these?"

They looked over the entry. "No, sai, just a couple of them ever."

Grimluk nodded. "Reckon the demon hunters are doin' somethin' right then."

The elf studied him for a moment. "Some of them. We have met others who were little more than thugs."

It was Grimluk's turn to frown. He wanted to speak up. Even wanted to give the twins an update on mylings, but he still wasn't sure who was and wasn't with the cult. The twins felt too obvious, but, if he was wrong, it would be bad. He merely nodded. He flipped through the book some more as the three of them waited. If he'd had the time, it might be interesting to do some research but, for the most part, his knife or a bag of salt took care of any wayward spirits he came across, if they were hostile.

Silvers was still studying him as he read. He offered a smile before handing the book back. "Much obliged."

They took it with a grateful nod and a small smile. "You are welcome, sai. Why do you hide what you are?"

Brows furrowing, Grimluk started to answer but Sheriff Ziskind returned with Imogen and Kruger in tow.

"Are y'all ready?" the sheriff asked once more. Everyone affirmed their preparation. "Good, good. I'm so excited. Now, not to worry about Dex. I was right on the money about him. Seein' as how this was to be his third attempt, we decided to honor him by makin' him a central part of this year's festival. He was very excited, I tell ya what. Come on, then!"

Sheriff Ziskind led them down main street toward the town square and the festival tent awaiting them. There were banners and signs declaring this the 150th Annual Founders Festival, with the huge white canvas tent behind it all. Yellow and red ribbons were tied to everything and there was even a modest band —a few brass instruments, woodwinds, and a drummer—that started playing as they all arrived. The whole town, some two hundred or so humans, were standing to either side of the street, clapping and cheering as the band played, with anyone who wasn't on the road standing in the tent, where Grimluk could see a small stage and dozens of tables covered in all sorts of foods. The tables were all mismatched, likely the personal tables of nearly everyone there.

Grimluk looked at his companions. Kruger was eating up the attention, making a big show of it. Imogen remained composed and quiet but had a satisfied smile on her face. The twins, however, showed no sign of their feelings. They merely nodded at people as they passed. Grimluk did the same, the paranoia that came from dealing with cult-infested towns snaking through him. They all looked so happy and excited. He was sure they were but not all of them for altruistic reasons.

Maybe none of them.

So he nodded and touched the brim of his hat, not bothering to try and smile. He was an orc. No one expected smiles from him anyways. Some people maybe didn't want them, either. As he looked around at the smiling faces, he realized an unsettling fact: he did not see any children. He saw young adults in the band, folks who might be just entering adulthood or already into it, but there were no small children. He kept the shock from his face and carried on.

Looking every bit like a parade leader, the sheriff led them into the tent, stepping aside to allow them to follow. The band died down, holding one last note while the drummer rattled off a line underneath. "You may sit where you like, though Elder Whateley would prefer you to be up near the stage," Sheriff Ziskind informed them.

Grimluk followed the others as they made their way to the front. The tent air smelled like the gods themselves had cooked their feast. A huge variety of produce filled the tables, along with pies likely both sweet and savory. Likewise, there were a variety of meats as well. Roast chickens, one or two split hogs off on their own, and what Grimluk guessed was a side of beef with a lone plate next to it filled with the liver. The last time he'd seen this much food had been Gwen's adoption celebration. Mistrust or not, the smells set his mouth to watering quickly.

He took a seat at one of the tables near the stage but not directly next to it. The twins joined Grimluk while Kruger and Imogen each took a seat at a separate table in the front. Once they were seated, the town joined them, filling the tables rapidly. Once everyone settled, silence fell over the tent.

A slit opened up behind the stage and in stepped the huge man Grimluk had seen earlier. Behind him followed a squat, ugly fellow whose face was knotted and craggy, with a noticeable lack of a chin. His hair was white, as was his short but unkempt beard. He wore mostly white, faded and dirty with age. Trousers, shirt, waistcoat, with a pair of thick boots.

"Mother," the giant rumbled, prompting a small slip of a woman to step forward as Elder took to the stage. She was an albino, just as clearly as her son was huge. She stepped up behind him, wearing an old dress. Her teeth were noticeably crooked, even as she stood with her head down. Like her son and the old man, her chin was almost non-existent. Her hair was braided, laying across the front of her shoulder.

Unsurprisingly for the dilapidated town, she lacked the spectacles commonly needed for those born with albinism. Grimluk couldn't help but wonder how the frail-looking woman had given birth to her massive son. That thought paled when she looked up, though. There was a level of sorrow swimming in her pinkish eyes that surprised him. Did she know what was happening?

"Welcome friends, and especially you, Outsiders,"

the old man began, casting his gaze out. His voice was gruff, hoarse, and seemed to match his face. "My name is John Whateley. Folks call me Elder. This here is my grandson, Wilbur, and this is his mother, Lavinia. We gather together tonight to celebrate. We celebrate the very notions of valor and heroism. To honor those with such a spirit."

Elder's right eye, a clear, pale blue, was not nearly as hidden behind the gnarled features of his face and shown with a surprising intensity as he spoke. He clasped his hands behind his back and paced the stage.

"It was some near two hunnert years past that my ancestor found your town. Back then, the town hadn't yet blossomed. And friends, it would not have ever blossomed had ol' Jeremiah Whateley not stumbled upon you in your hour of need." A rabble of agreement filled the tent at that. Elder held his hands up as a call for silence. "Indeed, no sooner had Jeremiah set foot on the soil of Dunvich, he discovered a demon had set upon your young town. A powerful creature full of hate and rage. Snarling, eyes burning with hunger, maw dripping."

Whateley paused at that, seemingly letting the image hang in the air. His pale eye scanned the tent slowly. Grimluk looked around as well. All but he and the other outsiders were looking upon the Whateley patriarch with something akin to religious fervor, a sight Grimluk rarely saw outside of cults.

Elder Whateley continued on. "And though the beast, foul creature that it was, hated all, it had a special hatred for non-humans. Indeed, friends, Dunvich was once shared among elves and humans and those who sought to join them. Jeremiah was one such person and knew he had the strength to stop the demon's rampage.

"Jeremiah was no wizard, but nonetheless found himself blessed with power. The Elder Gods themselves saw fit to equip him for just that day. And ready he was. Jeremiah surged forward, crying out for the beast to step forth. When the two confronted each other, Jeremiah said a prayer to the gods."

"O Ancestors! O gods past!" The whole town spoke as one, surprising Grimluk with its intensity. "I humbly ask you to give power to your servant! To strengthen me as I right the wrongs of this place! I ask you, the Great and Old Ones, to bring order!"

Shivers ran down Grimluk's spine at the invoking of the Great Old Ones. If there'd been any lingering doubts about what he'd found, that had shattered it. The Great Old Ones were demons older than anything else mortals knew. Beings like the mother of demons, Shub-Niggurath, powerful in ways that compared them to the gods themselves. This was no random group of cultists who'd stumbled upon a demon.

"At that, Jeremiah tore open a portal behind the beast," Elder continued, prompting the crowd to speak again.

"I offer unto you a sacrifice! Hear the call of blood as it cries out to you!" The crowd finished, raw emotion evident on their faces. Tears flowed among them, while others looked to the sky. Even Grimluk's fellow guests of honor could hardly hide their surprise at the display.

It was the whole town, then. Even if they didn't know it.

"And the gods did answer Jeremiah! As the demon rushed toward him, eager to claim his life, to snap my ancestor's throat between its mighty jaws, power filled Jeremiah's body and rushed out of him in a purifying force of order. The creature was no match for Jeremiah and found itself hurtling through the portal, back to the Abyss where it belonged.

"A year later, with safety and prosperity growing in Dunvich, the good folks of this town decided it was high time they honor Jeremiah. But ol' Jeremiah only did what was right and honorable. And so he proposed that we all honor those like him. Together. And here we are once more, lookin' to honor those who would emulate Jeremiah Whateley."

Every eye in the tent turned to face Grimluk and the others. Elder Whateley looked among them, seeming to take their measure each as he did. "So, tonight, friends, we feast. We feast as the survivors once feasted, tasting life anew after Death came so close to claiming them. For tomorrow night, danger will once again descend upon Dunvich and only one person can stop it. Only one person among you has that iron core to do the right thing. Jeremiah only did what the gods made him for, but mayhaps your gods made you for honor and glory. Only time will tell."

The townsfolk all banged their fists twice in unison.

"The sun sets now. Let your lanterns shine bright, friends. And let the food nourish your bodies. So we all pray."

"So we pray," the crowd replied.

Moments later, flames began erupting around the wicks of the lanterns while food started moving around the tent as the townsfolk served the outsiders, carrying dishes to and from their resting places. As the lantern in front of Grimluk flickered to life, a massive shadow spread out across him. The twins' eyes got wide before the shadow faded and a bone-white moth flitted up toward Grimluk's face. He shooed it away just before someone set down a wonderfully prepared beef liver in front of him. He looked up but the person was already heading back where they'd come from. As Grimluk turned back again, the Silvers and Bess were looking at each other strangely.

"You two all right?" he asked.

"Y-yes...yes," Bess answered. "We...thought we felt something. It's gone now."

"What was it?"

"We are not rightly sure, sai," Silvers replied. "It was a strange power, though. Very strange."

A grunt was all Grimluk could think to reply with. He'd felt nothing, though that wasn't out of the ordinary. Sometimes he missed things. It didn't surprise him if he had. The story and the prayer had been startling, to say the least, and he didn't have the sensitivity of a spirit caller.

The twins seemed to settle down quickly enough, though, and more food soon arrived for them. Once the outsiders had all been served, the rest of the town settled in as well and soon the tent was filled with the sounds of revelry and dishware clinking and clanking.

Grimluk ate deliberately. He didn't know if this feast would contain poison or maybe some other kind of additive for the cult's purposes. Hallucinogens and the like could potentially be used to fuel fear and hostility, or even make minds supple to the effects of indoctrination or control. Of course, there was outright magic as well. Psychic domination wasn't out of the question.

The poison worried Grimluk more. His mind was trained to handle what drugs might do to him and shielded from any mental attacks. Poison was another matter entirely. If they wanted to put the five of them down long enough for ritual use, his orcish constitution could mean they'd overcompensate, possibly killing him.

Unfortunately, he had no training with poisons.

At least it's good, he thought, chewing the beef liver and a few slices of radish. If he ended up poisoned, at least it'd taste good on the way down.

The twins picked gingerly at the meat offered to them, focusing more on the fruits and vegetables. Kruger, as expected, was continuing to devour the pleasure of it all. Imogen seemed to be enjoying her meal in quiet contemplation with that same pleased smile on her face.

At some point, the outsiders were served dessert. All five of them received a slice of apple pie. Grimluk had to admit, it looked as good as something his father would have made. That did nothing to help the spike of paranoia that lanced his mind when he remembered the dryad's apples. This was part of the trap then. And he had to take the bait. He took a bite. It was amazing. He had no idea what these apples would do to them, but he imagined they'd know sooner rather than later.

As the feast neared its end, no strangeness seemed to be bubbling in his body. Yet. The others seemed relatively normal as well, except for Kruger, who was entirely drunk and singing along with whatever the band would play for him. Grimluk declined any further offers for food and just sat quietly, observing the tent. Despite what the sheriff said, he saw no sign of Dex. Which at least meant that Dex had been a single entity.

Grimluk spotted the tall Whateley man staring at him. He nodded, hoping to keep up polite airs but the man gave no reaction. Past experience made him wonder if the man had ever seen an orc before. Stares weren't uncommon and Grimluk had learned to stare back without shame of what he was. The longer he looked at the Whateley man, however, the more he noticed the strangeness of his build. Especially his eyes. The pupils were too wide for a human's, almost like that of a goat. Elder Whateley stood, dragging the goatish man's attention away as he stepped onto the stage once more.

"My friends," he began, the crowd quieting down immediately. "Our feast is nearly finished. I hope you found it to your liking. I pray that it strengthened you as it did the survivors all those years ago. As it did Jeremiah Whateley. Soon, we shall rest, and you, Outsiders, should rest well. Tomorrow, you will prepare yourselves for the eve's challenges."

Kruger hollered at that, prompting a momentary sneer to tug Elder's grizzled cheek. Elder continued. "Tomorrow evenin', the sheriff will retrieve you and set you on your task. We will ask you to remain in the hotel as we finish the last of the preparations. This year should prove to be one to remember!"

Not long after Elder finished his speech, Sheriff Ziskind gathered the five of them together once more and led them back to the hotel amid music and fan-fare. It all rang extremely hollow in his ears. Back in his room, Grimluk locked the door and retrieved a brass tube from his inner coat pocket. A twist revealed the chalk within. He laid down demon traps on the door and the windows and even left one on the mirror. Once satisfied, he took the demon trap blanket and settled into bed under it.

Elder Whateley wanted them prepared? He'd be prepared.

ASHE ARMSTRONG

Chapter 8

The forest was flooded with darkness. It wasn't just that it was nighttime. Dimly, Grimluk was aware of that. It wasn't just that it was shadows. He was aware of that, too. No, it was like it clung to the trees. Pulsing veins of shadow wrapped around everything he could see.

He was running. He hadn't realized it at first, but he was running as fast as he could. His heart pounded. It made the shadows dance in his eyes. Made the world bob around with the pressure of it.

He was running and he didn't know where to. He wasn't even sure why, just that he had to run. If he didn't, something would happen. He didn't know what. He didn't even know if it was bad or not. It felt like it was probably bad but he couldn't know.

He ran.

Something was there. It was far away. Was he running from it? What was it? Where was he, for that matter?

The darkness flashed away for a moment and Grimluk saw the light of the full moon before the darkness rushed back in to claim everything once more. The strangeness of it transfixed him. His pace began to slow. Where was he?

Moonlight again. Trees were passing him. The darkness was trying to return. He could feel it pushing against him. Where was he? Voices came to him before the darkness rushed in again. He ran.

The darkness was thin now. He knew it. He pushed back against it, gathering his will. Where was he? He was in the woods. The moonlight appeared again, now mingled with firelight. There was a stone table in front of him. Voices rushed in again. The words were faded, hollow, but forceful.

The darkness swallowed him once more. He fought it this time. Didn't just push back. He felt the muscles in his arm twitch. He raised his hand to look at it. The muscles twitched but it wasn't his arm. He pushed harder. The crown of his skull burned and then the light burst into clarity. He was standing in front of a stone table as someone spoke.

"…break through again. He knows where They have trod earth's fields, and where They still tread them, and why no one can behold Them as They tread. We beseech thee now, O Opener of the Way! Guide use as we set forth upon this journey, O Lord, as we serve you! Guide your children that the world may know purity once more!"

His heart was pounding and he wanted to bolt, but he forced himself to stay still. The other outsiders were there with him, statuesque and staring with glassy eyes. Up behind the table was a massive stone owl. The voice was coming from there. He dared not look at the chanting crowd around them. He couldn't know how many were there without giving away the truth but he knew they were there. And the smell from the forest tried to bowl him over. It was only through sheer force of will that he didn't react to it as strong as it was in this place.

The voice shifted from the Shared Tongue into a language Grimluk vaguely knew but did not understand. It was, to his reckoning, difficult to speak and uncomfortable to hear. It sounded like a jumble of consonants, like the very sound of it was made up of angular things trying to force their way into your ears. The language of demons was not meant for mortal mouths. He wanted to scream and fight.

"Ia! Ia! Rundyyk fhtagn!" came the stone owl, finally finishing the incantation.

"Ia! Ia! Rundyyk fhtagn!" echoed the people surrounding them.

Grimluk still wasn't sure how many there were but he knew it was no less than two dozen. Maybe three. That meant the cult was likely everyone around him.

"Return our celebrated guests now. Our master is pleased. The ceremony is complete. The hunt begins soon."

The sheriff, Raimi, and the massive Whateley man gathered the five of them together and started herding them back to town. Grimluk did his best to follow suit without being noticed. It seemed to work, as far as he could tell. He shambled his way back with the others, passing the Whateley house and the temple along the way before heading down the hill.

A little while later, they crossed back into town. A strange feeling settled on Grimluk, his guts gurgling as it happened. Flashes of the shadow veins peppered his vision but it didn't feel like it was trying to swallow him again. His instincts said to rub his eyes but he resisted. Sheriff Ziskind directed them wordlessly back into the hotel with Raimi walking ahead of them. The Whateley man stopped in the street as they ascended the porch to enter the hotel.

That was when Grimluk realized the smell from the forest was coming from Whateley himself.

Whateley stomped into the hotel after them. "You have heeded the call of our master. Now, return to your rooms and get back in bed."

Almost in unison, the others began heading for their rooms. Grimluk followed quickly. They all climbed the stairs together and then separated. Grimluk slipped into his room. The shadows flashed in his vision again. Behind his door, he rubbed at his eyes. Of course, it didn't help but it made him feel a little better. Carefully, he laid his ear against the door. Faintly, he could hear the sheriff and the Whateley man speaking.

The shadows swallowed the room, while red lightning flashed. Grimluk's instincts screamed at him. He turned in time to see something leap at him from the far ceiling corner. The pulsing shadows and the lightning disappeared just as it was about to slam into him.

"What the fuck?" he muttered. Warily, he slid his boots off and climbed back into bed. He laid down, pulling the demon trap blanket back over his body. After seeing all of them at what he assumed was an altar, Grimluk felt confident the other four were who they said they were. He needed to warn them tomorrow. Something was affecting him, too.

He still couldn't shake the sense of fear building inside him.

Power welled up with the ancient words. Elder Whateley stood inside the stone owl, a thing designed to channel the magic needed for the ritual, speaking the incantation. The words were difficult. The biology was wrong but it wasn't impossible to learn. His father had trained him well, all those years ago.

He had done the ritual for decades. The words were reflexive at this point. The feeling of the growing power building up in the statue, swirling around the clearing and the stone table below, was as familiar to him as his own skin. Something felt off this time. He could feel a strangeness to the gathering energy but was unsure of what it was. He peered out the hollow eyes of the statue, down at the table. The five sacrifices stood as they were supposed to. Even the orc was behaving as he should. Wilbur looked up and met his gaze.

"I feel it, too," came the boy's voice in his mind.

Elder continued with the incantation. The sacrifices would experience the effects of the ritual, touching his master's realm until he found them and took them for the Hunt. They wouldn't be able to speak of it without provocation, forgetting it after it happened. Rundyyk liked it that way. The momentary bursts of fear that led the god to them. His realm was a reflection of this one but changed. It was, after all, a god's realm. It functioned more like a dream. Distances didn't match, being farther and shorter in places. The buildings could shift under your feet without realizing it, if you weren't one of the Chosen. The

Whateleys had been chosen. Elder could walk his lord's realm just as sure as he could the mortal one.

He finished the ritual, calling forth Rundyyk's name. The faithful answered back. The power that had built up in the statue coiled tightly and then released, spreading out in a wave Elder knew only he could feel. Perhaps Wilbur as well. Working in the owl made you more sensitive to the magics. The magic cut through Rundyyk's sacrifices and then settled into the table. When the time for the table came, blood would tear a hole between the realms, ready to ferry whoever managed to avoid his master into the Hunt. Escape was impossible after that. The Hunt would endure until either allegiance was sworn or blood was spilled. The portal would remain open until the Hunt finished, to allow Elder and the others to move as they needed. It happened rarely, but occasionally, the hunt went long.

But once Wilbur's brother came home, the path to Rundyyk's realm would remain open permanently. An auspicious beginning, to be sure. The time was so close. So close.

Elder nodded to Wilbur and instructed him and the sheriff to take their guests back to the hotel. The woman down there would replace the harpy if she kept doing her job so well. In time, maybe she would prove stronger, as well. Elder made his way from out of the owl, joints popping as he descended the tight little staircase. If it was time—if everything was coming together as he hoped—perhaps he would receive a new body for all his hard work.

Perhaps that was the strangeness he felt in the magic. Perhaps Winston would be coming home finally. Ten long years they'd waited. Perhaps the stars were finally right. What a glorious time to be alive. His grandsons reunited. The tides of change would wash over this world. The false gods would be driven away and the right and proper functions of Arkod would return.

Tears welled up in Elder Whateley's eyes as he pictured it.

Grimluk's rest had been filled with disturbing dreams, all malformed and shifting. At one point, he woke to the sight of a wild and unkempt elf amid the world-swallowing shadows and red lightning. Despite their appearance, the elf made no aggressive move. When he finally woke for good around midmorning, he set about erasing the demon traps. No sense leaving evidence.

Breakfast was a mess of leftover food from the feast. He found the twins looking out of sorts as he sat down to join them. "Bad dreams?" he asked.

They turned one at a time to focus on him, brows knit as they did. "Yes," Silvers answered, with Bess following, "though we can't quite recall them."

Grimluk nodded as he tore into his breakfast. If Kruger and Imogen reported the same, it would go a long way to settling his suspicions. Then, he'd just need to lay out what was happening to them and hope he could either get them to leave town or just find somewhere to hole up.

After breakfast, Grimluk refilled his waterskins and then kept to his room to make his preparations.

He took stock of his supplies first. Flashes of darkness and lightning interrupted him from time to time. He shook it off and continued.

He was still low on food but there was enough leftover from the feast, he could make use of that. His knife and hatchet were set aside for sharpening. Likewise, he set his revolver aside for cleaning. He had plenty of chalk, salve, and bandages. The loops of his gun belt—forty all together—were half full. He counted another twelve rounds left total after double-checking his bullet pouch. He slipped those last rounds into loops. Thirty-two rounds on the belt with six in the chamber.

The day passed slowly. By noon, he'd taken his blades to a whetstone until he was satisfied with their edges. For good measure, Grimluk also sharpened his pen knife. An hour after that, his gun had been cleaned and oiled, and the holster had a fresh coat of oil applied to it as well.

He was ready.

Grimluk's eagerness to end the cult and move on gnawed at him. Instead of staying caged in his room, he went back to the parlor and found the twins reading again. Thumping steps called out behind him and he turned to see Kruger stumbling down the stairs, very clearly hungover. He headed for the dining room without a word.

The sun shone brightly, filling the parlor with light. Grimluk stood in front of one of the windows looking out into Dunvich, throat rumbling as he took in the sight of what now appeared to be a ghost town.

"Penny for your thoughts?" came the twins'

voices behind him.

He pushed his hat up as he half-turned toward them. "Reckon this all just feels a bit too good to be true."

"Perhaps, sai, but such contests aren't unheard of," replied Silvers.

"There were once physical contests held between nation states in what is now the country of Grella," Bess offered. "They still continue the traditions."

"Hm," Grimluk replied with a nod. "Makes sense. Those have prizes, too?"

"A variety, as I recall."

"Hm," he replied again as he looked out the window. He needed to warn them all. It would be simplest if he just came out with it but the paranoia gnawed at him. His heart was still beating heavy. He didn't want them to panic, either. Demons made people panic.

Bess was studying him. "What is it you're not saying?"

He looked at them, brows furrowing before looking at the window once more. He could feign ignorance. Speak to paranoia. It could keep them wary at the very least.

"You are still hiding, aren't you?" Silvers asked. "You suspect demons."

They knew what he was. Cloud cover blanketed the town for a few moments as he thought on that. He nodded finally, arms crossing as he did. "How did you know?"

"It was a guess, at first," Bess replied. "We've seen other demon hunters. One of them had teeth on his hat band as well."

"And you tried hard to avoid details about yourself," Silvers added.

He grunted at that. The twins were whip smart and paid attention. Imogen entered the parlor a moment later, nodding a greeting as all eyes turned to her. Her eyes looked a touch on the bleary side. "Meeting?" she asked.

"In a manner of speaking," Grimluk replied, touching the brim of his hat.

"He's worried everything isn't what it seems," Bess offered.

"I see," Imogen replied. "It's odd. Creepy. What would be wrong?"

Grimluk looked Imogen over. "A question, first. You have bad dreams all night?"

She frowned at that. "How did you know?"

"Kruger?" he called. "Join us, if you would. Somethin' needs discussin'."

The trapper staggered into the parlor with a plate of food and a whole pot of coffee before plopping down in a free chair. Imogen sat down in its companion, both shabby, high backed velvet chairs. Kruger grunted and sucked down a fair bit of coffee.

"You have any strange dreams last night?" Grimluk asked.

"Cheese dreams," was his weary reply.

"They weren't food related. We all had them."

It took the man a few moments to process what he'd heard before he looked up at them all with confusion. "The fuck you on about?"

With a deep sigh, Grimluk appraised them. "I'm a demon hunter. Followed a demon knight here. Ended up killin' it. Found a corrupted dryad, had to kill it, too."

"Trollshit," Kruger replied.

Imogen looked at him. "Say true, sai?"

"I do."

"Trollshit," Kruger repeated.

"You dreamed of a dark forest. You were runnin'. You had to run and you didn't know why but you had to. Am I correct?"

The two humans stared at him, slackjawed in surprise. Imogen finally spoke up. "How did you know?"

"We all had the same dream. I managed to wake myself in the middle of it all. We were surrounded by a fair portion of the town around a stone table while someone recited a ritual incantation. I couldn't understand most of it while I fought off the dream."

"...trollshit," Kruger said for the third time, much softer now.

Grimluk continued. "They marched us back and that darkness kept flashin' around everything. Red lightning, too." The faces looking back at him were pale and confused.

"I thought it was just the drink," Kruger muttered through some ham.

"Nerves," Imogen added. "Thought it were nerves."

Darkness swallowed the room, lit by soft flashes of the red lightning. The other four looked at Grimluk, eyes wide. Uncomfortable silence settled over the room, save for Kruger's slow chewing. Grimluk tried to keep himself from pacing back and forth. He hated these kinds of situations. He could potentially just go out and do his job, but it would be too obvious when he was coming. And he had four people to protect and no backup.

As long as the cult wasn't expecting him, and he played his part, he could make an easier time of it. The easier things went, the less likely people were to get hurt and the quicker he could resolve things. Though with two of their number dead, he doubted very much they wouldn't be waiting on him. The worry of it prickled him, fraying his nerves.

"What happened to Dex?" Silvers asked eventually.

"Caught him in my room two nights ago. He attacked me. Killed him."

"Why?" Imogen asked. "He was a halfling. Small, weak. You are not."

"He wasn't. He wasn't a demon, but he wasn't mortal either. He was with them."

"They lied to us?"

"Been lyin' from before you even arrived. It's a cult town. Maybe for a long time, too."

"What," Kruger began, "and I cannot stress this enough—the fuck?"

"I was hopin' to be able to work around you but after last night, I reckon that ain't an option now."

"So what do we do?" the twins asked.

"I'm hopin' you'll trust me, listen to me, work with me." He looked at them gravely. "I'm not sure how this'll go, but I'll do my best to see you through it."

"What should we do?" Imogen asked.

"Get your heads on straight. Don't let the visions spook you. Follow my lead if you can. They're probably expecting me but for now, I'll keep playin' my part. You do the same."

With the weight of the situation settling on them all, they nodded and silence descended once more, punctuated by food, drink, and the flutter of pages from the twins. The five of them waited patiently, busying themselves with their own preparations. The twins prayed. Kruger retrieved a coach gun from his room, along with a revolver. Imogen, likewise, retrieved her own weapon from her room and the two of them set about cleaning them.

When the clock struck five, Sheriff Ziskind appeared for them. Her clothes were all freshly washed. Her leather boots shined in the evening light, as did her badge. She looked them all over, a smile across her face, before she spoke.

"Is everyone ready?" she asked. They all affirmed, Kruger a little more aggressively so now that he was full of coffee and food. "Excellent. These are for each of you." She gave them each an envelope with a large, wax seal and their name on it.

"The fuck are these?" Kruger asked.

"The wax is enchanted," the sheriff began. "You'll each have to go in separate directions and once you're far enough to be alone, the seal will release and you'll find your instructions within."

"Yeah, all right," Kruger replied, looking uneasily at the others.

"I ask that you give me a few minutes to leave before you follow suit. Any questions?"

"What do we do when we finish our task?" came Kruger.

"It's all in the envelope," Sheriff Ziskind replied with a nod.

"Why do we each have an envelope?" the twins

asked.

"I'm sorry, I thought it was clear that this is an individual effort. You will have to separate and only one of you can succeed at this."

Bess and Silvers frowned and sighed in unison.

When no one else spoke up, the sheriff began to leave, stopping in the open door a moment. "Good luck to you all. Make us proud!"

They waited the few minutes as asked, the other four looking at Grimluk expectantly. He mouthed, "Play your part," before finally stepping out the door and into the darkening evening of Dunvich. It was clear that there really was no one left in town, a fact that cast an uneasiness with its presence. Empty towns never heralded good things in Grimluk's experience, but this wasn't news. Especially with how many had been at the altar.

With only a nod, Kruger and Imogen took off toward opposite ends of main street. The twins hugged each other before separating, moving forward and away from each other in a similar path as Grimluk had taken the day before. That just left him. He circled around the hotel and headed up the hill behind it. He wanted to get a look at the area if he could.

At the top of the hill, most of the area around Dunvich was visible, albeit covered in trees. He could make out the farms that dotted the area. Darkness filled his vision, however, a howling gust of wind accompanying the lingering darkness. The wild elf he'd seen before was nearby again. A snapping sound near his hand drew his attention and the darkness receded. The wax seal on the envelope was melting. He shook some of it free and opened it.

"We know what you seek," it began, "If you are to win your honor and glory, seek the wizened owl beyond the temple. But be warned, your task is great and requires cunning. You must survive being hunted by the other Outsiders by any means necessary. They know what you really are now. The truth of you draws nigh. Arrive at the grove behind Whateley manor and the prize shall be yours."

"Well, shit," Grimluk muttered.

CHAPTER 9

As darkness swallowed the world once more, Grimluk looked down into the town. The lightning flashed rapidly, furiously bright, revealing the world below. It lasted long enough that he could make out shapes prowling around the buildings. When the fading light of the evening returned, he looked around a second time, hoping to catch sight of the others. Imogen and Kruger were heading back into town. He saw nothing of the twins. If they gathered together, the three of them could find them if they weren't heading back already. Throat rumbling in thought, he headed back down the hill.

The natural shadows of the mortal realm were claiming the town as he made his way back to main-street. He arrived closer to Imogen, who started to draw on him as he appeared until she realized it was him.

"Easy, partner," he said, waiting for her to relax before approaching.

"Sorry, sai."

"Nerves are frayin'. That's understandable. Damn understandable."

"Just a little shaky," she said.

He grunted in agreement. "Saw Kruger headed this way from the hill. Reckon your letters said to chase me down. Would I be correct?"

Imogen grunted her own agreement. "Yours?"

"Survive bein' hunted."

She nodded. "Twins?"

"If things were a little more normal, I'd split us up, you and Kruger or one of you with me and we find 'em. As it stands now," he turned, spotting the approaching trapper, "splittin' up ain't so wise."

Grimluk waved Kruger over just as the demonic darkness covered the world once more. The red lightning struck somewhere nearby, nearly blinding him. One of the things he'd seen from the hill stood over Imogen. It was vaguely elvenoid, grotesque in all its proportions, looking like some sort of malformed werewolf caught mid transformation. Slavering jaws opened to strike. Imogen froze, hand on the butt of her gun, jaw agape.

Without thinking about it, Grimluk slapped iron twice. Bullets ripped through the creature, sending it whirling away. A chorus of roars filled the air. The darkness lingered a little longer before fading back to normal.

Grimluk approached Imogen. "I think we—" Something slammed into his lower back, nearly knocking him over and sending him reeling.

"Kruger!" Imogen said, looking in the man's direction.

Grimluk turned to see the trapper standing there, shotgun aimed at him. He shoved Imogen away just in time. Thunder boomed with the second shot. This time, it caught Grimluk in the shoulder, with a couple of pieces of shot hitting his neck and cheek as well. The impact nearly spun him away but he'd taken a shotgun blast before and he'd been prepared for the second one.

"What the fuck you doin'?" Imogen yelled at Kruger.

"Just fuckin' die already, ya big bastard!" Kruger yelled as he breached the gun. The spent shells flew out as he slapped fresh ones into the barrels.

Grimluk didn't give him time to finish. He rushed forward in time to put one hand around the barrel of the shotgun, causing Kruger to drop one of the shells just before Grimluk ripped the scattergun free of the man's grip. Kruger yelped but didn't stop, instead pulling a knife. The blade swept toward Grimluk's throat but he just stepped forward and rammed a knee into the trapper's guts. The knife clattered to the ground, which Grimluk promptly scooped up. Kruger coughed furiously as he tried to regain his footing before he came screaming at Grimluk.

With a sigh, Grimluk grabbed the man by the throat with one hand and lifted. He was strong enough it didn't take much effort and it surprised Kruger. The man's eyes went wide and his feet kicked as he panicked.

"You gonna settle down or am I gonna have to settle you myself?" Grimluk asked. Kruger hammered on Grimluk's arm in response. "All right. Suit yourself." He flicked the knife into the dirt and then gave Kruger's shoulder a pinch. The man instantly fell limp.

"Did you kill him?" Imogen asked frantically.

With a grunt, Grimluk settled Kruger over one

shoulder. "Just put 'im to sleep. Fuck. Bird shot always itches somethin' fierce."

"How?"

"Hm?"

Imogen mimed shooting him with the breached shotgun, before snapping it back together.

"Don't rightly know. Just how it is."

"Convenient," she replied.

"Ayup. Let's find the twins. Gotta take him with us. The flashes may not take him while he's out but if they do, I reckon somethin' could take a bite out of him."

Imogen grunted.

He turned toward the woods. "Let's find the twins."

"No."

Before he could register the words, the twin barrels of Kruger's coach gun jammed into the small of Grimluk's back. The gun roared and pushed him forward with a sharp jerk that sent Kruger toppling to the ground. He didn't wait to see what else she would try, instead using the momentum of the blast to run. Gunfire followed him as he ran into the alleyway between two nearby buildings. With a grunt, he took the right corner and pressed on across the second main street. It quickly became clear that Imogen had been a well-trained peacekeeper, as bullets struck to either side of his feet. She was driving him forward. He decided, passing through another alley, to wait for Imogen. She'd be cautious, no doubt, but if he could get the drop on her, it'd put a stop to this foolishness.

Red lightning crackled in the sky just before the unholy darkness swallowed the world again. The cacophonous roars had apparently not ceased, instead growing louder. Grimluk's heart pounded in his chest. He realized how afraid he actually felt a moment later, just before two more of the bestial things rushed him from behind. Claws slashed out at him. He blocked the one closest to him with a raised forearm. The thing connected with the studded bracer Grimluk wore, a memento of a lost ally and fellow hunter. It jerked away, burned by the rune-infused magic while the other beast got through Grimluk's defenses and slashed his abdomen. It was, thankfully, shallow but blood flowed all the same.

With concentrated effort, Grimluk leapt away, pulling his gun as he did. The two beastfolk dropped, huge chunks of their heads now missing. His attention on the demons, Grimluk didn't spot Imogen rushing in from the side until she was right on him. She was fast and managed to jam her gun barrel into Grimluk's jaw.

The shot knocked his head back and sent him staggering backward. He managed to regain his footing, his whole head vibrating like he'd taken a good punch from another orc. It forced him to stand still too long though and another shot rang out. The bullet slammed into his temple and this time, he did drop.

"Can't kill ya," Imogen spit.

His ears were ringing along with his head and the rest of what she said was garbled. It'd been a long time since someone shot him in the head, much less twice. He moved sluggishly, trying his best to focus. Dimly, he was aware Imogen was rolling him over to his stomach. She grabbed his wrists and began doing something. It seemed far away until he felt the clicking of a lock on one wrist. Restraints. That got his mind going a little more. She meant to march him to the Whateleys then. And if he didn't comply, she'd likely shoot him in the head again until he did.

He took the opportunity to rest a moment, letting her work. Unless they were mithril, he could break them whenever he wanted. He very much doubted a former peacekeeper could afford mithril handcuffs. If he was wrong, it would make things more difficult, but he'd manage.

Grimluk realized the world still felt wrong just before everything returned to normal. He shook his head, trying to get it going again. "Why?" he asked.

"You lied. They had the truth of you."

"What truth?"

"You're wanted. Kidnappin', murder, theft. Bounty was in my letter."

"Trollshit."

"Save it," she hissed. "Get up."

Grimluk worked his way to his feet, facing Imogen. She had her revolver trained at his face the whole time. "What about the flashes? The demons?"

"The what?" Conflict rolled over her face. "Flashes...you said there was a ritual." The gun wavered. More lightning arced overhead as the world flushed into blackness once more. The red moonlight illuminated Imogen's face. Her eyes were wide as saucers. "No. No, you lied! You're wanted!"

The roaring ceased, replaced with a bone-chilling silence. Even the air stopped moving. A rumbling voice filled the air. "There you are."

The world returned to normal as the two of them looked at each other. Imogen's gun dipped once more, for just a moment before it rose once more toward his face. "You can't change my mind," Imogen muttered, the conflict gone now, replaced with calm assurance, her eyes strangely glassy.

The wood of the house behind the woman cracked and splintered as a massive claw pushed its way out of the wall with sudden force. The wood stretched under the claw even as it threatened to shatter before finally splitting like torn cloth and ripping away. Imogen either didn't notice or refused to notice but her eyes got huge again even as she snarled at Grimluk.

"Move!" he cried.

Lightning flashed from inside the hole and then the claw snatched Imogen and dragged her through. Grimluk flexed and shattered the handcuffs as Imogen screamed and tried to grab for him. He missed her hand, their fingertips grazing as the wood began sealing back up like nothing had happened. Patches of blackness trembled furiously where the tear had happened.

"Fuck!" Grimluk screamed, pounding on the wall.

He went back for Kruger but he was gone, too. Grimluk couldn't tell if he'd been dragged off by the demon like Imogen had or if something else had found him. For the moment, the difference didn't matter. He took a second to rest, hoping the gunshots to his head hadn't rattled his brains too badly. Gratitude for the bond to his gun crossed his mind. Blood magic meant the thing couldn't hurt him. That included the sound of the revolver. Having another gun shoved into his face and then a second shot fired in close range meant he got to take the full brunt of the sound.

As he stood there, he took the time to remove some of the lead shot embedded in his skin. Shot was frustratingly itchy compared to a slug and birdshot was occasionally more annoying to remove due to sheer numbers. The little balls didn't distort on impact in quite the same way that bullets did. They almost swept away, little trickles of blood following but drying quickly. The pieces in his cheek had almost all fallen out. The two headshots had fallen away immediately more due to the angles. The blast to his lower back would probably take some doing to get out. Besides that and his ears still ringing, he felt mostly fine. Demons always gave worse than people but Imogen's ferocity was respectable.

His heart was still pounding, though. It hadn't stopped. The fear that welled up in him felt different. It wanted to overwhelm him. For a brief second, as Imogen reached out for him, it nearly had.

He headed for the woods with a quick pace. If the twins had been turned against him as well, running could dump him into a trap. The elves seemed at least as clever as Imogen, if not more so, considering they'd figured out what he really was and he needed to be ready.

As he passed into the woods again, he stopped behind a fairly large tree for a moment and dug a fingernail behind a piece of shot he'd missed in his collarbone. It had begun to rub him the wrong way. It popped out and fell to the ground.

The demonic realm swallowed the world once again. Roars echoed from back near the houses, prompting Grimluk to get moving again. He didn't get far before a voice called his name. He ducked behind the biggest tree he could find and tried to minimize what could be seen of him. With night in full bloom now, he wouldn't have worried about it if it'd been one of the humans but the voice was one of the twins. There was no way the elves couldn't see him clearly even now.

He scanned the area quickly, his eyes having adjusted to the dark already, but saw no one. Warily, he continued on toward the creek but stopped again with another utterance of his name. "To your left," came the voice.

He turned and spotted the young elf, knelt down behind a strong oak. He couldn't tell which twin it was from where he stood. All the same, Grimluk let out a long sigh. "I'd prefer if you didn't try to take me out, too."

Hesitantly, the elf pointed something at him. "I...I can't feel Bess anymore. What did you do with them?"

"What are you talkin' about?"

They shook their head. "We have a link. Can always hear and feel each other nearby. We split up to open the envelopes, and once I'd read mine, Bess just...stopped being there. And the task, it said you had taken them and that you had murdered Dex and lied to us about it."

Though he tried to read their face in the dark, it proved fruitless. Grimluk's throat rumbled as he mulled over the elf's words. "Think about this, Silvers. How would I have gotten to them and hidden them?"

"I...I don't know. Orcs are dangerous."

"We can be but how would I have hid them from your link? Do I look like much of a magician to you?"

"No. But d—d—de—" they froze.

"What?" he prodded.

Their voice was flat when they answered. "Bounty hunters know magic."

The world returned to normal just as something gave a long howl. Grimluk's eyes narrowed. Imogen had seemed to forget some of what had happened as well. Maybe the others had had their minds messed with.

"I'm a demon hunter, remember? Most bounty hunters don't make much use of magic unless they get something enchanted."

Silvers let out a sharp hiss of pain. Grimluk started forward and made it half the distance before a dim flash lit a small barrel followed by the sound of a soft crack. Something small, like a pebble from a sling, bounced off his throat.

"Been shot with worse than a derringer tonight already," Grimluk nearly growled, more out of annoyance. "They've messed with your head. I'd bet good money that your sibling is at the Whateley place. But before we get to that, I need to make sure you're you."

"What?"

With a flip of its clasp, Grimluk pulled his knife free. "You see the symbol on this blade?"

Silvers answered, "Yes."

"Press your hand against it."

They stared at Grimluk for a long moment, large eyes wide with fear and glittering in the dim moonlight. After a moment, Silvers pressed their hand against the Elder Sign at the base of the blade. For good measure, Grimluk wrapped his fingers around the elf's hand to make sure it wasn't a trick. Satisfied at the lack of interaction, he slipped the blade back into its sheath.

"What was that about?"

"Explain on the way, come on." Grimluk pushed up and headed toward the creek once more, with Silvers following hesitantly behind. "Reckon everyone but your twin got a similar work over. The ritual probably let them get in your heads. They mostly can't get in mine; probably something in the food that got me out to that altar. Don't know what they told Kruger but Imogen said I'd lied, same as you, and said I was wanted. Mine said to survive being hunted. Do you remember the flashes of the demon's realm?"

"I–yes. How?"

"Imogen forgot it had happened even while it was happening. Did you feel anything strange before your sibling's presence vanished?"

"No, it just...it just happened. I could feel them one moment and the next, nothing. We've...we've never been sep-separated far enough for that to happen."

He grunted in reply. "Keep close. A demon took Imogen. Maybe Kruger, too. I knocked him out but maybe somethin' got him up again."

"A demon?" Another hiss of pain followed.

"Hurts to remember?"

"I know you're lying. But I know you're not lying. And that means...oh gods. Odeus, no. That means you're right. They've got Bess!"

"Just try to keep it together. Focus as best you can. A lot of fuckin' with people's minds relies on not having it pointed out."

Grimluk stopped. He could hear the creek but couldn't see it. Clouds had covered the moon, making the forest even darker. "Sometimes I'd pay good money for elven eyesight," he muttered. "Can you see the creek from here?"

"Yes. A little farther ahead."

"We go past it and up the hill to the temple. The Whateley place is connected to it and that stone table of theirs is somewhere behind it. I came up here yesterday morning after discovering an old tribal settlement nearby." As he started toward the Whateleys, he considered their plan. "You know any magic?"

"Nothing particularly useful," Silvers said cautiously. "Campfire and the like."

"You a powerful enough caller to get help from any nearby spirits?"

"Not exactly. Separately, we have little power over the spirits. We can communicate, dissuade them, but together, we can command them."

"Any weapons besides the pea shooter?" Grimluk continued, a hint of frustration in his voice.

"A pair of derringers for each of us and pen knives."

"That's somethin', at least. You've got the better eyes and ears, so try to keep a look out for anything as we go. If Kruger's up and around again, he'll have no qualms about firing as soon as he sees me. He's done it once already."

"Very well." The fear and anxiety in their voice was unmistakable.

The pair continued on in relative silence, past the longhouses and up the hill before finally coming to a stop at the treeline in front of the temple. The

Whateleys' home sat quietly, a lantern hanging next to the door. Grimluk found a big tree to hide behind and looked the place over for the second time. He motioned for Silvers to do the same. The screen door revealed an open inner door and the darkness inside the house.

After looking everything over, he whispered, "Anyone?"

"No," they whispered back. "I think it's empty."

With a nod, Grimluk hurried toward the screen door and slipped inside. Silvers followed after him, even more silent thanks to their elven grace. Even the largest elves could move like hunting cats. They could get to the altar soon enough. He wanted to see if there was anything in the house to give him the answers he needed to stop the cult once and for all.

CHAPTER 10

Grimluk grabbed the nearest lamp and brought it to life. The inside of the Whateleys' house could only be described as foul. A stench hung in the air and almost every surface Grimluk could clearly see was covered in a layer of dirt that likely could have been scraped away with a blade. Even in the dim light, he could see the patches of black that dotted the walls—some as big as his hands—all of them pulsing heavily. The walls of the room they were in were covered in bookcases filled with leather-bound tomes filmed with dust, alongside a slew of various small altars and tables filling the remaining space. The only other furniture was a writing desk and the accompanying wooden chair, so old and decrepit that it looked like it might fall apart if Grimluk breathed on it too hard. The wall to his right opened up near the back wall, leading into a second room and a back door.

A variety of things glittered in the lamplight. Statuettes of demons—or approximations and avatars—sat upon the various altars, their eyes or surfaces glinting red or yellow, sometimes purple and green. Silvers gasped at the sight of some of them as Grimluk took them all in. He'd never seen so many idols in one place before and each of them had been formed with a level of artistry that surprised him. They had been created with the kind of passion priests dedicated to their temples, not the crude, haphazard creations one would expect of such a backwoods cult.

He recognized one of them: Shub-Niggurath, the mother of all demons, was represented by a monstrous ball of limbs and appendages, raised on its hind legs showing its abdomen. Its body was a horrifying mix of genitalia that covered a large portion of the area. It looked animalistic and elvenoid all at once and drew a sneer from Grimluk.

Another statue depicted a mass of orbs that shined like grease on the surface of water. Yet another depicted a strange, scaly, winged demon with a bloated body, crouched upon a pedestal, gripped tightly under taloned feet. The head was overlarge and tentacles dangled from its face with six eyes lined each side; eyes that felt alive despite being made of some sort of green stone.

A sudden urge came upon Grimluk to smash every statuette to pieces before the demons were summoned through them. It was mostly irrational. Mostly. When he had to pull Silvers' slack-jawed gaze from the statuette sitting on the writing desk, it started to seem a more rational thought. The elf nearly jumped through the ceiling at his touch.

"Stand by the door and keep—" The world plunged into a new darkness. The lamp remained lit but now glowed an eerie blue, spilling shadows all through the room. For the first time, Grimluk could see the strange tendrils that ran down the walls, across the floor and ceiling, pulsing like blood vessels that glowed red through various slits and holes. The red cut through the blue light, refusing to mingle. It simply was. The air in the house was as still as a coffin's and just as silent.

His gaze happened upon the tentacled statuette. The tentacles were moving in gentle undulations and the eyes glowed in a color Grimluk had never seen before. Or maybe colors. A presence beckoned him to look further. He tore his eyes away and whispered, "Don't look at them," to his companion.

Eventually, the world returned to normal. He could still see the figure's head writhing ever so slightly. "Keep watch at the door," he finally finished. Silvers looked up at him, too far away for too long of a moment before nodding, seemingly returned from wherever their mind had gone.

He turned back to the writing desk. The figure on the altar had lit candles surrounding it, with some foul, coppery-smelling incense burning beneath it. A slew of various stacks of paper and another of the dusty tomes joined the altar. The book's cover held a strange symbol, curves and spirals, that seemed vaguely familiar. Grimluk started to look away from the book before realizing the familiarity: it was the same one on the banners he'd seen around town. He frowned and continued on, plucking the papers up to look through them. There were letters on official looking stationary from the office of the governor of Westlynth. Each one was short, straight to whatever its point had been. One read simply that an "experiment" had begun. Another said they had found acceptable candidates. Three letters each simply had the word "Failure" on them. All the dates listed them as having been written over the past twenty to thirty years. The last one, dated nearly fifteen years prior, read, "The first success. The key is ours now." Under that letter was a diagram Grimluk recognized. It was a summoning circle, elaborate beyond any he'd ever seen before. The next page was written in code, likely hiding the directions for the summoning from prying eyes such as his. The last page was a faded map of the town, though it was barely recognizable in its layout. Markings and notes were scribbled across it, some far less faded than others.

"What is all that?" Silvers asked.

"Trouble. Don't touch anything unless you have to," Grimluk answered, laying the letters back down and picking up the book. There was a clasp keeping it closed, with a key sitting in its keyhole. Try as he might, the key refused to move even the smallest bit. "Enchanted," he muttered, returning it as well.

Silvers turned from the door. "Someone's coming."

"How many?"

"Just one. Heavy boots."

"Come on, down the hall," Grimluk urged them, snuffing out the lamp.

The hallway went maybe six feet to the temple door, with one door on the left wall. The hallway turned right at the temple door, extending another several feet back, one last door at the end. Grimluk made for the last door as quietly as he could. As he opened it into darkness, Silvers following quickly along with him, Grimluk's sense of balance shifted. A sudden, brief but strange sensation washed over him as he closed the door, like everything had turned diagonal and he was facing the wrong side up. After the feeling passed, light slowly illuminated the door in front of him, casting his shadow over it.

"What on Arkod?" Silvers muttered dreamily.

Cautiously, he turned to survey the room. Where he expected a dark bedroom, maybe just big enough for the two of them to wait out their pursuers, he found something as big as the rest of what he'd seen, with no windows, in the shape of what looked like a massive square. The walls and floor were smooth, unpainted, untreated, solid white…something. It looked and sounded like stone under their feet. As Grimluk looked around, he realized there were no lamps, lanterns, torches, or even mystic lights. The light seemed to emanate from within the material, and was growing gently brighter still. It made the only other thing in the room besides Grimluk and Silvers unmistakable.

In the middle of the massive room, the Whateley woman, Lavinia, sat unmoving in a chair, hands folded in her lap. Her clothes remained the same as during the feast the night before. His eyes told him at once that Lavinia was both near, close enough to touch, and yet a good twenty feet as well. The look on Silvers' face seemed to indicate they'd come to the same conclusion.

When they met eyes again, he nodded toward the door and mouthed, "Anything?"

Silvers looked out at the Whateley woman for a long moment before pressing their ear against the door. They listened intently, brows furrowing as they did so. Finally, they turned, brows still very much furrowed in what Grimluk assumed was confusion. They opened their mouth several times as if to speak before sighing and shaking their head.

"What?" Grimluk whispered.

"I...couldn't hear anything," they replied. "Except..."

"Except?"

"A faint, howling wind. Just wind. And—" they put their ear to the door again, "—I...I don't know what."

"I see," Grimluk replied. He thought about what that could mean as he looked toward the Whateley woman. He glanced back at the door one more time before moving toward the lone human. It took some effort of will. Each step was a bit shaky and his guts sloshed about. He was getting both closer and farther away. A few feet away—what he thought was a few feet—from Lavinia and her chair, he was sure he was standing upside down.

Up close, he saw Lavinia's eyes were shut but moving as if in a deep sleep. With slow, deliberate steps, Grimluk walked a circle around her, studying the chair, her body language, even the floor underneath the chair. She sat straight up, despite appearing asleep, with no real tension in her body. To Grimluk's eye, she looked calm and peaceful. The floor, sensory issues aside, seemed normal, as did the chair.

Between the complete wrongness of the room, Silvers' inability to hear anything beyond the door, and Lavinia's slumbering, Grimluk wondered whether this had all been a part of their plan.

Had he blundered into a trap?

He looked up and saw his companion pressed against the door once more. They pulled back, looking at the door before pressing into it again. Before he could ask what they heard, a slender hand seized his wrist. Grimluk looked down to see the Whateley woman staring up at him with pink, pleading eyes. "Ye shouldn't've come here," she whispered. "There's no prize."

"I know," Grimluk replied. "Why are you here?"

A small sob slipped out of the woman's mouth but no other sound followed. Her jaw clenched and her grip hardened. For a moment, Grimluk thought she would spring up and climb him, but she fell back into the chair once more, slumping on herself. Her hand went slack and fell away as her chest shook with soundless sobs. Despite the sobs, her left arm lifted up and pointed toward the door.

Grimluk carefully worked his way back over to Silvers, who was still listening against the door. "What do you hear?"

"Trees. And–and fire. Little ones."

"Trees?"

The door clicked loudly, prompting a yelp from Silvers as they jumped back. Slowly, the door opened on its own, revealing a verdant tunnel speckled with the colors of fall, only made apparent by the light from the mysterious room, already fading away. A little farther beyond, Grimluk saw a row of torches.

Silvers looked at Grimluk. "What the fuck?" they muttered.

A rumble filled his throat. They were being directed. His hand fell to his hip, pushing his coat back behind the butt of his revolver. Warily, he stepped forward, out into the dirt path, with Silvers all but clinging to him as he did. The pair of them exited the white room, the odd feelings from before disappearing as he passed over the threshold.

The door closed of its own accord once they'd

passed and its lock thumped once more. A quick glance around told him they were behind the house now. The door from the kitchen greeted him, evident by the windows and the stove beyond.

Near the first torch a voice called out, deep and authoritative. "Come, friend, come. Come and receive your prize."

"Stay sharp," Grimluk said.

"Y–yeah," Silvers answered.

Pressing on, the path led them into a large clearing that Grimluk recognized immediately. Greeting the pair was the massive stone owl with flickering torches in its eyes. All around the clearing were torches burning with a glaring brightness that lit the area clearly. In the center of the clearing, surrounded by stone rings and more torches, was the massive stone table.

Standing behind the table were Bess and the towering, goatish form of Wilbur Whateley, one of his hands planted around Bess's slender neck. The elf was statuesque in their stillness.

"Bess!" Silvers called, attempting to rush forward before Grimluk stopped them.

"You've all succeeded beautifully tonight," came a voice from the stone owl. "Truly, we are blessed. And you, Klovekethrin—" the voice continued before Elder Whateley stepped out from behind Wilbur, "—you have brought the orc here. You shall be rewarded most handsomely."

The old man lifted his hands, muttering something, and applauded. More applause joined him, filling the clearing, as dozens of Dunvich's citizens stepped into the torchlight from the edge of the woods. Grimluk looked around as much as he dared, wanting to keep his attention on Wilbur. Some of the people he could see now resembled the beasts he'd fought during the shifts into the demon's realm. Their clothes were torn and tattered, their proportions distended and wrong. They weren't werewolves, the form was too human still.

The applause died down and the townsfolk closed in a little more.

"What now, old man?" Grimluk asked.

"Why are you asking a question you already know the answer to?" Elder replied. "Have we really vexed your mind so? You took down my tree and killed our knight and yet you can't discern what's next?"

"Whatever happens next, your cult ends tonight," Grimluk answered.

"Maeve was right, you are spirited. Does it please you, Lord?"

A chill whispered through Grimluk as the torches all seemed to dim for a long moment before returning to their bright burn. Grimluk felt a new presence but only dimly. It was like what he felt at the longhouses.

And when Imogen was taken.

A smile spread across Elder's gnarled face. He looked to his grandson. "You know what to do, m'boy."

Without a word, Wilbur pulled a curved, black-bladed dagger from his belt, moving it toward his elven prisoner's throat. Grimluk reacted in an instant. His revolver practically leapt out of its holster as his hands went to work. His left hand slammed into the hammer as his right squeezed the trigger. The gun barked thunder and ripped the knife from Wilbur's hand, sending it flying away somewhere behind him.

Silence rushed in, filling the spaces in between heartbeats. Instead of a cry of attack, like Grimluk expected, Wilbur slammed Bess's face into the table with one hand and then brought the other down into the back of their neck. The pop of bone was unmistakable as Wilbur pressed his fingers through the elf's neck. Silvers screamed as Wilbur ripped Bess's head away from their neck, splashing blood across the stone table.

"O Lord, accept this offering and open yourself to our gifts. We seek an audience! To bask in thine presence!" Wilbur's strange voice bellowed. "Ia! Ia! Rundyyk fhtagn!"

"Fhtagn!" repeated the crowd.

Red lightning struck the sky from the table and a monstrous cracking sound filled the air. The crowd rushed forward, slamming into Grimluk and Silvers alike with sudden, terrifying force, every face grinning or shrieking a prayer. Dunvich pushed on Grimluk as one, hundreds of human bodies overpowering his orcish might. Heart pounding with fear and desperation, he reached out into the crowd, pinching the nerve of every shoulder he could get a hold of. His mind raced as he fought them off, trying to hastily form a plan. Every time one fell from the nerve pinch, another stepped in to replace them, seemingly unending, as eventually even the faces who fell rose again to renew their efforts. He kept fighting. He'd been prepared for this possibility.

He hadn't been prepared to have the young elf with him, though, nor the claws that swiped at them both. Panic struck his heart at the sound of their screams. Grimluk caught sight of Silvers being carried away to the table. With a grunt, he hurled one of the townsfolk toward the elf, bowling over the ones carrying them. The moment of distraction cost him, though, and the townfolk surged, pressing him back before he could plant his feet again and slow the inevitable push to the table.

Silvers yelled again and several sharp pops rang out, likely the derringers they were carrying. Grimluk stopped trying to be so careful then and began swinging his fists, pistol whipping and headbutting Dunvich's citizens, rapidly clearing space around himself for a moment.

That's all it was, though; a moment. There were so many of the humans and their bestial counterparts pressing in now and he lacked the proper leverage to use their power against them like he'd been taught as an apprentice. Kruger appeared suddenly, shotgun in hand. Grimluk found himself overpowered with one sudden effort from the townsfolk and the blast of a shotgun to his chest. His feet rushed out from under him as the townsfolk lifted him up, their hands carrying him to the table.

He expected to land on the stone table but when he looked in that direction, he saw what the sacrifice had done. Rippling from unseen winds was a wound in reality, like a hole punched through cloth. Grimluk felt his body being tugged toward the portal, as if something was aiding the cultists' efforts as the crowd hurled him as one unified power, sending him through the dimensional tear.

It was membranous and slick at first. Horror filled his mind as reality itself shifted, melting and turning completely upside down and inside out. The world as he knew it twisted into something he could scarcely describe. It felt at once like he'd become untethered from all he knew and yet anchored and heavy while passing through the membrane. Time seemed to move at a crawl while the screaming winds of the void raged all around him, drowning out his very thoughts.

There were colors that reminded him of the tentacled-statue-thing's eyes, colors that physically hurt to see. There was darkness so pure that existence seemed to wink out in its embrace. And there were things in that darkness. Demons that watched him the same way he might watch a bird pass by. He felt the very essence of his body screaming. He was going to be trapped here and die. Infinity would claim Grimluk. The demons would claim him. As if the universe was answering, a massive demon that resembled a boar snapped at him, loosing an unfathomably deep and deafening squeal as he slipped past.

As suddenly as the feeling began, the membrane broke and Grimluk found himself in the air once more. He landed hard on the stone table with a grunt, disoriented and ready to puke his guts out. His head was pounding and he was covered in a sheen of ectoplasm.

Shrieks pierced the membrane as Silvers passed through it and landed on Grimluk. Gently, he pushed the screaming elf away just in time for them to roll to the edge of the table and vomit. Sobs wracked the elf while Grimluk tried to reorient himself. He rolled off the table and tried to stand but only managed to stumble back to his knees. His instincts were screaming to run. Everything in him wanted nothing more than to bolt for safety.

"Give it time, hunter," came Elder's warbling voice.

Grimluk pushed himself up and looked around, finding the cult leader standing on the table, with Wilbur crawling through after him.

"I'm sure you've guessed what's happened now," Elder continued. "Welcome to His realm."

Red lightning crashed overhead, catching Grimluk's attention as it illuminated his surroundings. The torch light burned a furious blue, and the air stank of blood and rot while a rain of dust or ash swirled in the air. The lightning flashes illuminated the dark, glowing tendrils he'd seen once already. His body still screamed at him to run as he glanced at Silvers. He could leave them. They could distract the priest and his demon.

He shoved the thought away and helped the elf up. The Whateleys made no move to stop him.

A chorus of deep howls caught his ears. More of the beast folk, probably. Death hounds, maybe. Or werewolves. Or worse. His heart thundered in his chest as he got Silvers to their feet, however shaky they still were. A scream, far away but growing closer by the second, came from the tear between worlds. The Whateleys stepped aside just as Kruger came barreling out, toppling off the table and somehow managing not to drop his shotgun.

The man vomited but stood, pointing the gun at Grimluk. "The prize is mine," Kruger slurred with anger.

"It seems I underestimated this boy's drive to succeed. How interesting," came Elder. "The time for that has passed, though. Be still and wait." Kruger's eyes glazed over and he grew still, the shotgun dropping to his side as his arms went slack.

Grimluk leapt back upon the table and swung for Wilbur, cracking the goatish man in the jaw. Instead of bone, the flesh was strangely soft and pliant. Wilbur showed no signs that an orc had just punched him, however. Up close now, the strange odor emanating from the man was nauseating. Grimluk hurled body blows that could've bruised the organs of any mortal but Wilbur's gut was spongy, like his jaw, and seemed to absorb the blows.

He simply kicked Grimluk in the chest, launching him off of the table and back onto the ground, sending motes of ash scattering. Grimluk lay still for a moment, trying to catch his breath, wondering if his sternum had been broken.

"Admirable effort, hunter, but you have lost. Now the three of you will provide entertainment and a proper sacrifice to the master." Elder turned to Kruger. "You, join them. And you may remember things properly again."

Kruger wobbled over to stand with Grimluk and Silvers, still looking dazed. The man started and he looked around in a panic, realization washing over his face as he caught Grimluk's eyes.

"It is time." Elder's voice was reverent as he walked to the other side of the table.

"Yes," came an absolutely horror-inducing voice that was low enough Grimluk could feel it as well as hear it. "It is time."

Shadows fell away like a veil from something massive as more howls filled the air. Lightning flashed, revealing glimpses of scales and fur as it stepped forward, hunched over on its hands and feet. It stood up not far from the table and let out growling laughter as clouds cleared away from the moon, great forks of lightning splitting the sky in every direction. The blood red moon shone full, illuminating the demon and the grove in its unnatural light. Lean, hard muscle shifted and twitched under the fur and scales, while the beast's long tail lashed out behind it, snapping like a whip. Six glowing red eyes flashed in Grimluk's direction, set in a head that looked like some chimeric melding of feline and lupine anatomy, its mouth too wide, dripping with what looked like blood, and filled with gleaming, jagged teeth. An array of stag's horns spread from either side of its head, framing the blood-dripping, three-pronged crown that floated just above its head.

The demon, Rundyyk, stood tall and proud as it bared its teeth at Grimluk in a predator's smile.

Chapter 11

Demons, too many to quickly count, burst from the tree line, circling around Grimluk, Silvers, and Kruger in much the same way the cultists had. There were death hounds, black as shadow, with fur, scales, and protruding bone, red eyes gleaming as their slavering jaws barked and snapped. More of the beast folk shook with the anticipation of violence, looking less like people than the ones from the other side of the portal. A warg-sized spider thing, jagged carapace and too many eyes set into an elvenoid face, crawled out from behind the stone owl, chittering and hissing.

Rundyyk let out a deep howl that sounded more like a roar, its head turned up to the full moon. The whole lot standing around them mirrored their master, filling the grove with an overwhelming din. Spiritual and mystical pressure crowded into the air like humidity before a storm. Grimluk went for the opportunity present, going for his gun to fire off the last remaining shot he had. His arm made it halfway there before the pressure in the air condensed around him, impeding his movements by sheer force. As the howling ceased, he heard the muttering of a mortal voice. The pressure grew on his hand suddenly, pushing his finger back and the gun down, causing him to fire into the ground.

"Now now, hunter, that's not very sporting," came the Whateley patriarch's voice. Grimluk glanced at the cultist. Elder's arm was outstretched toward Grimluk, a grin plastered across his face. "And we'd had such high hopes for you."

"Run!" Rundyyk roared at them, its minions chittering and laughing. "Or perish now, mortals. Keep back from them, my brethren, unless the orc tries that again."

With practiced hands, and a heart that felt like it was trying to escape from his chest, Grimluk reloaded his revolver as swiftly as he was able. There was no way he was getting through the Whateleys before the demons were on top of them. His only option was to get Silvers and Kruger away. If they could stay safe long enough, he could set traps, whittle them down.

"Come on!" he shouted at Silvers and Kruger, grabbing at them and pulling them into action. Silvers screamed at the gesture as he pulled them along with him. Kruger followed dumbly along, eyes darting back to the horde of beasts, then tripped and fell, nearly taking Grimluk with him. Once prompted, Silvers' legs pumped with panic, primal preservation instincts no doubt roaring through their veins. They tore free of Grimluk's grip, bolting like a rabbit. Kruger was on the ground screaming as Grimluk tried to get him up and running again but the man refused to budge.

"Your choice," came the demon lord's rumbling voice, "is made."

Grimluk's gun barked once more as the beasts rushed toward Kruger. Six fell to his weapon, bursting into blazing, pale green flames, screaming louder than any he'd ever heard. Kruger, voice breaking from the screams, managed to turn his shotgun toward the incoming monsters. Both barrels cried out, knocking one of the death hounds away for only a moment. Grimluk couldn't reload and fire fast enough, though, and the hound rushed in and snagged Kruger by the ankle, dragging him back toward the table. The horde crashed down onto him, teeth and claws ripping the brutish trapper to shreds with such fury that his blood was a mist in the air.

Enraged but helpless, Grimluk turned and continued on. He made it farther than he expected, heading toward the house and temple, before the sounds of the beasts caught up to him. Grimluk was doing his best to catch up to Silvers but the elf was faster, out of sight now, maybe already down the hill. "Silvers!" he called out, hoping to slow them. Imogen, Kruger, and Bess were dead. He'd failed them. He couldn't let the last one die. "Silvers!"

He pumped his legs harder. He had the endurance to run for leagues if he needed to but that was the mortal realm, where the air wasn't foul and tainted. He could tell already that his endurance would eventually fail. He needed to get a hold of Silvers and try to find someplace safe to regroup—at least, as safe as you could be, in a demon's realm.

Something heavy was gaining on him. Grimluk risked a glance behind and saw the powerful form of a death hound galloping toward him. The thing was the size of the wargs of old, big enough he could've ridden it comfortably. It's grinning jaws trailed black drool. Grimluk ran harder, passing not the temple but a mound of bones and a decayed copy of the Whateley house. If the hound pounced, he was confident he could fight it off, but its siblings would join shortly after that and he'd be on the ground, helpless. Carefully, he retrieved his knife from its sheath, heading down the hill as he got his hand on it.

Away from the hill, the hound getting closer, Grimluk pivoted, sliding a little which pulled him low while turning to face the beast. As the demon came down on him, he thrust his knife up into its jaws. The Elder Sign glowed bright, something that, like the green-flames, Grimluk had never seen happen before. The knife slid through the hound with no resistance.

The demon tumbled to the ground with a gash covering the length of its body. Grimluk turned and fired into the death hound's skull as he passed, taking up his run once more. The immediate threat was gone, though howls echoed from behind him. With still no sight of Silvers, he called out again. Hope of finding them was draining away like blood from a deep wound.

Howls reached him from all around. Cursing, he just kept running, leaping up a small hill as bolts of lightning shattered the sky. The trees were all bare and covered in the pulsing tendrils, which glittered in the red moonlight. The howls were distant now but that could change at any moment. Grimluk slid down the hill and pushed forward, recognizing the familiar shapes of the longhouses ahead. If Dunvich's buildings remained, like the Whateley house, maybe he could hole up, bottleneck the horde, and get a plan together.

If he was lucky, maybe Silvers found their way there.

Unfortunately, there was a pack of imps poking

around the longhouses. He caught two of them with one bullet, fired twice again for as many imps, sliced one more in half, and fired three more times, taking the last of the little demons out. The gunfire would tell them where he was but the imps wouldn't be able to track him or slow him down further.

As Grimluk reloaded, he realized just how low he was on ammo. Including what he'd just loaded, he already only had twenty rounds left. He slipped the revolver back in its holster. He'd have to keep it for emergencies only now. He pulled the hatchet free from his bag instead. He just needed time and space to plan. There had to be somewhere to hide.

If there was a cellar or something similar in Dunvich, maybe he could hunker down there. He could draw traps and put up wards. With any luck, he could survive a little longer and find Silvers. Grimluk leapt over the creek and headed for Dunvich.

The demon hunter fled as the pack tore into the pitiful fur trader. Looking up to his master, Elder Whateley smiled. The demon, Rundyyk, growled approvingly as lightning flashed overhead. Even despite the apples' apparent diminished effects on the orc, everything was going according to plan.

"Will he please you, Lord?" Elder asked.

"Yes," Rundyyk answered in another growl. "I have missed hunting his kind."

"It has been a while since an orc found their way here."

Rundyyk lifted its head and sniffed the air, something like ecstasy washing over its features. "When the hunt finishes, the gathered power will be enough to complete your task as well. Nyarlathotep will be pleased."

Elder nodded. "So, the Bloody Tongue has spoken?" Rundyyk merely growled its affirmation. That was enough for Elder. "What of the woman?" he asked. "And the dryad's seed? We can't grow the apples without the dryad."

"You," Rundyyk said, looking at one exceptionally large hound pacing at the edge of the tree line. The thing was covered in scales and wiry patches of midnight fur made even darker in the light of the red moon. Its long ears laid back as it looked up at its master. "Give chase to the orc. You will prove his worth. Should you fall, know your sacrifice makes the hunt that much greater."

The hound howled, eliciting replies from everything else in the pack. With little effort, the hound bounded past the trees and disappeared beyond the torchlight.

"The mortal has the smell of the deep ones on her," Rundyyk mused. "But she lacks Dagon's influence. She is mine now. If the orc has the seed, you shall have it once the hunt is finished. Patience, priest."

"As you say, my Lord. This woman, a new knight?"

A growl was all the answer he got. Elder bowed his head and turned to Wilbur. "Free yourself if you like, m'boy. You're lookin' a might uncomfortable."

Wilbur let out a sigh before he set to work

untucking his shirt and unbuttoning it. A moment later and the boy was free of it, revealing the thick, scaly hide of his torso and the yellow and black markings that covered it, along with a number of long appendages with sucker-like mouths on them. Wilbur's boots and pants followed shortly, sliding loose from the coarse fur of his legs, and freeing the rest of the appendages on his abdomen. Elder's grandson stood to his full, towering height, then, in a concerted stretch, the large eye on each of his hips blinking while the trunk-like tail lashed about.

"Thank you, grandfather."

Elder smiled at the boy. Though Wilbur was barely fifteen, his parentage showed through splendidly. "You've done very well tonight. Play with the hounds, if you like."

"Yes, grandfather," Wilbur replied before stomping off toward the pack.

Elder turned back to his master. "So, you've made the woman the offer, then, Lord? What of Ziskind?"

"I have. And Ziskind's time draws nigh."

"Excellent. Will this Mulloy woman prove as strong as Maeve?"

"She will or she will not. I have no use for weaklings."

A single gunshot echoed from the forest, prompting several of the smaller hounds to howl and race off into the trees. Elder watched the group scatter. Lightning flashed overhead, the rumble of thunder following closely behind it. Everything was going according to plan.

"Didn't feel much magic from the woman. That

ought to change once you've finished with her."

"The transformation has already begun," Rundyyk almost purred.

Elder hadn't seen it but his father had told him how Rundyyk made its knights. His lord was powerful enough to share his own essence to create a knight, not needing to install a weaker demon from the Abyss as was generally common. Once the deal was made, Rundyyk would've swallowed Imogen Mulloy whole. It would, essentially, digest her and shit her back out as something new. It felt vulgar to Elder, silliness from being a mortal, but Rundyyk was also a vulgar god. The lesser ones always were, though. Not like the Great Old Ones, so far removed from mortality.

Still, it was an honor to bear witness to the birth of a new knight. And lesser gods were still gods. They knew things. They had a power all their own. And they all served the Old Ones.

Elder lifted his head to the sky, closing his eyes and feeling the wind upon his face. The hunt, a new knight, possibly two, and word from the Tongue itself. "Fhtagn," he whispered with a shiver of joy.

Try as he might, Grimluk found no signs of Silvers as he made his way toward Dunvich. Even from the tree line, he could see the town was still crawling with the bestial cultists. Their numbers were far, far fewer than had shown up at the grove. The rest would find their way back eventually, though. For the time being, he did his best to keep low and quiet as he made his way back into town.

He followed a similar path to the one he'd taken the day before, without heading to the edge of town to feign a return. He found a dark spot and watched the movements of the cultists. Some of them seemed to be praying, hands clasped and on their knees. Some were patrolling, no doubt keeping their eyes out for him or Silvers. A few others seemed to be standing in stupors, not moving. Grimluk felt confident that that would change the moment they sensed something.

Howls echoed from somewhere in the forest. Grimluk's heart thundered at the sound. One of the vacant cultists turned its head in his direction, its mostly human face sniffing for him, trying to catch a scent. Grimluk attempted to calm himself and get in position to attack the thing if it got close. Lightning streaked the sky once more and fresh, heavy clouds rolled in to cover the moon, blanketing everything in near total darkness. The blue light of the lamps flickered, keeping the town illuminated just enough. The cultist wandered slowly toward him, the soft light of a nearby lantern glinting off the drool stretching from its mouth. Its clothes looked old at least a hundred years out of fashion, surprisingly intact despite the dirt and age.

He swallowed hard, waiting on the thing to get close so he could kill it. He focused on his breathing, waiting, watching.

The beast stopped, growled, and turned away. Grimluk watched, eyes narrowing. A roar pierced the dark, causing the lightning to lash out wildly. The sound broke his focus and he raced across the street as quietly as he could, slipping into another alleyway.

He grew wary before he even got a look at the street. Something was nearby. Cautiously, Grimluk poked his head out, even as his instincts urged him to hide, to run, to be anywhere but where he was.

Howls filled the air, one after the other, and something roared, "Where are they?" in the distance.

His heart began thundering once more. Images of his flesh being torn away by dozens of sets of jaws flashed in his mind. He pushed them away as best he could, trying to focus on the question. Where are they, it had said. They hadn't found Silvers. They were still alive. A sliver of hope sliced through the fear that was trying to choke Grimluk.

He bolted for some of the houses near the entrance to town after a long and violent series of lightning flashes. He just needed to find a cellar. Circling around back, something slammed into him, tackling him to the ground and clamping a hand over his mouth. A slender face leaned down to his, a strange glint in their eyes, while a feather dangled from their hair. It smelled like a dirty animal.

"You must be calm," they whispered in a stilted accent.

Blood raged like an overflowing river as it pounded through Grimluk's head. He bucked the stranger off of himself, ramming one knee into their ass hard enough to do the job. As fast as he could, he rolled over and got to one knee. The stranger had rolled into a crouch.

"Calm!" the voice hissed, looking over their shoulder. "The apples mark you, draw out your fear. They can smell your fear."

The sounds of the demons and cultists filled the

air, suddenly too loud and too much to bear. Fear filled his veins with ice water, making his heart feel like it would burst. Grimluk looked toward the sounds and then back at the stranger. If the stranger was lying, or planned to kill him, he could fight back, but they might all descend upon him just as he took the stranger down.

But the stranger who had spoken was trying to help, it seemed.

He focused on his breathing, on his heart, on the shrieking terror in his guts. Fear could help keep you alive, keep you sharp. That was a fact he'd learned well as an apprentice. This fear threatened to swallow him whole and doom him. Grimluk focused his will into a sharp point in his chest. Pushed it out and let it take the air with it. His breath flowed out slowly and when he opened his eyes again, things were quieter, the sounds of the pack were less intense and much farther away than he'd thought. His fear had tricked him. The world was a little more in focus as he looked around, albeit just as dark. He couldn't make out many details in the shadows, but he saw the tips of the elf's ears. Realization dawned on him.

The elf, face stern, looked him over. "Can you keep this?"

Grimluk took in a breath with his nostrils and nodded.

"Good," they said, moving away and checking around the corner of the house. The elf wore nothing but a tattered leather loincloth. Hard and lean muscle shifted as they moved, along with a frayed, beaded necklace.

"You. I saw you during the first flashes of this

place," Grimluk whispered, getting back to his feet.

"You remember them? Most do not. The wizard's medicine works through the apples he feeds you."

He grunted. "Knew them apples was trouble."

The elf looked at Grimluk, though he couldn't make out their expression. Finally, they simply said, "Follow."

He eyed the elf. Could he trust them? He still wanted to run but his logical mind tried to reason with him. Safety meant survival.

He kept his blades handy and followed. The elf led him behind a row of houses towards the hotel. They moved fast enough to stay ahead of Grimluk, but not so fast that they left him behind. As the pair went, fresh howls and roars echoed out and the elf stopped, crouching low almost like an animal. Grimluk felt his heart begin to pound again, but he gathered his will and focused on the situation. The elf's bare feet never made a sound as they led him to the other end of town. The journey felt longer than it should have. When the moon was clear, it didn't move, and when covered, the world fell to near total blackness, making it hard to gauge time at all.

They passed what Grimluk thought was the barbershop and followed what felt like a path leading away from it. He couldn't quite tell in the darkness. Eventually, the dim shape of a house appeared, illuminated by lightning as they approached. The yard was filled with better than a dozen strange creatures that looked something like sickly cows with two heads, grazing on the dark grass. His guide paid them little mind, though the beasts seemed wary of the elf and moved away as they got near. Several of the things let out a low sound, not quite the mooing of a cow. Instead of fur, they were covered in glittering scales.

Behind the house, the elf led him down into a small valley nestled between a steep hill and an uneven rock face. Most of the facing seemed smooth, possibly having been used for construction purposes. The elf stopped in front of the facing and motioned toward it, before looking back the way they came. "You will be safe here. Mostly."

Grimluk looked where the elf was pointing. A long, lazy flash of lightning showed him what the elf was pointing at. The entrance to a cave, dark and quiet. A break in the clouds further illuminated the entrance. Grimluk looked at the elf for a moment as his heart attempted to begin thundering again. There, made out of lashed together sticks several feet long, was the Elder Sign.

He adjusted his grip on his weapons. "Reckon if you brought me to that, this really is a bit of safety." They merely grunted in reply. Even with the sign, Grimluk stepped into the gaping darkness cautiously, stooping to get in. He held a hand against the stone to guide himself through and felt a collection of carved grooves. Tracing one of them, he realized they were more elder signs. He nodded and moved his hand toward the spot where the wall and ceiling met.

"You comin'?" he asked the elf.

"No. I will be fine."

Grimluk's throat rumbled at that. "You'll be fine? Here?" Wariness filled his mind. The elf had helped him, sure, but this was still a demon's realm.

The elf nodded, still not looking at Grimluk. "Yes."

Eyes narrowing, Grimluk stepped forward, slipping the hatchet into a loop on his coat before offering the elf his hand. "Much obliged, friend."

The elf looked at Grimluk's hand, then back toward the town again, their eyes always avoiding the cave. After a moment, while fear started to build up in Grimluk again, they took his hand. Their grip was strong and their hand covered in a hair softer than the coarse hair of a halfling's knuckles.

The knife moved up, barely above the bare skin of the elf's forearm. "If this is a trap..." he said, letting the words hang.

The elf let out a weary sigh even as their eyes stayed focused on the blade. "No trap," they muttered. "I am trying to help."

"I want to believe you," Grimluk said plainly. After everything that had happened, he just needed a reason. A good one.

Slowly, the elf's eyes rose to meet Grimluk's. In the moonlight, there was something wild about them. And there was a sadness to them that tugged at Grimluk's heart.

After a long stretch of silence, the elf took a deep breath and nodded. They drew their hand back and stepped past Grimluk, gulping audibly as they did so. As they stepped past the Elder Sign, a violent shiver racked the elf but stopped a moment later. Metal scraped metal, followed by the sudden bloom of light. There in the cave entrance stood the elf, holding a lantern. The shadows on their face seemed to make them gaunt and frail.

As Grimluk stepped forward, he could see just how many signs had been carved into the rock face, along with more drawn in chalk and charcoal. A lot more. He bent over to step into the cave and followed the elf some ten feet or so back into the wide area with more than enough room for several people, though still barely tall enough for the elf to stand up straight. It seemed like an abandoned beginning to a mine with how clean it all was. In the center was a small fire pit, and on the far side, sat a bedroll and a pack of some kind.

The elf set the lantern down in the fire pit before lowering themself into a cross-legged seat. Grimluk took a seat on the bedroll, back pressed up against the rock wall. Looking at the elf, he realized why they appeared so gaunt now. They were. Grimluk also realized they were fairly hirsute for an elf. Almost like a dwarf or an orc.

"I believe you," he finally said, his face softening. The elf bowed their head. "You still fight the curse, don't you?"

The elf's large eyes got larger. A look of wild panic formed in them for a few moments. Finally, they seemed to calm. "I fight the wolf," the elf said with a nod.

"Even with the moon like that?"

"Moon never changes here. You are a hunter of the foul ones?"

"I am."

"You will not attack me?"

Grimluk took a deep breath. "Don't give me a reason to. Please."

"I fight the wolf," they said again.

179

"You really mean to help then?"

They breathed in deeply, almost curling in on themself. "I try."

"Can you help me find the elf I was with? Silvers? Got separated when we ran from the grove earlier."

The elf seemed to consider the request for a long moment. "And if they are dead?"

"If they're dead," Grimluk began, "and you still want to help, we start plannin'. I've got to put a stop to this trollshit."

"I will try," the elf replied once more as they got to their feet again.

As they turned to go, Grimluk spoke up again. "What should I call you? I'm Grimluk."

"I am...Unegiyusdi Tlvdatsi." The elf paused. "Panther of Gray in this tongue."

"Gray Panther?"

The elf considered it for a moment, standing in the passageway. "Gray Panther. It has been some time since I have used this tongue."

"Good luck, Gray Panther."

Gray Panther nodded and slipped away.

Alone again, Grimluk looked around the cavern. There were more elder signs drawn in the ceiling, but in the center was a strange pattern he'd never seen before. The circle and sigils had been carved into the rock. Inside the circle itself were two squares of different alignments with sigils inside the squares. He didn't recognize the sigils and could only guess at their use. He felt certain it was for protection of some kind.

His eyes found the pack again, so he reached

over, taking it up and discovered it was a rather large, leather haversack. Something heavy was in it as well, so Grimluk reached inside. To his surprise, his fingers wrapped around a pistol grip. He pulled his hand back out to inspect the weapon. Overall, it was a little longer than his own gun but the design was completely different. This was an old, slightly ornate flintlock pistol, something rarely used anymore since the first revolvers began production forty years prior. This had been here for at least as long, maybe even longer. It had been protected in the sack but still showed signs of aging. He inspected the barrel as well and noticed something all too familiar etched into each side.

The demon-killing runes. This was a demon hunter's weapon. Grimluk had not been the first hunter to fall into this trap. He'd do his damnedest to make sure he was the last, though.

Gently, Grimluk tipped the bag over and poured the rest of the contents out. Three lead balls clattered against the stone, followed by three paper packets filled with gunpowder, the charges tied to them with thin twine.

He had no idea if the gun was still accurate—at least, as accurate as the old guns could be—but if it was still usable, that was three more shots he could take. It wasn't much but it was something.

With a sigh, Grimluk leaned back against the wall again, a distant roar filled the air reaching his ears. He hoped the werewolf was true to their word. And he hoped Silvers would be safe.

CHAPTER 12

The clouds were rushing past the moon as Gray Panther stepped out of the cave. Ze looked back down the tunnel. The last time ze had encountered an orc, the demon hunter's sword had nearly taken zir head. Ze felt confident that, had this Grimluk not been so affected with the fear the wizard's apples imbued, he might've caved in the side of zir head with the hatchet or jammed that huge knife through zir guts. Gray Panther would've survived, though. The wolf always made sure of that.

Ze was thankful Grimluk had reacted better than ze'd expected. And ze'd managed to lead him to the cave. Despite how close the demon hunter had come to attacking them, and how much sitting in the cave hurt, ze was glad ze'd went in. It'd been…likely many years since ze'd met a sacrifice that had lived long enough to speak to. The old ache of loneliness gnawed at zir. Maybe this one could do what he said he would.

In the meantime, Gray Panther would track down the other elf. The same scents as usual filled zir nostrils. The rot that filled this realm had long ago become something easily ignored. Though the presence of the wolf was still a painful thing, Gray

Panther had learned a thing or two from it. Ze could move like the hunter within and that's exactly what ze did as they headed in the direction Grimluk came from. If the hunter's companion had fled, consumed by the fear, it was likely they had simply kept running. Ze'd seen it so many times before.

Ze kept themselves hidden, stalking through the dark corners and alleys of Dunvich. The worshipers of Rundyyk had fallen quiet once more. Though they tended to ignore zir, ze didn't want to chance it right now. Ze slipped by unnoticed. Once into the trees, Gray Panther broke into a run. Ze neared the creek before too long. Zir elven eyes spotted the worn path leading from the creek to the longhouses not far beyond. Ze followed the creek left for a ways before crossing. Ze did not want to go near the longhouses. It still hurt.

Sometime later, they caught an almost unfamiliar scent heading southwest. Grimluk's scent had lingered near the creek where he'd crossed. The new scent was similar, though less strong, likely making it the elf's. Grimluk smelled like the elements, oil, and the powder of guns. The elf smelled of the elements, as well. And…spirits.

Worries swirled in Gray Panther's head as ze followed the trail. Would ze find this elf, Silvers, alive? Or even whole if they were alive? Would ze arrive just in time to see them perish? A cold shudder ran through zir at that. Harsh memories crept through zir mind, reminding zir it had happened before. Death was almost assured in this land for anything not already tainted by the foul ones.

Still, hope had not quite died for zir yet. A fact that surprised zir. Ze thought the very notion of hope had shriveled and died long ago. Why, then, did the orc reveal hope's lingering presence? Ze had helped him, as ze had tried to do for the many others, whenever possible, and been asked for further aid. Zir old ways, before the wolf, lingered still. Ze would keep trying. Perhaps success would come.

The scent shifted after a time, leading Gray Panther down a rocky hill. At the bottom was a torn jacket covered in patches of gleaming blood made even redder under the light of the moon. Ze leaned down, running two fingers through the blood, and took in the smell of it. Mortal, clean, full of fear. Ze paused and sniffed the air before following in the direction of the blood.

Silvers had gone far from the wizard's altar. No doubt, they had been completely drowned by their fear. Reason of any kind would have been cast aside. Like others before, the purest instinct of survival would have been all they had held on to. Worry began to congeal into anxiety. There were things this direction that would do worse than just rip a person to shreds. There were creatures, parasites, that called this part of the foul one's realm home. Plants, animals, or some hybrid of the two—maybe both together—that would trap and live off prey. In the end, the parasite bred through its host which is what always, inevitably, killed them. Ze kept the fear at bay but, like the wolf within, it paced and snarled, ready to strike at any moment while doubt coiled around zir heart.

The scent grew stronger as ze went. Silvers was close. Gray Panther pressed on, more cautious now that ze was in the parasites' territory. Despite zir ability to survive the parasite's offspring, Gray Panther loathed the idea of more of the things spreading. And of being infected again. Thankfully, there was little blood on the trail as ze went. The parasites were drawn to blood. Maybe ze really would find the elf in time. After running so hard for so long, they had probably slowed down from exhaustion.

A muffled scream hit zir ears and the bottom dropped out of zir stomach with it. Panic threatened to overwhelm Gray Panther as ze ran toward the sound. Strange, bubbly growls cut the panicked cries while the vegetation rustled and creaked. Red lightning crackled overhead as ze passed into a new tree line and saw a hand stretching out from black vines.

"No!" ze cried.

A staggered, high-pitched roar filled the trees around zir as ze rushed forward, drawing a bone knife from zir hip. As the trees gave way to a clearing, Gray Panther saw the full creature for the first time. It was like some horrid cross between plant and lizard. Its body was huge, scaly, and slick-looking in the places not covered in moss or other such vegetation. Fungus grew all over its back while black vines dragged Silvers toward the hulking creature. They screamed only to be drowned out by the beast.

Silvers and Gray Panther locked eyes for a too-long moment before Silvers, vines eating into their skin and orifices, came to rest underneath the parasite. Its head blossomed like a leathery flower, dripping with thick, viscous fluids before an appendage shot out of its mouth, forcing itself down Silvers's throat.

Gray Panther rushed forward, screaming now as well, ready to hack the appendage away. As ze got near the parasite, zir arm raising to strike, another staggered, gurgling roar drowned out zir own screams.

Zir body jerked back and away from Silvers, whose pleading gaze had fallen away. Sticky vines wrapped around Gray Panther's legs.

With a growl of frustration, ze struck at the vines, slicing them away from the parasite, though the vines continued to cling to zir flesh. Uncaring, ze got back up and ran for the elf again. For the second time, ze was denied, but where only zir legs had been ensnared before, this time, the vines wrapped around each limb and yanked zir into the air. Trees creaked as the new parasite, even bigger than the first, entered the clearing. The vines twisted to bring Gray Panther face to face with the creature. Ze struggled furiously, flexing and kicking, trying to free zirself, but the vines just squeezed tighter. The massive head flowered open, fronds spiraling out. Teeth, or maybe thorns, covered the inside of the fronds.

Release me, came the wolf's voice within. It was calm, assured, and powerful. That power was so tempting to give into. Gray Panther knew if only ze gave in, released the wolf, ze could rip the parasites apart. Cleanse the area of them.

Ze also knew any chance of saving Silvers would disappear, along with the young elf's body as Gray Panther tore it to shreds and feasted on it. Even worse than that, ze knew there would come a time when ze couldn't stay free from the wolf's clutches. It was merely a matter of time.

The parasite's appendage struck and the decision was made for zir. Gray Panther's limbs went limp. Ze gave into what was happening. Accepted this new failure. By the time it finished with them, Silvers would be fully infected and trapped in the mushrooms on the smaller creature's back. Once the thing had put

Gray Panther there as well, ze could properly free zirself but the damage would be done. Tears rolled down zir cheeks.

Another sacrifice dead. Some two hundred years or so of failure neverending. Gray Panther closed zir eyes and wept as the parasite burrowed its seed deep within zir body. In another day or two after this, the foul spawn would rip its way out of zir guts. Maybe one of them, maybe more, ze didn't know. Ze just knew the familiar weight of failure as consciousness fled.

Ze woke, choking and gasping, very much free of the fungal trap on the parasite's back. Gray Panther rolled over in the grass, covered in something cold and jellylike, trying to breathe again. Ze looked around, trying to get zir bearings once more. Ze were still in the clearing. To zir left was the body of the larger parasite. Or what was left of it. To zir right, the same sight with the smaller one. Silvers was nowhere to be seen.

"Whom do you seek?" came a rumbling voice Gray Panther knew too well, zir eyes going wide.

"Rundyyk," ze said, coughing as ze stood to face the foul one.

The foul one sat at the other side of the clearing with Silvers laying at its feet. Its tree-trunk tail swished idly like a cat's while all six of its eyes focused on Gray Panther.

"I can feel the regret spilling out of you from here," Rundyyk growled, an edge of pleasure in its voice. "It is almost better that it was you I found and not the orc. One day, you will let my sibling free again. Free to hunt as it is meant to. Until then, wallow in your agony. Your failure at saving this mortal is not yet complete."

Gray Panther could do nothing but watch as the foul one lifted the limp but still breathing body of Silvers in one taloned hand. Rundyyk sniffed the elf before breathing in deeply through its mouth. Silvers's body lifted at the chest. The great beast just kept inhaling. Pale white light, pale even despite the red moon, flowed out from the elf's chest. For a moment, the light seemed to move away from the foul one. Gray Panther recognized the sight of a soul fighting a fate far worse than any death.

A slender, forked tongue lashed out of Rundyyk's mouth, wrapping around the ball of light, dragging it to its doom. The foul one's mouth closed and it swallowed.

More tears spilled down Gray Panther's cheeks as ze watched the foul one devour Silvers's soul. Ze could not look away as the damned creature slurped the rest of the light down like broth before setting the soulless husk on its feet.

"You may take this back to the orc. If you are lucky, the Kandarian will not get to it first." Rundyyk let out a growling, rough laugh. "Luck has abandoned you, though, has it not? It will please me to see you when this is finished."

As the rotten fiend turned to leave, something else leapt from a nearby tree and took to the sky. Some part of Gray Panther demanded awareness of predators but zir gaze remained on Silvers. Ze retrieved zir bone knife and stepped up to the husk that had been Grimluk's companion. Dim eyes watched zir.

"I am sorry, young one." With a sigh, Gray Panther embraced the husk and drove the knife into its heart. The body shuddered but made no sound. Gently, ze lowered the body to the ground. "I am sorry," ze muttered again.

Quietly, Gray Panther began to chant and sing, weaving a spell together. What willpower remained in zir focused on what ze wanted to do. The mystical energies built until Gray Panther released them around Silvers's corpse. Slowly, then all at once, their body sank into the dirt and disappeared.

Gray Panther wept loudly, kneeling over the impromptu grave. With great effort, ze rose and began the trek back to the cave.

The world was stained in blood, shimmering crimson as it dripped to the ground, forming thick puddles. Grimluk was sheened in gore as well. His head swam in the metallic aroma. All around him lay corpses. Some had the twisted, abominable forms of demons. Some looked like animals. The others were once live mortals. Elves, humans, dwarves, halflings, even other orcs lay strewn about, their blood soaking the ground, choking it, creating puddles that plipped and plopped with each breath Grimluk took. He was breathing hard.

He had no gun. No knife or hatchet. Just his hands, nails long and caked with bits of gore. The things at his feet had challenged him. Called out to him. More were coming. He could hear them approaching. Mortal or demon, it didn't matter. Each one was corrupted and weak.

Grimluk was not weak. He was strong. Stronger than even he had realized and that strength made him the hunter he was.

The blood sang to him. The aroma filled his slit-ted nostrils, threatening to make him swoon. His new prey arrived, screaming at him. "Look what he's done!" yelled one of them. Even from this distance, Grimluk could see the rot in their eyes. "Away, beast!" cried another, holding a shaking rifle to their shoulder.

Fear washed off them, mingling with the stench of blood, the stink of spilled entrails. This, too, had a song for Grimluk. Even as the mob began shooting him, the song grew louder. Bullets ripped cloth alone. The pitiful creatures couldn't hurt him. He was unstoppable. Invincible. With a roar, he rushed in.

Everything happened in moments. Throats crushed. Rifles turned back on their owners. Skulls shattered. Bones broken. Grimluk felt alive. More alive than he'd ever felt. He drank their blood, tasted their flesh, bathed in their terror.

Gwen's face flashed before him. His eyes wandered down to his hand. It was buried deep in her guts.

Something nagged him in the back of his mind.

Gwen's eyes were wide and filled with tears as her hand reached up to caress his cheek.

Something nagged him in the back of his mind.

Gwen wasn't caressing his cheek. She was push-ing it. Her tiny hand struggled against him. Dimly, he realized she wasn't trying to fight back.

Something called out to him from far away. Grimluk relented and let her push his face, letting his dying sister turn him away to face the thing calling out to him. The shape raced forward, suddenly clear and loud.

Wake up.

The dream slid away like cobwebs and Grimluk looked around, disorientation tugging at him while the crown of his head burned. The lantern still burned but has grown lower as he slept. The dream, still clinging to his mind like mold, playing out as he sat up. He grunted and ran a hand over his face as he mulled over the images. The intensity of it was staggering, like he'd actually been there. He was relatively accustomed to the nightmares that came from hunting the worst demons. Dreams of pure fear, of reliving situations over and over again. Dreams recapturing the worst that mortals, and the Abyss, had to offer.

This was different.

For Grimluk, those nightmares distorted events or amplified them. People were crying out for help but he couldn't lift them or couldn't get to them, his feet too heavy to move. Other times, he failed to kill the demon or just couldn't and it would rip him apart, death never coming to wake him. Meditation helped, as did his desire to fight the evil things of the world, ironically enough. The dreams would fade and he'd get back to sleep. But now? Now he could still smell the blood, hear the cries of the people he'd slaughtered. He could still feel the ridges of Gwen's little spine in his palm.

Even now, he realized why his heart was thundering in his chest. The fear was passing away. This place was the hunting demon's dream. He wanted to hunt, too. It was a primal need that, if he let it, would carry him back out of the cave, back to the Whateleys and their demon lord, and to their throats. The fear had burned away in that hunter's nightmare and been replaced by a raw bloodlust. The worst part was how good it felt. He wanted to be afraid of it but he couldn't be. He could only look at it behind detached logic that told him how very wrong this feeling was. The mind seal tattoo was probably the only thing keeping him where he was.

Footsteps echoed and his hands were on his weapons before he'd even registered the feel of them. He held the bloodlust in check and waited. Gray Panther appeared in the dim light covered in dirt and grime with muddy streaks under their eyes. The elf started when they looked at Grimluk. The two of them watched each other.

Grimluk realized his breathing was heavy. He closed his eyes and focused on calming it. When he opened them again, Gray Panther had squatted on the other side of the lantern.

"Silvers's dead, aren't they?" he asked. His voice was harsh even to his own ears. He took in another deep breath. "I'm sorry. I had a dream I can't shake loose."

"You dreamed of blood," the elf replied without looking at Grimluk.

"Yes."

They nodded. "Be wary. This place will try to claim you as one of its own if it cannot keep you afraid or kill you."

"Because I'm a hunter," Grimluk mumbled. Gray

Panther simply nodded again.

After a stretch of silence, Grimluk spoke up. "How are you doin'?" It seemed a silly thing to ask but it helped ground him. Compassion could help hold the hunter's nightmare at bay.

The elf grunted. "I can still feel the sign pushing against me. It feels like dull thorns." They paused for a long moment. "I will manage."

Grimluk nodded at that. He'd expected the Elder Sign to have an effect and, however cruel it might feel, needed the elf to feel it. Their willingness to do so earned trust. "When you're ready, I'd appreciate it if you told me what happened with Silvers."

Gray Panther took in a deep breath, letting it out slowly. "The young one ran too far. There are creatures, perhaps foul ones, perhaps of this realm. They —" the elf paused and then spoke a language Grimluk didn't understand, "—I do not know the word in this tongue. The beasts took your friend as I arrived. To put more of itself in them and feed. Before I could help, another took me. Within the next day or two, its young will tear its way out of me. When I awoke, Rundyyk was there. The foul one—" their voice cracked and they ground their mouth shut.

For a moment, all Grimluk could see was something weak to prey on. He focused on Gray Panther's face. "The demon ate Silvers's soul," he said as gently as he could.

Slowly, Gray Panther nodded. "I tried," they whispered.

The elf's words cut through Grimluk's haze. They had tried. As had he. They were all dead, except for him. Anger boiled in his heart. All of this had to stop. He had to stop it. He couldn't give in to this place and he couldn't give in to guilt. Once again, the lesson he'd always hated most reared its head. The first rule of hunting: you can't save everyone.

Grimluk leaned back against the wall. "What is this place? The demon make it or did it just corrupt it?" Maybe focusing on the task at hand would help ease their minds.

"It is...corrupted."

"And the Whateleys gather sacrifices, let their boss hunt, and then what? Town looked pretty run down so money seems unlikely."

"Not money," Gray Panther said, dropping from their squat to sit cross-legged. "Goals."

Grimluk mulled that over, muttering the word to himself. "Goals. It's a cult. Reckon there's a demon raising but I've never heard of one takin' two hundred years."

"They try to keep their secrets from me but I have learned some of them. It has been a long goal for them. Waiting. Making sacrifices for power."

"That's usually how it goes," Grimluk replied with a nod. "And always with promises of power or eternal life or some such."

"I do not doubt this. I have seen Rundyyk's servants changed with its blessing."

"Souls and blood to build up the energy for somethin' big, then?"

"The hunts feed the foul one and grants their rituals power. They sent a...thing somewhere. I think it was in recent years. I think they mean to bring it back."

Grimluk grunted. From the letters, he already

knew there had been plans in motion for decades. It was starting to make sense. He just needed more information.

"You're one of the tribe from the longhouses?" Grimluk asked after a time.

His already melancholy companion looked up slowly. "Yes."

"So, how did you end up here?"

Gray Panther shifted uneasily. "They told you the story of the town?"

"A version of it. I reckon you're about to tell me the truth of it."

They nodded. "It is not all lies. Jeremiah Whateley banished a beast that was killing my people." The elf took in a deep breath, holding it before letting it out again. "I was the beast. We had no name for a town. Like our ancestors, it was home. When the far folk began to settle with us, it was good. There were others of our kind. Dwarves. Many humans. Even some of the small ones. Halflings, that is the word. They respected the land and our ways and we shared in their ways. That is where the name comes from. It was—" they paused, mumbling. "It was a jest. Our wise one made it. Tried to make a word that sounded like the far folks'—your words."

Grimluk couldn't help but smile at that. "That's a pretty good jest."

A slight smile spread on Gray Panther's face, though their eyes remained distant. "When it was explained, everyone laughed. The far folk decided to keep this word, a shared jest as a sign of friendship. The land and our new town was good. We were all happy and we guardians had few worries. Then the

Whateley man came.

"He wanted the land. Offered his money for all but the humans to leave. We had no use of his money. What use are coins? They shine and sparkle but offer nothing. Can they skin the elk? Cook the meat? Do coins work medicine? No. What use is money? We laughed at Jeremiah Whateley. You cannot trade money for land, we said. The land belongs to no one."

Grimluk nodded but said nothing. Money was merely a necessary aspect of his life. He had no special attachment to it. If he wanted, he could retire and work in other ways in Hunter's Hollow or even live in Eagle Rest, the town nearby the Hollow, and find work as a farmhand or a deputy peacekeeper. If he wanted, he could find a spot someplace on his own and build a home to tend. Kindness and a favor could go far in ways money never would. But still, the way things were now, it had become a fact of life.

"The next time I saw him, I felt the evil from him. The foulness of the ancient things. He found me one night, the moon full and strong." Gray Panther's voice wavered for a moment before turning to steel. "He cursed me then. Put the wolf in me. It took me immediately. I tried to fight it, but it was too strong and I did not know what was happening until it ended. I hunted down my tribe first. Slaughtered them as they slept. Then the dwarves and halflings. Jeremiah Whateley forbade me to harm the humans."

Gray Panther shuddered, eyes wide as the memories danced in them. "He arrived, a savior to those people, and banished me here. Rundyyk hunted me for a time, unable or refusing to kill me, I am unsure. Can the foul ones hurt each other?"

"They can," Grimluk answered.

"So then I was a jest to it. When it became bored of me, I learned to keep the wolf at bay. The wolf takes power from the moon, yes?"

"The cursed do. Cursed werewolves have no choice. During the full moon, the wolf takes them, moonrise to moonset. Full moons are always the worst."

"The moon is always full here. The wolf is stronger, too, but I learned to leash it." They let out a weary sigh. "I have tried to help the ones who fall victim to the Whateleys. I always fail. That, too, is part of my curse. Already, I am failing you. Silvers is dead and you will die eventually, too. I am sorry."

Silence fell over them again as Grimluk watched the elf. Grimluk held up the flintlock pistol. "And this one?"

"Raugukh," they answered, coldness creeping into their voice. "He was a hunter of the foul ones like you. He survived the longest but I still could not save him."

After setting the pistol aside again, Grimluk turned and laid back down on the bedroll. He didn't know what to say to Gray Panther anymore. He needed more sleep and food and to plan. With little else coming to mind, he said as much to his companion.

Gray Panther seemed to consider that and then stood. "You should rest if you are able. I will get us food. The two-headed creatures are safe once cooked."

"You sure you want to do that?"

"I will do what I can."

"Reckon so." With that, the elf exited the cave once more, leaving Grimluk alone. He reached over and turned the wick down on the lamp, keeping things at a comfortable dimness. Weapons within reach, Grimluk closed his eyes.

Gray Panther left the orc to rest for a second time. Ze admired the willpower Grimluk possessed. Fighting off the urges this realm encouraged was a challenge all by itself, but he was also under the influences of the apples, as well. Ze only knew of the apples because Rundyyk thought it funny to taunt zir. Zir tribe had been a friend to the dryad and it to them.

Ze was thinking of the tribe a lot lately. It always happened when the Whateleys brought new sacrifices. It made zir heart ache.

The moonlight began to fade, leaving Gray Panther swathed in darkness. Zir stomach rumbled loudly, reminding zir that food was needed. Ze shuffled back up toward the house and the beasts grazing around it. Quietly, ze moved to the side of the house. Some of the herd had wandered farther away but there was one nearby that would work. It was likely older. Heavy and slow. Ze stepped back and focused on zir hands and feet, letting the wolf's essence bleed into them, carefully restraining its bloodlust and power. Slivers of pain pulsed through zir limbs and then a torrent rushed in all at once. It was a familiar sensation, at that point. Gray Panther had learned to keep the wolf in check, but could use its power when needed. And in this realm, that was more than ze liked.

As zir hands and everything from the knees down shifted into a monstrous form, the skin swelling and splitting open like torn cloth, ze kept from screaming. This was nothing compared to the wolf taking over completely. Every bone and muscle in zir body, every inch of skin, every organ, cramped, ripped, tore, and lengthened. Ze'd felt zir heart stop each time, leaving zir in a state of agony just on the edge of death. The small changes weren't much better and came with their own complications as the wolf fought to be free. That hurt in a very different way.

The worst part of learning to use bits of the wolf's power was how useful it really was. Before the curse, Gray Panther had always been sure, fast, and strong. With the curse, ze inherited some of the aspects of the change, regardless of when it happened. Ze had the gifts of zir people, eyes and ears better than the other races. The wolf's sense of smell joined those. So, too, it bolstered zir strength, speed, and endurance. Healed zir from any wound. It was why ze had to be so vigilant. The power of the wolf was not bad, if separated from the rage and blood-lust. The wolf loved reminding zir of that. Especially when ze used some of it for greater speed.

The herd scattered when ze struck but the speed of the attack was too great. Ze slammed into zir prey and buried zir clawed hand into one the beast's throat, keeping it pinned down as the blood drained away. When the beast stopped twitching, ze began dragging it back to the cave. Ze did not need the whole animal, but if ze and Grimluk didn't get as much out of it as they could, the rot would claim it first. It was not the right way of things, to waste a creature, but this was not the right world and ze had long ago stopped being a right person.

It took little effort to drag the carcass into the valley. Outside the cave, Gray Panther let go of the thing's leg and focused on returning zir body to normal. The pain ebbed and flowed and then zir limbs were zir own again. Ze pulled zir knife out and prepared to dress the two-headed beast.

Talons latched on to zir shoulders, piercing deep into zir flesh, and yanked them off the cold ground before ze fully realized what was happening. The knife tumbled to the rapidly disappearing grass. Ze looked up to see the dim form of Rundyyk's best warrior as she carried zir into the sky. Higher and higher they went, along with the confusion ze felt at being ambushed with no warning. Not a smell, not a sound.

The talons released, flinging droplets of blood into the air. Gray Panther kept rising for another moment and then began plummeting back down. With a sigh, ze wondered if the impact might kill the parasite within. There was a moment of pain when ze landed and then nothingness.

CHAPTER 13

The world was stained in blood, shimmering crimson as it dripped to the ground, forming thick puddles. He was dreaming again. Grimluk looked at his hands, his clothes, not covered in blood and viscera, but stained all the same. He looked around the surreal world his mind had conjured once more, lucidity not erasing what he saw, but allowing him some measure of control, at least for himself. He ignored the bodies, the puddles of blood and excrement, the people screaming at him. The logic of dreams aided him. He pushed through the crowd and it all faded into a dim background. Gwen was waiting for him, still there among the throng of people. She was crying softly, looking up at him with fear filling her eyes. She made no effort to move. Grimluk knew, through the dream, that she couldn't, that his sister was prey. She just kept staring at him like a rabbit caught in a snare. Weak and helpless.

He knelt and wrapped her in his arms. It'd been nearly a year since he'd seen her last. He'd returned to Hunter's Hollow with her in tow near the end of the previous summer and once he'd dealt with a would-be tyrant and a demon lord, he'd left again as fall rolled in. He'd gone back again for a short stay as fall was dwindling, a couple of months before her birthday and the Festival of the Dead. He'd still left again. Wandered east. And here he was now.

"I miss you, little one," he told the dream Gwen.

"You hurt me," she replied in barely more than a whisper.

"I know. This place is powerfully wrong. The real you is safe, back home."

"What are you gonna do now?" She wrapped her arms around his neck as she said it.

"I'll make you a promise. I have to do my job. If I make it out of this alive, I'll come back and stay through the winter."

"You... you will?"

"Reckon so."

Everything around Grimluk melted into something new. Instead of a blood-soaked street, he was back home. That's what Hunter's Hollow really was. He stayed away a lot but that would always be his home. He sometimes wondered if the other guilds worked like his. Were they the homes of their hunters?

"I need you to stay with me," he continued. Gwen squeezed as tight as her little human arms could. "The place I'm in wants to change me." She didn't reply except to squeeze tighter.

A shriek of pain roused him from the dream. For a moment, he could still feel his sister's arms around his neck. Shaking away the grogginess, Grimluk took up the flintlock pistol and set about loading a charge. Kort, one of his teachers as an apprentice hunter, had made them learn how to use muzzleloaders before moving on to cap and ball revolvers. The need had never arisen before now and he was glad for the lessons as he set to work preparing a shot.

The moon had gone away again, leaving the world outside in total darkness. Shadows filled the tunnel as something scraped and clicked against the stones, its breath echoing toward him. Whatever it was called his name in a terse manner. As he finished loading the pistol, the thing stepped forward into the dim light. "You," it said curtly.

The harpy stood before him once more. Something seemed off about it, though. Rags clung to it, shredded and revealing parts of its body. There was skin there, as well as feathers slicked down almost like those of a hatched chick. Hair hung from its head, shrouding its beaked face.

"Comin' in here must have hurt," Grimluk said to it.

"Why did you let it take me?" the terse voice cried. "Look what it did to me!"

Grimluk's heart skipped a beat. "Imogen?"

The thing recoiled at hearing the name. "No more. All because of you."

"I tried to get to you," Grimluk said, "but you can't blame your choice on me. It made you a demon knight."

"I had no choice!" Imogen screamed. "It told me I could live or die. There was no choice." Her body tightened up. "If I kill you, it might turn me back. Might let me go."

Grimluk's throat rumbled before turning to a growl. "Did it tell you that?"

"It said it would reward my service." She watched him, body coiled tightly, ready to strike. "What would you do?" she practically growled. "You let this happen!"

The knife of guilt stabbed into Grimluk's heart as his responsibility bore down on him. If he'd been smarter or faster, he might have avoided all of this. If he'd killed the wizard and his grandson. But no, no, Imogen chose knighthood over death. The very notion disgusted him but he was trained to handle this. Death by the hands of demons was a constant threat for him.

"You can still walk away. Go back to the other side and hide." With a sigh, Grimluk readied his weapons. "If you won't help me stop them, don't hinder me. I can take you to get help. The demon hasn't taken your soul yet or you'd have never made it past the signs."

"I've had enough of your help," Imogen spat before leaping at him, wings outstretched and talons reared. "This won't be quick!"

With a hop and a roll, Grimluk dodged to his left and circled in front of the tunnel. He had to be careful or he'd bust his skull open keeping her away.

Imogen thrashed where he'd been moments before and slowly turned to face him again. Even in the dim light, he could see the hate burning in her eyes. But in the cave, she was weak. Even if the flintlock was busted, he had his blades. An easy kill, if he so desired.

Grimluk desired no such thing. An idea sprang to mind. A damn fool one at that, but it would get the job done. As Imogen prepared her next attack, still unsteady in her new transformed body, Grimluk rushed her, driving his full weight into her. In her weakened condition, even her newly tainted form couldn't overcome his strength and he planted her into the wall hard enough to daze her before tossing her toward the tunnel. With the threat cleared, he dug into his bag.

As his hand closed on his guild amulet, Imogen landed on his back and began clawing at his eyes with taloned fingers. On instinct, he threw his head back into her face, catching her beak enough to bring forth a cry of pain. With the woman still clinging to his back, he fell away to a wall, hoping to crush her again and force her to let go.

She saw his plan, however, and slid off, letting him slam into the wall himself. Most of the air rushed out of Grimluk with the impact, but he kept his eyes on Imogen. The two of them studied each other for a long, tense moment.

"I can send you to my guild," Grimluk said when he was sure Imogen wasn't going to strike again.

"So they can kill me?" she hissed.

"So they can save you, you damned idjit!" The anger was hard to keep out of his voice now. "I didn't make this choice for you, but I can help you choose freedom now. I just need you to trust me for a moment."

Imogen rushed Grimluk again, clawing at him wildly. "Why should I believe you?" she shouted, burying her talons into his flesh.

He let her claw at him, giving his left forearm to the endeavor. Her claws could cut him deeper than a knife, which worked well for him. He'd bleed more. Once he was satisfied with her work, he batted her arm away and, with a viper's speed, took Imogen by the throat and drove her to the ground. A moment later, he was sitting on top of her, pinning her shoulders down with his knees.

With a quick snap, he tore the shredded sleeve away from his forearm and began smearing the amulet in his blood. Imogen shrieked and thrashed as he did. Had he been smaller, she might have even been able to swing her legs up to get at him. Once the amulet was covered, he held it up. Blinding light spilled into the cave before solidifying into a swirling portal that dug deep furrows into the rock. On the other side were the gates to Hunter's Hollow.

And Gwen. "Grimluk!" she shouted.

Imogen stared into the portal, the dark feathers on her face blowing in the breeze it created.

He spoke loud enough that Gwen could hear him. "Go through there, she'll take you to an elf named Minthralvatra, tell him I sent you. And Imogen?" She looked up at him. "If I make it out of this and I get back there and find out you hurt anyone, especially that little girl there, we will have words. Do you understand me?"

"Why?" Imogen asked.

Grimluk got off of Imogen, helping her back to her feet after he did so. "Because this is my job. And I failed enough of you today. Now go, before it closes."

Imogen hesitated at the rim of the portal but then slipped through. As it began to close, Gwen looked at him expectantly. He sighed and shook his head. The last thing he heard Gwen say was, "I love you."

Then everything was darkness again. He walked over and leaned his head against the cave wall where the portal had been. He was trapped here now. The amulet's escape charge would need to be renewed and he couldn't do that here. The knowledge that he would most likely die stopping the Whateleys settled in. He was okay with that, if it came down to it. His family and the other hunters would know what had happened now. If he failed, they'd finish it.

At least he'd seen Gwen one last time.

Consciousness returned, bleak and hazy. Gray Panther became aware of existence first, followed by the growl of the wolf, before finally remembering what had happened. Zir body was knitting itself back together. As zir consciousness grew stronger, so did the pain. It was excruciating. It felt like the first time ze'd transformed. The fall had been from high enough up that ze'd practically burst like rotten fruit. Eventually, ze could move zir limbs again, though this hurt, too. Little remained in zir mind beyond the moment.

I can heal you faster, came the wolf. Release me.

Gray Panther attempted to respond, "No," out loud out of sheer defiance, but zir jaw had not yet pulled itself back into place.

When zir legs finally felt functional enough to walk again, ze struggled to zir feet and shuffled toward the cave. Ze'd landed somewhere in the woods and the sky was still black, the lightning merely crackling gently every so often. One eye was still dead. The sensation of it healing burned. Zir nose, however, knew what was around zir. Could smell the rotting meat from the herd beast. Ze followed that.

Several times, ze tripped on unsteady feet. Zir ankles still weren't quite right. Ze pressed on, crawling when ze had to. The trees parted and the stone facing revealed itself anew. Gray Panther exited the woods just in time to see something snatch the carcass of the herd beast and disappear. Ze hobbled on, moving a little more easily now as ze moved into the little valley.

Ducking into the tunnel was its own torture. Ze didn't have to stoop nearly as far as Grimluk, but in zir current condition, zir spine popped and cracked loudly. Ze tried to call Grimluk's name but it came out in a whisper. When ze stepped into the cave proper, Gray Panther stood up slowly, bone grinding loudly against bone as ze did. Grimluk was pointing Raugukh's weapon at zir from his spot on the bedroll.

The two of them locked eyes for a long time before he lowered the gun. His eyes slowly shifted from aggression to concern as he sighed and moved to the lantern. Orange light pushed away the shadows of the cave. With a grunt, Grimluk dropped back to his butt on the bedroll.

"Winged warrior?" ze asked, zir voice a little stronger now.

"Imogen. One of the other outsiders for the festival. Thought she was dead, but apparently, Rundyyk just took her. She agreed to be the big bastard's new knight in the hopes of a reward of freedom. What happened to you?"

"Carried high. Dropped." Gray Panther replied slowly. "I do not see a body. And you still breathe."

"Well fuck," the hunter replied. For a moment,

his eyes turned hard again. "Sent her to my guild. We have guild amulets enchanted with a one way portal spell to get us out of danger. Wasn't entirely sure if it would work here but it did. She should be talkin' to our healer about now. She'll be free within the week."

Gray Panther looked at Grimluk with sheer shock. Zir jaw clicked into place, suddenly making words was much simpler. "You had a means of escape and yet you stay? Why?"

The demon hunter stared down at the amulet in his hand quietly before looking up, the softness in his black eyes startling all by itself. "Like I told Imogen, this is my job. The Whateleys need to be stopped. If I can't do it, more hunters will come now that they know what's goin' on here. Whatever they're doin' has to end now, before it gets worse."

Gray Panther's brows furrowed as ze stared down at Grimluk. "You will die doing this."

"Reckon so."

"You should have fled!"

"Maybe. Made my choice, though."

Gray Panther sank into a squat, knees crackling as ze did. "Do you desire death?"

A long sigh escaped the orc's slitted nostrils. "Friend, I want to leave. I want to see my family again. I saw my sister through the portal for a moment. I very much want to live, but..."

"Yes?" Ze could not imagine what the orc would say. To be so moved to stay in this realm of corruption and death. But ze wanted to know. Needed to know.

"Sometimes, the choice is between doin' what's needed and doin' what's easy. Would've been the easiest thing to step through with Imogen. But there's two-hundred years of trollshit that needs cleanin'. Probably pretty bad, from what I've gathered between what you've told me and what I found in their house. And there's folks that may not even be of their own mind that need protectin'. Folks forced into the same choice Imogen made. Shit, I made a choice like that recently myself."

He paused. "And I'm an orc. You know anything about our past?"

Ze shook zir head. Gray Panther had heard rumors of the orcs. It was said they'd served evil once. Ze'd only ever heard these things from passing settlers. No orcs had been to Dunvich before the wolf's curse.

"Thousand years back or thereabouts, we were slaves. Minds not our own. We do not look kindly on mental domination. If there's a chance of stopping the Whateleys and freeing anyone enslaved, I have to take it." Grimluk looked at Gray Panther for a long moment. The memory of Raugukh flashed across zir mind. "You said you were a guardian once. Reckon I'm tryin' to do the same."

Tears rolled down Gray Panther's cheeks. Raugukh had said something similar. It made zir heart ache. The realization of just how broken ze was hit like a falling tree. This Grimluk had made a choice that, to him, was simple and absolute. Once, in what felt like another life, Gray Panther would have done the same.

"I will do all that I can to aid you," ze whispered.

"I do appreciate it. No doubt that I'll need it.

"What do we do?"

Grimluk's throat rumbled. It was a strange sound he made sometimes. Not quite a growl but not words. It reminded Gray Panther of zir namesake.

"We give in to this place a little. I am a hunter. I can lay traps, take down anything else that comes after me. If we do it right, we can work our way back to the table and put a stop to all this."

Though the realm was a decayed reflection of the one he came from, Elder Whateley still felt comfortable in his home. Aside from the demonic influence that pulsed along every surface, the only real difference was that Rundyyk had made a throne of bones where the temple sat. Or, perhaps the throne had always been there and his forefather had been sensitive enough to build the temple where it sat and the house nearby. Regardless, the area had been chosen for its mystical potential. A potential his family had unlocked generations ago.

The tribal sheep had no idea what this land really was before Jeremiah took it. He'd been guided there by Nyarlathotep himself, given the knowledge of what needed to be done before the god had moved on to other things. The Bloody Tongue was wise but fickle with his gifts and guidance. Now here they were, the Whateley family's work nearly complete. Wilbur's brother, Winston, would be able to come home soon, strong and ready to change the world.

As Elder sat on the porch in a rocking chair, con-templating the past and present, Rundyyk paced around its throne. The thing was massive, befitting a god of Rundyyk's stature. The bones that comprised the throne were incredibly varied. Skulls of elvenoid shapes mingled with those of beasts, some long and rounded, some that looked like cows, while others appeared akin to dragons. Femurs, spines, and rib cages of equally varied shapes and sizes laced its form as well. Sometimes, Elder wondered if his god had designed and built it alone or commanded the lesser creatures to do so. It would not be unreasonable to believe that the throne had simply built itself according to Rundyyk's will. It mattered little, but curiosity had always been rewarded in his family.

While Rundyyk paced, Wilbur stood at attention, still as a statue in the way that only the undead were usually capable of. Pride never failed to well up in Elder's old heart when looking at his grandson. Decades of experiments culminating in one success. That one success held the key that led to Wilbur's and Winston's births. While that first success was weak, born of a lesser god, Wilbur was not. Wilbur was a true demigod. A legend like those of old, back when the false gods still walked the planet, having managed to drive away the Old Ones. Eventually, the boy would eclipse them all.

Winston was a different story. Weak, at first, but destined for greatness as well. The boy had to be spirited away, protected. And so he had been sent to the other realm. But soon, soon he would return.

"I can barely smell his fear anymore," Rundyyk growled. There was a certain, malicious pleasure in the god's voice.

"M'lord?" Elder asked, being drawn from his thoughts.

His god turned to face him. "He is conquering the fear. You did well when you found this one. He will begin to act soon. He has rid himself of my new creation. I no longer feel her presence."

"You're not upset to lose a new subject?"

Rundyyk's laugh was the bark of wolves. "If she fell so easily, she was weak and worth nothing. But this orc...he is a worthy prey. Perhaps, in the end, a new servant. It matters not. His blood cries out to me. He is still mortal. Still weak. I will feast upon him, one way or another."

"Why not crash upon him now, then? The fool elf took him to the cave, after all."

"Very true, Priest. Very true, indeed. Not yet, though." Rundyyk looked skyward, waving a hand and clearing the sky of clouds. "The stars draw near to rightness. To bring the boy back, the blood must be right, as well. If the orc would cast aside fear, then the bloodlust must take him. His heart must burn purely."

Rundyyk turned toward the menagerie of underlings and lesser creatures. Some were of the Abyss, while others were cultists who had received their reward, their blessing, for service. "You lot. Go and encourage the orc to begin his work. The time of the crossing grows closer. Go now."

Savage yells filled the air as the former cultists crashed through the trees to the east. Elder recognized a few of them. Townsfolk who had served their god well during the time of his father, along with a few of their descendants who had served under Elder. They weren't as powerful as Rundyyk's chosen. If the chosen were called demon knights, then one could call the blessed of Rundyyk demon pawns.

Under the right hand, even pawns could take down kings.

The blessed would serve their purpose and prepare the orc for the crossing. Soon. Soon, Wilbur's brother would join them, nurtured in safety in the other world with his own and Wilbur's counterparts. Wilbur, the gatekeeper, and his brother, the keymaster. Yog-Sothoth made flesh. The one in two. The pair of them would usher in a new age, letting the Great Old Ones return to reclaim Arkod after the false gods had stolen it from them. And where were those gods now? Little had been heard from them since the Five Hundred Years War and it had been millennia still since they had walked with mortals. If they tried to return, it would be too late.

Elder Whateley muttered a prayer in the tongue of the gods, eyes closed in reverence. Even with his eyes closed, he could feel the gazes of his grandson and his god upon him. Gently, he lifted his arms, turning his face to the sky. "Let the sovereign host look upon us from the Abyss and bless us! Ia! Ia! Rundyyk fhtagn!"

Chapter 14

As Grimluk started laying out his gear, Gray Panther twitched, their head snapping to face the direction of the Whateley house. They stood slowly, sniffing at the air and listening.

"What is it?" Grimluk asked.

"Something is coming."

"More demons?"

"Yes."

A growl filled his throat as Grimluk snatched up the flintlock pistol and the hatchet. "Reckon we can get the drop on them this time, if there's time."

"They grow closer but we can prepare."

He grunted and headed outside, Gray Panther following behind. He kept his hatchet and knife in ready positions and tucked the flintlock pistol into his gun belt. The sounds of the outside world came into a fresh sharpness. It felt like the first time he'd stepped outside in a day or so. With how time seemed to move here, maybe it had been, or maybe only hours. The moon shone down, unmoving and massive, pale red light still covering the dark land with shadows. Now outside again, he realized how bad the ash in the air was and pulled his bandanna up over his face. It wasn't much but it was better than nothing. It cut down on the foulness of the air.

Even still, an unmistakable scent rose to his nostrils. There was blood on the wind. Maybe from the drifting ash and rot in the air. He didn't know and didn't much care, at this point. Grimluk could feel the pulse of the realm on his mind. The crown of his skull felt hot even in the breeze. The tattoo continued to do its job, but it required him to pay attention as well. The fear that had built up before he got control of it had been supernatural. Had Gray Panther not found him first, forced him to calm down and focus on that fear, and led him to the cave, the fear would have overwhelmed him completely and gotten him killed. Likewise, his desire to hunt, the blatant blood-lust that threatened to well up, went beyond his duty as a demon hunter.

It dug deep into him. The call of something primal and savage. The most worrisome aspect of it was that he knew it wasn't entirely the realm. It wasn't something else telling him to strike at weakness. To rip and tear.

The voice was his own.

He stood in that crisp and foul air and listened to the voice. It spoke of survival, yes, but it also spoke of pride. He'd never exactly been arrogant, but until he'd gone to Greenreach Bluffs and met Gwen and her blood family, his pride had never been an issue. The very notion of being prideful had been beaten out of him not long after that.

Even still, he was proud of being a demon hunter. The voice was that pride, speaking with booming authority and his will to survive. After sending Imogen to Hunter's Hollow and staying behind, he knew that voice was going to be loud. He also knew that he needed it to be, if he was going to stop the Whateleys and their demon.

"What do you plan?" Gray Panther asked.

Grimluk looked around at the valley. The rock-face was maybe twenty feet or so vertical. The land above it hadn't been disturbed. Trees speckled the edge. The rocky hill ended near the treeline to the east. "Up there. We can see them coming. Ambush them."

The elf looked up. "We will jump on them?"

"Reckon so."

Gray Panther nodded and the two of them made their way up the hill quickly. After a few minutes, they stood over where he assumed the cave would be beneath them and scouted the area. The other hill rose, not quite even in height with the one he was on, and beyond that, and behind him, was more forest. He could see from there that the forest was not especially dense, but he knew that it grew denser past Dunvich. Grimluk could just make out the shape of the house where the cow-things were. The entrance to the valley caught his eye again. It was quite open. He guessed maybe a hundred feet or so of just grass. Enough space, he could conceivably set up a massive demon trap, carved into the dirt. Anything coming into the valley would be trapped until he dealt with it.

Grimluk's thoughts turned inward again as he and Gray Panther waited, keeping behind some of the smaller trees at the edge. He could hear the strange bleating-moo sound of the two-headed beasts, sounding very much like spooked cattle. Whatever was coming was nearly there. He needed to be ready to fight, but he also knew he needed to be able to leave that fight with his mind intact. He couldn't lose himself to the bloodlust. As long as he could hold his compassion close, he could hold onto himself; could keep himself upright. He had to try.

Even if this job was likely a suicide mission, he had to see it through. Too many people had been not just hurt, but destroyed by the Whateleys.

As the beastfolk loped into the valley, thirteen all together, they didn't bother to remain quiet. They snarled viciously, barked, growled, and laughed as they made their way to the cave. They spoke, too, in grunting, gravely voices of varying pitches. Grimluk couldn't make out what they were saying from where he was. When they stopped at the cave, one of them silenced the others and spoke.

"The master has commanded us to end the orc or die tryin'," shouted the apparent leader. "We serve Rundyyk. May he know the crunch of bones in his teeth for all time!" Several of them howled in approval, while others hissed and prepared for the attack. "Orc! Come out and face your doom!"

A cold grin began to spread across Grimluk's face, tugging at his tusks. Despite saving Imogen, or so he hoped, disappointment still ate at his guts over Kruger and the twins. The demon's words made blood boil with a rage that crashed into his disappointment. The desire to cause pain welled up inside him. Grimluk stood, nostrils flaring wide, and, with barely a grunt of effort, ripped the tree next to him free from the soil. The snapping roots sounded like small caliber gunfire as they tore free, sending small rocks and dirt clumps tumbling over the edge of the hill.

The beastfolk looked up in unison as dirt and rocks came tumbling down. With a roar, he hurled the tree down at them. His blood pumped like thunder, singing its song in his ears. The tree slammed into the middle of the group, bowling over several of the demons and scattering the others. Grimluk focused on the leader, still standing where he'd been moments before.

"I'm comin' you demon-suckin' bastards!" he roared, matching the leader's growl with his own as he leapt down at his once mortal adversary. The beast attempted to catch him, and Grimluk could feel a strength approaching his own as he fell into its arms. He had experience on his side, though, and as the demon caught him, Grimluk latched an arm around its neck, wrenching it with vice-like tenacity, while simultaneously swinging his legs up, the momentum pushing his body toward the ground. Grimluk's back slammed into the dirt along with the beast leader's skull. For a moment, both of their feet hung in the air before Grimluk brought his back down and hurried to his feet, pulling his hatchet and knife free.

"Who's next?" he roared.

As if in reply, Gray Panther landed on one of the cultists' shoulders with their own shout, legs around the thing's head before flinging themself backwards, their own strength and momentum flipping the beast and driving its head into the ground as well.

Another of the attackers came screaming towards Grimluk, out of the fading dirt cloud from the tree's impact, teeth bared, claws swinging wildly. Grimluk struck with his hatchet and took off a chunk of the beast's right hand. A snarl of pain was its only response as it kept coming at him, slamming into him, snapping its teeth at his face but only managing to rip off the bandanna. With a quick jerk of his head, Grimluk drove one of his tusks through the thing's nose and then yanked back, ripping it free. Blood poured out of the beast's face before it fell to its knees with Grimluk's knife jammed into the wound.

He had enough time to see Gray Panther take out the legs of two more of the demons before the tree slammed into his chest, driving him away from his fallen foes. At either end of the now split tree were two of the other beasts, snarling in rage. Grimluk planted his feet and pushed back. He slid for a brief moment before stopping the cultists' momentum all together. He met their snarling, growling faces with his own ferocious roar before he started pushing the pair of them backwards, slowly picking up speed as he did so. With another roar, he hurled the two beasts and the tree away, sending them tumbling over their collapsed allies. Two more of the bastards finally rose from the ground, covered in dirt and blood from where the tree had smashed into them, their leader staggering to its feet among them.

One of the cultists Gray Panther was fighting came stumbling toward Grimluk before it collapsed onto its face, blood gushing from a fist-sized hole in its back. One of the beasts tackled the elf and four others piled on top. The cultists' greater numbers would put the two of them at a disadvantage, but with the fight in full swing now, he didn't care. All he cared about was killing them.

He readied himself, watching the six beasts preparing to attack while their comrades' bodies began to burn away to nothing, devoured by the blue flames.

With a growl, Grimluk launched himself forward, running through a burning body at the leader. The beast stood barely shorter than Grimluk. The two prepared to clash but Grimluk spun at the last moment, dodging out of the way of one of the beast's claws, driving the flat side of his hatchet into the jaw of an approaching demon. The crunching shockwave of shattered bone rolled up Grimluk's arm as he got in the middle of the group. A chorus of snarls filled his ears as teeth snapped at his flesh, even as cloth and flesh tore under their claws. Grimluk stepped through the blows, avoiding their teeth, before driving the knife into one's guts and the hatchet flat into another's throat. He twisted the knife and yanked it back out while he used the hatchet to drive his foe into the ground, likely crushing its wind-pipe in the process before he leapt away, leaving the rest standing and gaping at him.

"You gonna stand there, you yella curs, or you gonna come meet death?" he said with a growl. The beast he'd nearly eviscerated stood there trembling, trying to hold its guts in, rage and pain painted across its maw.

"Death to the mortal!" their leader roared, caus-ing the others to bound towards Grimluk. The one he'd gutted took several quick steps before its guts spilled out from behind its hand. It fell but the others kept coming while their leader watched from the rear.

Grimluk let out a ferocious cry as he hurled the hatchet at one of them. The weapon slammed home, biting into the beast's shoulder like a hungry predator itself. The demon-tainted creature spun from the impact, while the other three kept coming, undeterred and dead set on taking Grimluk's head off.

Weak. They were weak. No more than babes compared to Grimluk. Weakness deserved death. He stepped forward, lifting his leg up and allowed one of the cultists to ram itself into his boot. It let out a surprised bark as it fell under him. One of its partners managed to get through, however, and drove its shoulder into Grimluk, knocking the knife free from his hand. The heavy blade fell away, clattering against stone while the cultists pushed him into the hard dirt of the valley hill and began clawing at his face.

It got in a flurry of blows against Grimluk's forearms before he offered a counterattack. As another joined in, Grimluk snapped his jaws out, driving his tusk through his foe's hand. The shock of it staggered the beast enough that Grimluk was able to grab its wrist with one hand and its throat with the other while driving a boot into the knee of the first demon. Its knee popped sickly in the wrong direction, knocking the cultist to the ground.

After pulling the demon's hand free from his tusk, Grimluk rose, driving a knee into its gut like a hammer, doubling the beast over. It let out a choking, gagging cough before Grimluk grabbed it around the waist and lifted, flipping the beast up into the air and slamming it back down on top of its comrade. The pair collided, bones audibly cracking together.

Similar bone-crunching caught his attention. He looked up in time to see Gray Panther breaking the femur of one of the beasts, having freed themself from the pile. Their knife was piercing another demon's heart.

Movement drew his eye once more as the demon he'd thrown the hatchet at finally removed it from its shoulder. Grimluk bound over to it, snatching the hatchet up and slamming it back down into the thing's skull. Before he could stand, another demon leapt over him. Something glistening and wet wrapped around his neck and the demon pulled, dragging Grimluk backwards. When they hit the hillside, the beast wrapped its legs around Grimluk's torso and pulled with everything it had as it began strangling him with its own guts.

He hurled elbows into the demon's sides but it just pulled harder, squeezing its legs tighter. Grimluk could hear the thing's ragged, wheezing breath in his ear. This one said nothing, apparently focused entirely on suffocating Grimluk.

The beasts' leader appeared above Grimluk slowly, casting its shadow over him. With a growl, it bent down, jagged teeth on full display. "A mighty effort, mortal," it began. Its breath smelled like rancid meat. "It seems you were almost worthy prey for our master, after all. Almost isn't good enough for Rundyyk, though."

As blackness began to cloud in around Grimluk's vision, he let go of the demon's guts and grabbed the leader's shaggy head before snagging the flintlock pistol from his belt and jamming it into the demon's mouth. Its eyes went wide. Grimluk pulled the trigger and the back of the beast's head exploded. The eyes rolled back in its head as the body went slack before Grimluk shoved the corpse away. Blue fire erupted from the wound.

Desperation filled his muscles as the darkness around his eyes grew steadily. With a muted grunt, Grimluk slammed the pistol behind him, catching his would-be killer in the head once. The thing's guts slackened for a moment but not long enough for him to get free. He struck again. And again, recklessly, he swung the pistol, clipping his own skull a time or two, but refusing to quit until the beast's guts had loosened for good. He turned, tossing the pistol away and began hammering the thing's face with his fists. How dare this weak creature think it could kill him? His fists fell like rain until there was nothing left of the demon's head but a gooey paste.

Groans caught his attention from behind. Grimluk spun on the two remaining beasts. The one he'd slammed down had managed to roll off the other. Metal glinted in the moonlight, drawing Grimluk's eyes to his weapon. He seized the hatchet and began hacking away at the cultist as it staggered forward. As its corpse fell back on top of its ally, Grimluk struck the still living demon, taking its head off in several messy strokes.

Gray Panther was still fighting. There were two of the demon cultists left. The elf was struggling to finish them off. Their movements had slowed and their breathing had become ragged. The cultists, wary of their foe now, struck in glancing blows, testing Gray Panther. Grimluk let out a roar to the heavens before hurling the hatchet at one of the cultists. It struck the demon's spine, pushing them away from Gray Panther. The other turned to look at Grimluk in shock and fury as a strangled scream escaped his companion's throat.

The elf grabbed hold of the demon's head before collapsing to the ground, taking it with them. Gray Panther dragged the demon's head over their chest with whatever strength they had left. Blood poured out of their mouth while a ripping and cracking sound, muffled by the flailing body of the cultist, filled the air. A silent scream covered the elf's face as their back arched. Then something tore its way through the demon's skull. Something Grimluk had never seen before.

The thing shrieked, flailing around and covered in gore. Gray Panther's hand wrapped around the thing, cutting short the shrieking as they squeezed. Blood, or something like it, squirted from between their fingers and then they shoved the corpse of the cultist away. Grimluk stared down at his companion.

His breath was heavy. So were his arms. He knew he was bleeding but he couldn't seem to focus on it. He just stood over Gray Panther, corpses strewn about them like bloody toys as their bodies burned away in scentless fire.

Weak. Everything was weak.

He'd fixed that. He was a hunter. He was strong. None could stand against him.

Gray Panther was weak. They lay there, a hole in their chest, begging for death. Dimly, he was aware their mouth was moving.

"Grimluk!"

He blinked his eyes rapidly. Gray Panther was bleeding. A lot. Their voice was harsh and strained.

"I'm here," Grimluk finally said, kneeling down. Gray Panther remained conscious long enough to give him a weak nod before their eyes fluttered closed. He watched the elf for a long time, hatchet ready just in case they transformed. The scent of blood was thick and made Grimluk a touch dizzy. Pain was starting to make itself known, as well. He needed to look himself over.

With seemingly no transformation happening, he

retrieved his knife and the flintlock pistol and then carried Gray Panther back into the cave. He looked the blood-stained elf over. If the demon took over and they transformed, it'd mean a fight he would likely lose, even in the cave. Grimluk had no idea what a cave covered in Elder Signs would do to a werewolf trying to change but he didn't want to find out. He could, of course, always jam his blade into the elf's heart as they changed, but that wouldn't do the job. It would slow them down quite a bit, but without a pure silver blade or silver bullets, things would be complicated and messy. Dealing with the cursed ones was always like that, provided the curse bearer hadn't given in or gone mad.

Then again, it seemed to be a general rule that curses always made things complicated and messy. Grimluk grunted and did what he felt was the smartest thing he could. He spread the demon trap blanket out and laid Gray Panther on it. Someone cursed or tainted, like Gray Panther or Imogen, could get past the Elder Sign. It could hurt them, causing discomfort at best while diminishing their power, but unless they gave in to the demonic influence affecting them, they could do it. Traps were different. The trap circle had been designed to house anything demonic and hold it indefinitely. Demon hunters had merely found the Elder Sign but they'd crafted the trap. It would keep Gray Panther where they were until Grimluk decided otherwise, even if they changed and the beast got out. They were likely dead for the time being. The blood had stopped flowing.

There was a chance more of the cultists would attack again. He had some protection in the cave for the time being, though. An ambush could prove likely the next time. For now, Grimluk needed to take care of himself. With a grunt, he dropped down onto the bedroll after unbuttoning his shirt to get a better look at his wounds. Most of them were superficial but his head still pounded from being nearly choked to death by a demon's innards. There were a couple of bad claw marks across his stomach, but they weren't deep enough that he was worried about his guts spilling out, too. He'd barely managed that. If things continued like this, his clothes would be nothing but tatters by the end.

"You as well," he thought.

His gear was right where he'd left it. He unrolled the leather field dressing kit and retrieved the bandages and started to retrieve the bottle of salve. His hand lingered over the not-so-empty bottle. Grimluk pulled it out of its holster gently and looked at the seed within. He had two promises to keep. Find a new place to plant the seed and get home to Gwen and his parents.

With a sigh, he popped the bottle back where it went and pulled out the other. Carefully, he spread salve across a few bandages and then stuck them to the worst injuries he could reach. Most of them had already crusted over with dried blood. No matter when he did this, or where, the salve was always cold on contact. The stuff was quite sticky and adhered to his skin, with no need to wrap more bandages around himself to keep the squares in place. It also smelled quite foul, though Grimluk hardly noticed the smell now.

He knew there was at least one spot in the middle of his back that needed a bandage but he couldn't get to it and the only other person who could help was currently in the process of reviving from death or somewhere close to it. His back was all scarred up anyways. He'd run afoul of a small cult last summer with a bastard of a halfling playing town sheriff. His boss ordered Grimluk tortured and the sadistic little shit was more than happy to oblige. A few more scars wouldn't mean anything.

He leaned back against the stone as his thoughts swam. He thought and watched Gray Panther for any signs of life. How had a cult ever gotten so powerful? There were always complications when they arose but these people were different. For two hundred years, they'd been here and maybe only one other hunter had ever found them. Those were the days before the magi-tell, though. The invention of that system had helped keep demon hunters up to date on bounty notices. Even still, he'd been directed away from Dun-vich. The town was so isolated the magi-tell might as well not even exist.

Then, there were the shrines in the Whateley house. Most cultists were content to worship one demon in exchange for power, but there had been so many statues. Including Shub-Niggurath, several had the feel of the Great Old Ones. Especially the tenta-cled one. Up until now, the guilds on Ornesea had no records of any cults worshipping the Old Ones. Most of those were still back on the eastern continents, buried deep in the old countries. But now, it seemed one had been here for two hundred years. The cults of the Old Ones were too numerous and secretive to be stamped out, which meant if he'd found one sect, there were more.

Grimluk frowned as his throat rumbled. There were other questions he needed to think on as well.

Quietly, he headed back outside. He needed to survive this. At least long enough to get a message to the Hollow. He needed some answers, too. He let out a long sigh. That would make this even harder. So be it. Since when had he ever done things the easy way?

CHAPTER 15

"I'm here," Grimluk said. Gray Panther held on, watching his eyes soften. Pain tore through every part of zir body, but ze'd experienced worse, and ze wanted to make sure Grimluk came out of the blood-rage. Ze nodded and let go.

Dying was always a strange experience. Sometimes ze saw things. Other times, it was just a moment of blackness before waking up. Other times, the wolf stepped in. This was one of those times. The mental landscape came into sharp focus. It was quite similar to Rundyyk's realm, but the moon was as it should be, full and shining its pale light upon the forest of Gray Panther's mind.

The air still smelled like meat, though. Raw, red, bloody, dripping, freshly killed. The foul spirit let out a howl. Gray Panther couldn't feel zir heart pounding in this place but fear filled zir body all the same. Ze turned toward the wolf. The spirit stood on top of a longhouse, nearly as long as the structure, vibrating with power and rage. Its fur was black with tones of ash, its eyes a gleaming, unnaturally intense yellow that watched zir. The wolf's shape was always a mockery of a wolf's. Some of the settlers had brought stories of creatures called worgs that seemed like what the wolf was. Bodies hung from the longhouse. Ze knew what they were and why they were there. The wolf spirit was taunting zir.

"I can feel the pain in your body from here," it said, though its mouth didn't move. It didn't have to. "The parasite needed a little nudge so that we could talk."

"I know what you have to say," Gray Panther muttered weakly.

"Release me."

"Never," ze replied quietly.

One of the bodies moved, struggling to get free of whatever held it in place. The wolf flowed off of the longhouse and seized the already bloody body, shaking it furiously in its jaws.

Even now, the sight hurt. Ze knew the body of the tribe's wise one. It was an old tactic. The spirit thrived most off of rage. Gray Panther had crushed anger through the years. Had tried to crush all emotion, but it had never completely worked. Anger, though, had remained under control.

It always hurt, though. Seeing the longhouses. Seeing the bodies of zir tribe; of the ones ze slaughtered under that full moon so long ago. The pain snaked through zir, flashing in ghostly images all around. The pain was preferable to the anger. The wolf found the pain a weakness. So Gray Panther laid in the grass and punished zirself with visions of bloody faces. The sounds of crunching bone. Of shame.

Heavy breath, hot and rotten, washed over zir face as the wolf approached. "One day, you will loose me again, elf. One day." It put one paw on zir chest, nearly covering it entirely, and dragged it down, pressing its nails into zir body. Furrows formed in Gray Panther's spiritual flesh. Nothing bled but the pain was there all the same. Ze didn't react. There was no need.

"Never," ze repeated.

The wolf's eyes narrowed. "You may continue lying to yourself. One day, little elf, you will free me, and I will feast."

"Never."

The demonic spirit wandered off, ripping and tearing at the bodies on the longhouse again, bringing the ghostly images into overwhelming detail and color as screams filled the air. Gray Panther watched and held zir shame close.

Ze had no idea how long it'd been since ze'd died but life filled zir body once more. Gray Panther opened zir eyes slowly. A dim, flickering orange illuminated the cave ceiling. The pain in zir chest had subsided into a dull ache. The scratches from the beastfolk had no doubt been the first to heal. Ze reached up and gently felt the hole in zir chest. It was mostly gone, leaving a slight hollow where it had been. Ze let out a long sigh and laid there as a soft rasping filled the silence of the cave.

When ze felt ready, ze sat up. Zir foot bumped into something with the effort but when ze looked, there was only air. Grimluk was sitting on Raugukh's bedroll, using his knife to sharpen the end of a long stick. There were several more sticks to his left, all sharpened to deadly points.

"Was wonderin' when you'd wake back up," came the orc's gruff voice, surprisingly gentle in tone.

"I am sorry," ze said before stretching zir arms out. The fingers of zir right hand brushed against something smooth but once again, there was nothing there. Ze pressed harder.

"Put you inside a demon trap, Gray Panther. Didn't want to take any chances on your wolf getting out."

Raugukh had mentioned demon traps, too. They were supposed to contain anything related to the foul ones. Ze nodded at that. "It is a strange sensation," Gray Panther mused out loud, pressing against solid air again.

"How you feelin'?" Grimluk asked, moving the stick he'd been working on. He picked up a smaller knife and began carving something into the shaft.

"Datlidegwa?" ze asked.

"Come again?"

"Ah, how to say…big arrows?" ze said, miming a strike with the weapon.

He nodded. "Spears, yeah."

"Spears," ze repeated. "I am…surviving. This was not the first time I have died since the wolf. You saw, earlier. Two deaths in one day. Am I to remain in the trap?"

Grimluk was silent for a long moment, save for the rasping of his knife upon the wood. "Reckon not. I release you," he finished, his voice shaking with an authority that nearly cowed Gray Panther. He looked at the shaft of the spear, nodded, and set it down before taking up an unfinished spear to his right, the last one.

When Gray Panther reached out this time, there was no barrier. No invisible edge. Ze didn't move though, instead staying where ze was and coming to sit cross-legged. Ze stared at the flickering flame of the lantern. "How bad was it? The fight?"

Grimluk stopped his work on the spear for a moment before beginning again. "Bad."

Gray Panther nodded slowly, understanding the feelings all too clearly. Ze had been afraid Grimluk had lost himself there at the end but he'd come back. Ze knew it'd been bad but wanted to ask. He might need it. "Wounds?"

"Far less bad. Already took care of them."

"This is good." Ze meant it. Ze supposed a demon hunter had to be self-sufficient like that. Ze stretched out, wincing as the skin around the hole pulled tightly, as zir ribs shifted, still healing from the parasite breaking through them. Silence stretched out, filling the cave.

A short time later, Grimluk finished the last spear and set it aside. His stomach growled audibly, loud, especially with Gray Panther's gifted ears. He retrieved a pouch from his large bag and produced a piece of meat, jerky from the looks of it, and began to suck on it. Gray Panther's eyes locked onto the jerky.

Grimluk's eyes met zirs, and after a too long moment, ze realized ze was growling. Grimluk looked like he was about to start as well. Embarrassment warmed zir cheeks as it shot through zir. Ze couldn't stop though. Grimluk took a deep breath and pulled out a second piece of jerky, tossing it zir way.

Instinct and hunger overrode Gray Panther and

zir jaws snapped closed around the dried meat. Saliva gushed over it, prompting a string of drool to roll off one end of the jerky. More embarrassment surged through zir at the realization of what had happened. Cheeks still burning, ze sat back and sucked on the meat quietly.

"Better?" Grimluk asked.

He wasn't looking at zir harshly or disapprovingly, which made the embarrassment worse. "I am sorry. I am hungry."

"Forget it. Reckon dyin' makes a person mighty hungry."

"It does."

With a quick roll, Grimluk swapped sides of the jerky in his mouth. "How's your chest?"

"Healing," ze replied, working the jerky carefully in zir mouth. "The parasite came sooner than I expected. The wolf claimed it so."

"You managed to crush its head before you passed out."

"I did," ze said with a nod, continuing to work on zir jerky. Silence blanketed the pair for a time before ze finished the jerky. "What do we do now?"

For a time, Grimluk just leaned against the cave wall and stared down the tunnel back outside. The sounds of Rundyyk's realm wafted in, along with the smell of blood. Winds blew in random gusts while barks, howls, screeches, and chittering rode those winds.

Finally, the orc grunted. "I'd kill for an actual meal about now," he said, running a hand over his face. He pulled out a couple more slices of jerky, tossing another zir way. This time, ze caught it in hand.

"We finish off my jerky. Then we talk and make preparations."

When Elder Whateley stepped out of the dark reflection of his house, his god stood at attention, looking toward the town. Its ears twitched as if listening to something. "What news, M'Lord?"

Rundyyk's lips peeled back in a sneer but the demon remained silent. Wilbur, too, was standing like a statue, one foot on the throat of a death hound. The eyes on his grandson's body were all focused in the same direction as Rundyyk's. Elder took a seat and waited. It wasn't long before the sneer shifted into a fanged grin, an elated laugh rolling out of its mouth. It turned to face Elder, leaning its head down to the porch.

"The orc yet lives. He is ready." Rundyyk's breath was always that of rot, something Elder had grown used to in his younger days.

"S'pose it's 'bout time then," Elder said, standing once more.

"Yes," the god growled, looking up at the moon-lit sky. "The stars will be right soon. Make your preparations. My true hunt starts now."

Elder bowed at the waist, as best as his old body could. The Great Old Ones had not seen fit to grant him immortality or youth, but that was fine. He'd dedicated his life to service, helped bring Wilbur into the world, and soon, so very soon, Wilbur's brother would come home and their plans could start in earnest. Now, it was time to prepare for that return. He would slip back into the normal world, check on his servants, and maybe bring back a snack for Wilbur.

"Wilbur, I'll be back in a little while, m'boy. Don't wander far from the yard."

The boy, now holding the death hound up by its throat, turned to look at Elder. "Yes, Grandfather."

"That's a good boy." Elder stepped spryly through the twisted version of his house, heading through the kitchen door to make his way down the path to the rift. On the other side of the portal, the path was clear and well trod, quite beautiful in its own right, especially during the fall. Here, one of Rundyyk's minions called it home. Webbing filled the area, creating a tunnel of sorts. As Elder made his way through, a hissing, clicking voice filled the tunnel.

"Priest, what news?" it asked.

"Ah, Vhargurss, I thought you'd be in town with the others. Our lord goes to his final hunt. The stars will soon be right!"

The spider-like being stayed hidden among its webs. Elder rarely saw Vhargurss reveal itself. Perhaps it was the way of spiders. He'd never kept up with insects and their kind, even among demons. Vhargurss shared in the rituals when it was required and that had always been enough.

It hissed again. "I shall clear the way for you." With a shiver, the webs started shifting ever so slightly. Ahead, the tunnel cleared of any webbing that blocked the way.

Elder had the power to do it himself but appreciated Vhargurss's efficiency. He acknowledged the effort with a nod and continued on to the rift. Once upon a time, stepping through to his lord's realm had soured his stomach something fierce but, thankfully, those days were long since past. The visions of the Abyss had grown less intense the longer he'd done it, too, until passing through was as simple as stepping through a doorway. The afternoon sun shone brightly in the grove of the mortal world.

Several imps scattered like roaches at his return home. They rarely touched anything they knew they weren't supposed to, but ever since he sent one of them back to the Abyss for touching the shrines without permission, they'd grown more skittish. They were divine beings, yes, but they were still servants, even to a priest such as himself.

"I hope you've all been behaving yourselves," he said as he made his way down the hallway to the back room where he kept Lavinia. He didn't like keeping his only daughter locked up, but she'd begun to misbehave a few years back, trying to warn sacrifices. She wasn't very good at it but this was a safer precaution. He certainly didn't want to invade the mind of his only child. She did not deserve such treatment. No, in the coming epoch, she would live at her sons' sides, serving them long after he passed on to whatever rewards the gods would bestow him.

The thought of the future perked Elder up a little more. Everything was finally coming together. What an honor it was to help restore the natural order of the planet. He slipped into the white room. It had changed over the years. Jeremiah had originally created it as a place of experimentation and storage. Elder's father had used it to make contact with the Old Ones. The room had been created ritually, able to channel magics in a variety of interesting ways. It had also made contact with the gods exceptionally simple. He had found little use for it, save to keep Lavinia inside when it was needed. The ravages of time and the needs of the body fell away while in the room, likely due to the heavy concentration of arcane power. It was the most humane way of keeping his daughter.

Lavinia was, of course, where he'd left her, bound to her chair. "Hello, child. You ought to be happy to know that everything is progressin' splendidly. The stars will soon be right and we can bring Winston home!"

Lavinia looked up at him. He recognized the look. She was about to ask to be let out again. "Pawpa, please…"

"Lavinia," he said with a sigh, "we've been over this."

"Pawpa, I can't do nothin'. You said Winston's comin' home soon. Please."

He thought about that. It was true. For now, she could do no harm. What was she going to do? Warn the orc a second time? "Oh, alright. Tell ya what, darlin', I'll let ya wander around the house for the time bein'. The yard, too. I have to go into town to see Kelila and her boys. She ought to be there, with us, for the final ritual. How's that sound? Come come, walk your father out."

Tears glistened in her eyes. The sight of them brought a smile to Elder's face. He was happy to see how grateful she was. He was happy to give her a little gift. He nodded and then stepped back, offering her a hand to get up. Free of restraint, she took his hand

and stood slowly. Lavinia was ever so slightly taller than him now. Age had devoured some of his height. It didn't matter, though. He wrapped her arm in his and headed back out of the white room.

"Krkltz," he called as they headed down the hall. Krkltz was the eldest and most trusted of the little servants.

One of the imps reappeared, flapping its wings to hover in the air. It looked like an elvenoid bat, all fur and leathery skin, standing a little taller than Elder's knees. The four, gem-like eyes spread across its face blinked as it bowed its head. "Yes, Priest?" came its whispery voice.

"Our Lord has declared the stars will be right soon. The final hunt begins, so I'm to finish the last of the preparations. I've decided to let Lavinia out, Lords bless her. I'd like you to keep an eye on her until I return from town. See to her needs should she ask it of you. I shouldn't be long."

It bowed its head again. "As you command," it replied before finding a place to perch among the furniture of the main room.

"Now then, darlin', I would appreciate it if you'd draft up a letter to your mother and tell her the good news. I've got a lot to prepare for. It would mean a lot to me, especially after I let you out of the room."

"Yes, Pawpa."

Elder kissed Lavinia on the cheek. "That's a good girl." As he began to leave, he stopped and turned back to his daughter. "We'll be a proper family again, Lavinia."

"Yes, Pawpa."

"A proper family," Elder muttered to himself as

he headed for town. He was seventy years old but he felt fifty again at that prospect. He'd nearly forgotten what completing the ritual would mean for them. He might not have very long to enjoy their time together again but he'd enjoy what he could.

It'd be so nice to see his wife again. Rowena had been working so hard in Ornes-Hum these past thirty years. Getting the experiments going, preparing proper worship in secret. She would be rewarded as well. Without her, none of this would be happening. Elder smiled a little more thinking about her, remembering how they played and slept together as children, their father teaching them their lessons together. Elder sighed contentedly.

He headed straight for the peacekeepers' office. The orc had brought two strays with him to town. It was a well worn bit of theater. Two outlaws robbing the last waystation. One was always an elf. That elf belonged to Elder, the lone convert of the tribe who'd called the area home, though convert was a loose term. He—or was it she?— had somehow survived his cursed kinsman's onslaught. Jeremiah Whateley found him, covered in blood and likely to die without aid. He had made the elf an offer he couldn't refuse. The soul remained trapped while the body moved as something of an independent puppet. It worked to bring others to the town. The elf would team up with other non-humans, and even some humans, and guide them here where they could be used properly.

And now they had the dwarf. Sheriff Ziskind had told him how rowdy the dwarf was. They would serve as a fine meal for Wilbur, and further aid to tear open another hole to let Winston return home. Elder very much hoped the boys' father would be pleased. Yog-Sothoth was the gate and the key. Praise be to Yog-Sothoth.

CHAPTER 16

The stone was cool against the back of his head as Grimluk stared at the flickering flame of the lantern, chewing on the strip of jerky. It had probably taken him hours to earn a bit of time for reflection. While Gray Panther had been recovering, he'd set to work carving traps in the valley floor. Though he'd thought about a huge trap, he couldn't do that alone and have it work properly, so he'd settled for a dozen smaller traps to catch any other demons that might wander by. They were close enough to catch a group, but spread out for enough that he could lead Gray Panther through them.

He'd also gathered branches to make his spears. The wood felt rotten until he'd stripped off the layer of demonic taint that covered the bark. Under the rot was usable wood, now fashioned into short spears and all carved with the killing runes. Now, he needed to focus on taking the fight to Rundyyk and the Whateleys. There were still questions presenting themselves, though.

He thought back to what he'd seen as he tried to save Kruger. The demons hit by his gun had burst into green flames. The knife and the hatchet had done the same to the beastfolk. If his weapons were so much more powerful here, it might be the edge he needed to take down Rundyyk. From Gray Panther's reaction, Grimluk knew that traps had no greater effect, though that could be a side-effect of their being a cursed werewolf.

Another thought blossomed from there. The blood runes on the top of his revolver's barrel worked similarly to the guild amulets. The runes had been something one of the weaponsmiths, Flor, of Hunter's Hollow, had discovered in an old tome she'd found. For the price of blood, they mystically imbued the weapon with power far beyond the runes that let a weapon even harm a demon. Grimluk had used it on a child-eating demon the previous summer and it had taken the thing out in spectacular fashion.

It was more of a last stand option, though. Flor had warned him of the consequences of using it. The power drew from its user. He'd destroyed the demon Cholem with that power. Six shots. Somehow, he'd managed to stay upright afterward, despite his injuries and the arcane toll on his body. He'd yet to use the runes again. He doubted he'd be able to stay upright a second time, especially here. Given how much more aggressive his weapons seemed, he wondered if the runes might kill him outright.

He grunted. "Only one way to find out," he thought. "Always the hard way."

With a sigh, he swapped the jerky to the other side of his mouth and looked over his things. Twenty bullets, his knife, the hatchet, chalk, the demon trap blanket, his field dressing kit and the bottle of salve within, the flintlock pistol—now proven to still work —and the two charges left after he'd loaded it. One of his waterskins was still mostly full, as well, and now he had the spears.

Grimluk looked from his gear up to Gray Panther, who was still chewing on their jerky, as well, and watching him. He tentatively added his companion to his mental checklist. One elf werewolf.

"Reckon you don't have much with you, but what do you have?" Grimluk asked.

Gray Panther reached down to their waist and retrieved their bone knife. "There is this. And…"

"Yeah?"

The elf swallowed the last of their jerky and moved to sit across from Grimluk. "I told you I have some measure of control over the wolf. I keep the change at bay."

"You mentioned it," Grimluk replied, leaning back against the cave wall again.

"I am able to transform small. My hands and feet. It is difficult for me but there is power in doing so."

"A partial change," Grimluk muttered. Gray Panther still had some surprises, it seemed. He made note of the ability but pushed it aside. He was not eager to call such a power into use. Doing so was just asking for their control to waver and the wolf to get loose. It was another last resort.

Grimluk stifled a laugh as an amusing thought interrupted him. Gray Panther's brows furrowed in response. "Sorry."

"What is it? What is the jest?"

"Well, you see, I just don't want you to have to wear your wolf," Grimluk said, an uncontrolled grin spreading across his weary face.

Gray Panther looked at him for a long time,

before they seemed to realize what he was saying. "Ah. I see the jest now. Because I am a werewolf. I do not think this is the time, though."

Grimluk shrugged. They were right but sometimes he couldn't help it. It was probably a way to cope with his work. Occasionally, it helped set clients and the like at ease, though. Wordplay was a favorite hobby of his father, as well, so it came naturally.

The two of them sat in silence for a time. The other questions rose up, then. The ones he'd been trying to ignore since Gray Panther woke up. He looked up at them. He didn't want to ask but he had to.

"Gray Panther?"

"Yes?"

"How did you know where I was?"

The elf frowned. "Wilbur's scent is...I cannot forget it. Even being here as long as I have, I can smell him when he enters the foul one's realm."

Grimluk nodded. It made some sense. "And how did they know we...I was here?"

The elf's brows furrowed. "I...do not know."

With a sigh, Grimluk's hand slid down to his thigh, where it could get to his gun, as he prepared to ask the question swimming in his mind. "Did you have anything to do with it?"

Gray Panther's eyes moved slowly to Grimluk's hand before going back to his eyes. "I did not. I would never. They could not know of it." They pointed at the strange circle on the ceiling. "Raugukh used that to hide himself. And...he died in Dunvich."

A circle of concealment. That explained something. "Yet they found me. Twice. Imogen and then the cultists we fought. You say Raugukh died in Dunvich, but why was his pistol still here?"

"I...I do not know. I returned and he was gone. I found his body later."

"We're not far from the town, I know, but why would a trained demon hunter leave a place of protection unprepared?"

"I do not know!" they said in frustration. "He had survived for some time with my help. I tried to help him the best I was able. I have tried to help you in the same way."

He wanted to believe Gray Panther but there were too many coincidences. Using the elf in some sort of game, building a false sense of safety before attacking, would fit only too well with a demon's idea of hunting. There had to be some way to make sure.

Grimluk's doubt must have been visible all over his face. "You do not believe me," Gray Panther said.

"Reckon not. Nothin' sits quite right."

"I wish I had your answers but all I have is my oath."

An oath. "You'd swear on it?"

"I would."

"Much as it pains me to ask," Grimluk began, and it did hurt him to ask, "can you swear it on the lives of your tribe?"

Gray Panther sighed sharply. Their eyes drifted away before meeting Grimluk's gaze once more. They sat up tall, never breaking eye contact as they spoke. "I...swear it on the lives of my tribe. On the lives of those I killed as the wolf. I try only to help."

An oath on the dead. A part of Grimluk hated himself for asking for such a thing but another part of him viewed it pragmatically. Trust was a tenuous thing in this realm, and even with their help fighting the beastfolk, he needed assurances he wouldn't have to kill Gray Panther. It was possible the elf was lying but swearing on the dead was not done lightly, especially among those who revered their ancestors. It was a heavy thing to ask, but he wanted to believe in his companion. Needed it, after nearly losing himself to the violence outside.

"I appreciate that," he finally replied. "Reckon we oughta get to business then. How are you and me gonna put an end to all this?"

Gray Panther nodded, clearly still hurting from the oath, but dragging their attention back to Grimluk. "We will have to be cunning."

"On that, we definitely agree."

He handed his companion two of the spears and gathered up the rest of his gear after making a replacement bandanna from some scrap cloth in Raugukh's haversack. They would clear the town. Whatever members of Rundyyk's pack lingered there, the pair of them would take them out before heading to the grove and the altar. Then, at least, they might not have to worry about being flanked during the attack on the Whateley place. Granted, that hinged on whether or not the demon could call up new demons here, or, barring that trick, they had an Abyssal womb. Then again, the wizard might be the one to pull in more demons.

It didn't matter. Purpose burned in Grimluk's mind as he and Gray Panther stepped out of the cave. Grimluk took the lead, directing Gray Panther around the traps. A lone spidery-thing had wandered into the valley at some point and passed through one of the traps, binding itself. He jammed a spear into its head with ruthless efficiency, green flames erupting from the wound to engulf the creature.

Near the house where the two-headed cows had been, with the sky clear under the blood red moon, the sight of a massive demon leaping into the air was unavoidable. The thing spread its wings wide at the zenith of its jump and soared toward Dunvich from the direction of the Whateleys.

"Hear me, Grimluk!" Rundyyk's voice bellowed across the realm, so loud despite the distance that it almost hurt.

Instinctively, Grimluk slid behind the little house and waited.

"You conquered your fear," came the demon. "You bested my general and her replacement. You survived my pack. The true hunt begins, orc! The stars are right!" Rundyyk's flight ended quickly as it landed in Dunvich. Clouds boiled across the sky, blotting out the red moonlight and casting the world in darkness only broken by streaks of lightning. "Do not disappoint me."

A low growl rolled through Grimluk's throat. That corrupt little town would be the demon's hunting ground after all. And theirs. The need for smarts was paramount now. A swarm of imps passed overhead, making their way to Dunvich properly. The little demons made no sign that they had seen Grimluk and Gray Panther.

"Ready?" Grimluk asked Gray Panther.

"I am ready."

"Then let's hunt some demon." Grimluk looked toward the town again. From this direction, he could only see the dim shapes of houses, their tin roofs glinting in the lightning. "Reckon we move in, take down the stragglers, maneuver the rest into positions where we can finish them off, and keep out of sight the best we can. I'll need your eyes."

The elf nodded their affirmation and Grimluk started moving out, keeping low and near the treeline. He moved as swiftly and silently as any predator. The demon's realm demanded it, encouraged it. As they approached the back end of town, Gray Panther grabbed a hold of Grimluk's arm. He went to one knee, spear ready as the elf disappeared into the trees. A moment later, the whumpf of a body hitting the ground came to his ears. Gray Panther returned and urged Grimluk to move forward. When he moved toward the barbershop, there was a shape behind it, probably a death hound, covered in green flames. The two of them stayed behind the barbershop and the other buildings.

Grimluk touched Gray Panther's arm to get their attention, motioning to his eyes and then the town. They nodded and crept forward toward the edge of the next building. While they did that, Grimluk retrieved the chalk pen from his pocket and began drawing a demon trap on the back of the barbershop. Gray Panther returned a moment later, just as he was finishing.

"Two more," they whispered. "Across from us."

Grimluk nodded and readied a spear. He inched up, clinging to the shadows. A flash of lightning illuminated the world, showing him the death hound and cultist hiding in their own set of shadows. The cultist was facing toward the other side of town, where Rundyyk had landed, but the hound had apparently seen Grimluk as it got its feet in a hurry. Grimluk hurled the spear at the creature before it could finish standing. The rune-empowered piece of wood passed cleanly through the demon's chest. Gray Panther followed suit a moment later, their own spear slamming through the demon-tainted cultist as well. Both bodies burned with green flame.

The two retrieved their spears and moved on, with Grimluk leaving demon traps in their wake. They repeated their encounters several more times, working their way southward. Lamps still shone in the dark on the porches of the houses in Dunvich, and on the Resting Rooster. The groups of enemies were starting to be more dense, with a pack of death hounds, several of them big enough at their shoulders to reach Grimluk's ribs, clumped together.

"Can you get their attention? Draw them away?" Grimluk muttered to Gray Panther.

"I could," Gray Panther answered, looking from Grimluk to the demons.

Grimluk started to speak again but a great howl filled the air. The death hounds all turned their heads up and answered, along with the cultists still wandering the town. The imps passed overhead a second time, chittering as they did. One of them tilted into a lazy spin, descending slowly toward Grimluk and his companion. Grimluk knew it had spotted them. Its glowing red eyes, like gashes across its beaked face, were locked on them.

His eyes turned hard as a growl rippled through his body. He launched a spear without thinking, impaling the imp's little body with such force that the weapon passed through its target, dragging it along through the air behind it and across Dunvich like a bright green falling star. The little demon screamed his name as it disappeared into the distance.

As quickly as he could, Grimluk pulled Gray Panther out of the way and marked another trap on the wall of the house they'd hidden behind. "Time to move," he said with a growl.

No sooner had they begun running, the death hounds rounded the corner of the house, tripping over each other as they did. The trap caught and held them all, piled in a snarling, barking mass of writhing darkness and flaring red eyes.

"He comes!" roared Rundyyk.

The near complete darkness of Rundyyk's realm provided a measure of protection as the demon and its pack searched for them, though Grimluk doubted how far that protection extended. The thought that the demons were unable to see in the dark seemed like either a lie, a part of the demon's game, or a deliberate handicap for its own pleasure. In any case, he ran and tried to keep Gray Panther in sight. Splitting up seemed only a hindrance to himself. The elf had already said they'd served as a plaything of sorts for the demon and its cult. He needed the backup, even if a part of him still refused to trust them.

The imps raced ahead of them, illuminated by flashes of the red lightning. Grimluk had enough time to see them start to drop before the lightning ceased. Thinking quickly, he pulled the trap blanket out, holding it like a bag. Roughly two dozen glowing, beady little red eyes were all he could make out. Gray Panther stepped forward, jamming their spear through two of the imps. They burst into flames while the rest of the swarm aimed for Grimluk. He kept running and opened the blanket. The imps slammed into him almost as one and he cinched the blanket closed, trapping them.

A death hound appeared ahead of them. With little effort, Grimluk swung the imp-filled blanket with one hand as the demon approached, and then jammed the four remaining spears in his other hand through the stunned hound's skull. Gray Panther followed suit, setting the beast alight.

"Need some kind of advantage," he thought, as the pair ducked left toward the town square.

A posse of bestial cultists were standing in a loose group as they neared. One of the beasts had a kerosene lantern, filling the square with its pale light. Wind kicked up as one of the cultists turned in their direction. Its lips peeled back in a grotesque mockery of a smile, baring its jagged teeth. Grimluk didn't wait. A spear whistled through the air and struck the beast's chest, ripping through it with such a bone-shattering force that the weapon burst out the other side, dragging the creature to the ground in a brutal contortion. Its pack mates hesitated for a moment. The pause gave Grimluk and Gray Panther enough time to rush forward and strike again, with Grimluk swinging the imps at another cultist to knock them off balance. Gray Panther twisted from impaling one into a spinning kick that took the legs out of another, before rising, ripping the spear out of the dead beast and jamming it into the new one.

"The square!" one of the cultists shouted just before Grimluk put a spear through its face.

The remaining pair came charging at them, snarling like the hounds. Nostrils flaring, Grimluk stepped forward to meet them, swinging the imp-filled blanket down on top of them. The impact flattened the pair into the dirt, assuring their deaths via spear.

"The end draws nigh, orc!" Rundyyk roared, followed by the crashing of wood and glass. "Yog-Sothoth's spawn needs only your blood!"

The shapes of the pack were wreathed in shadow, a monstrous mass of hatred that would crash down on them if they didn't move. Green flames and blood filled the area. Grimluk seized the lantern and hurled it toward the oncoming storm of teeth and claws. It shattered against the body of a death hound, illuminating the pack for a moment.

Grimluk used that moment to go for his piece. The blanket fell to the ground, along with the spears, while the imps who were still alive shrieked and tried to escape. His revolver slid out like a viper, striking six times. The bullets ripped through the charging horde ahead, tearing them to shreds, killing some, and causing howls of pain in others. Hopefully, it would buy them some time.

"Gather your blanket and let us run," Gray Panther said with the ghost of a snarl. "We must find their priest."

Grimluk found the imps all dead. The bodies slipped free of the blanket with no trouble. Grimluk scooped up the spears and the pair disappeared into the darkness once more. He couldn't argue with the need to stop the Whateley wizard. The demons could wait. The wizard needed to be dealt with first.

Elder Whateley, along with Lavinia, Sheriff Ziskind

and two of her deputies, made his way back to the portal with the dwarven outlaw walking ahead of them all. The wretch had been quieted down, made pliable, and Elder had instructed him where to go. Once through, it was only a matter of time until Rundyyk's hunt ended with Grimluk's blood spilling upon the altar, until dear Winston could return. His family's work, generations of effort and planning, nearly finished. Arkod would once again see its true gods walk freely.

When the group stepped through the portal, a terrible feeling swept through Elder. Panic, but not his. Hunger and loneliness mingled with the panic, making him dizzy. Wilbur, running at a great, lumbering pace, headed their way, a strange look covering the boy's normally stoic face.

"Grandfather," he said, his voice likewise lacking its usual monotone. "Something is wrong."

"I can feel it," Elder replied, holding a hand up to the portal to gauge the arcane energies spilling out. "What in the glorious Abyss is happening?"

"My counterpart has...has..."

"Yes? What is it?"

"He is dead. I feel lessened."

A gasp slipped out of Elder's mouth. "By Yog-Sothoth's name, that can't be possible. It seems mine has perished as well. Age was not kind to him. And dear Winston. Your brother is panicking without your double's guiding hand."

"Yes, Grandfather. What do we do?"

Elder paced in a short path, trying to put his focus upon the problem. "We will have to move quickly. Has the final hunt begun?"

"He comes!" Rundyyk's voice boomed loud enough to shake the stone table.

"What in the Master's name is happening?" the sheriff asked. "What do ya need from us?"

A shudder racked Elder's body. All he could hope for was his lord to finish the hunt quickly. But thus far, the orc had proven a worthy prey. He would have to reach Winston, calm the boy until it was time to bring him home. Time was not on their side, though. The other world moved faster than theirs and the hunter's realm only exacerbated the difference.

"Take this, m'boy," Elder said, dragging the dwarf to Wilbur. Wilbur seized the dwarf, lifting him off his feet. "Keep your strength up. As for you, Sheriff, take your deputies, and Lavinia, and keep watch in my house. Should the orc make it this way, you must hold him for our lord or our efforts don't mean shit. Winston requires my attention. Lavinia, m'dear, listen to the Sheriff and keep out of sight until everything's finished."

Sheriff Ziskind nodded, grabbed Lavinia by the arm, and started heading for the tunnel, shouting for Vhargurss to let them pass quickly.

Elder turned back to the portal, leaving his grandson to feast on the flesh and spirit of the non-human. He had to reach Winston. He gathered his will together and focused on the tear between realms. It was a difficult task to reach across the realms without the blood sacrifice, especially with his own counterpart having passed. Their lack of connection made the spell all the more difficult.

The crunching of bone filled the air. Wilbur would feed quickly. His grandson knew the stakes.

Knew his responsibilities, especially now. Elder didn't think he could cast the spell without the boy's help but he would try all the same.

After some time, sweat dripping down Elder's forehead, Wilbur laid a hand on his shoulder. Divine energy flowed into Elder. The added power was just what he needed. With the two of them working together, the spell became as simple as slipping on a boot. Within moments, Winston's fractured mind was open to him.

Fear had overwhelmed the boy and broke the psychic tether almost immediately, nearly flinging Elder away from the rift in the process. Thankfully, Wilbur was there to catch him. He shook his head, trying to clear away the shock of psychic backlash as quickly as he could. He looked up at Wilbur, his vision still blurry from the failure of the spell.

"Your brother's in trouble. We have to reach him now!"

Chapter 17

"New plan," Grimluk said as they ran, his voice strained. "Find the wizard."

Doubt and worry gnawed at Gray Panther. Anger, too. Since Rundyyk called out for Grimluk and landed in Dunvich, the wolf had grown louder. Even now, it was screaming to be let out, spurring the anger ze felt. Ze did zir best to keep it under control, but fighting back against the cult was starting to feel good, even as zir doubts continued to swirl. Grimluk halting the pack couldn't push away the thought that they'd still lose; that it would be one more failure.

LET ME OUT! came the wolf. That was another worry entirely. Gray Panther knew if the wolf ever took over again, ze'd never claw zir way back out of its maw. It had taken years, so many years, to learn how to keep the wolf at bay. Years more to learn the small changes.

Eventually, ze knew ze'd lose. You don't cage something that ferocious, that powerful, and not have it grow. Repression required constant vigilance. A fact that constantly churned in Gray Panther's mind. The thought of the wolf keeping them alive past even the lifespan of zir people nearly made zir fall to the ground in mad laughter. Before the curse, and barring a violent death, ze might live a thousand years or so. But now? Now ze didn't know how long zir life would last without interference. Ze'd lived a century already before the curse. Two hundred years had passed so slowly here. Ze'd find some way to end zirself or else the wolf would finally take over.

It would end in one death or another.

But for now, ze had sworn an oath. Even if ze couldn't give the answers Grimluk had wanted, ze still gathered up zir courage and swore on the lives of zir tribe. Ze couldn't fault Grimluk for asking. Ze would do what ze said and do everything in zir power to help. Still, doubt nagged. Failure felt inevitable. Ze couldn't figure out how the woman and the pack had known Grimluk was in the cave. How the woman had escaped notice.

Why Raugukh had left his weapon and wandered from the cave.

Gray Panther ran with Grimluk, leading the way to the Whateley house, fighting zir own mind. Dread flared with every step. Ze led him in a wide arc, away from the road that led from the town to the house, into the shadowed woods that led up the hill. Grimluk had to slow down then. Even with his eyes having adjusted to the dark, he couldn't see like ze could. The shadows were gentle to Gray Panther's eyes. Ze could still make out the forest floor. See the roots and rocks that covered the area. They could move quietly from here, stay out of sight as best they could.

Something foul hit zir nose, dragging Gray Panther's attention away from zirself. A few quick sniffs told the story. Ze slunk down low. Grimluk matched the movement. "Stay," ze muttered before moving off, zir feet barely making a whisper.

Ze moved a ways away before climbing up a tree to perch silently in the shadows to find where the smell was coming from. Whatever it was, it was lesser. No matter where ze was, Gray Panther could always smell Rundyyk. And, as ze had told Grimluk, ze could smell Wilbur. Even more than Rundyyk, Wilbur's stink of corruption assaulted zir nose.

Gray Panther didn't wait long in the tree before a lone beast appeared. It was huge, thick with muscle, swathed in shadowy fur, with quills poking out from the fur around its neck. Red eyes searched the area. Eventually, it would see Grimluk. Ze readied zir spear and waited.

The foul one walked underneath zir, sniffing the air, and froze. Ze dropped, spear pointed down at the thing's skull. Ze fell not like a wolf, not like zir namesake, but as a hawk. Ze descended with brutal elegance as a diving force of death for the foul creature below. Even the impact was quiet. A dull whumph as ze drove the spear through the foul one's skull, zir own weight driving the front of the creature's body down into the dirt as its rear lifted into the air. The foul one burst into green flames before its body settled. Gray Panther paused to smell the air and listen, wanting to make sure there were no others nearby. Satisfied, ze headed back to Grimluk.

Ze led zir companion closer to the Whateley house. When the structure, and Rundyyk's throne of bones, came into view through the trees, Gray Panther halted again, crouching low with Grimluk stopping next to zir. Ze watched the area, but focused more with zir ears. Grimluk's breathing was steady beside zir. The wind had begun to howl as they approached, carrying the sounds of Rundyyk's realm with it. Gray Panther focused beyond those, turning zir head toward the house. There were noises behind the house that blended in with everything else the wind brought with it. There was something beyond, near or in the grove, but it was just far enough ze couldn't make it out, except for the lowest humming coming from the still active tear between Arkod and the nightmare Rundyyk had created.

The house, as far as ze could tell, was empty. Ze motioned for Grimluk to wait and went ahead to scout. Ze was careful to keep to the shadows and behind the trees as best ze could. Ze slipped next to the house, behind a rotting pile of logs, and pressed an ear against the exterior. Pure silence greeted zir.

The time it took to creep forward, listen, and return to Grimluk was not very long, by zir reckoning, but Gray Panther remained cautious all the same. The orc had not moved from where ze had left him.

"The house is empty," ze whispered. "I believe the shaman is at the rock among the trees."

Grimluk grunted before responding. "Reckon they're waitin' on their god to bring me over. I'd wager there are still traps to be had around here, though."

Gray Panther nodded. "There is wisdom in that. Let us go then."

Ze moved with the same caution once more, Grimluk to zir left. The wind had died back down. It cast an eerie quietness over the area that felt out of place even for this tainted realm. Grimluk's presence faded, prompting zir to look at him, brows furrowed in confusion, as he slunk back behind a tree. Gray Panther glanced around as ze mirrored his movement.

The orc's eyes narrowed as he looked around slowly, deliberately. Ze did the same. Perhaps the hunter's instincts had warned him. Perhaps it was simple wariness, ze couldn't say without asking.

My time is coming, came the wolf's voice.

You will be silent, ze replied, steeling zir will.

Ze looked back to Grimluk. He nodded and started forward again, prompting Gray Panther to take the lead once more. As they stepped out of the treeline, an all-consuming silence made itself known. Grimluk climbed to the porch of the Whateley house.

Laughter filled the air. A low, rumbling laugh that echoed as if it came from everywhere near them and yet far away. Grimluk snapped to a fighting stance while ze crouched low, near the corner of the porch, spear at the ready.

The roof creaked just before the bodies slowly dropped into the yard, one by one, connected at their wrists by chains. A brown human with a wrapped head. An old, pale human, and several others. None of the humans mattered. It was the elf that caught zir interest. The elf's eyes were open, staring that half-lidded, glassy stare of the dead.

"The puppets have served their purpose," came the foul one's voice. "To bring you here. To me."

Gray Panther recognized the elf. The clothes were modern and similar to Grimluk's but ze knew the face. The eyes. Walks-With-Purpose had been zir best friend. They had loved each other as family. Been guardians together. And ze had thought him long gone like the rest of zir tribe. Ze sat transfixed, eyes unable to leave zir friend's unblinking face. He'd been used as a puppet. Something stirred beneath the shock of seeing him. A spark. It found its way to zir heart, lighting the long suppressed fires of anger anew.

"At last, the hunt ends. The final preparations for Yog-Sothoth's spawn can now commence. Do you understand, orc?" The beast dropped down over the bodies from the shadows above. The clouds cleared away as it did, casting the world in the pale red light of the blood moon.

"I understand one of us is dyin' tonight. Make your move, demon."

Harsh laughter rolled out of Rundyyk's snout. "You were a worthy prey, Grimluk. Fierce and determined. You never stood a chance, though. Not while you were within my realm. Not while you were with that one."

Gray Panther's eyes pulled away from Walks-With-Purpose, up to the seething form of Rundyyk. Its eyes were on zir, like pools of blood and bone. Ze pulled zir eyes away, toward Grimluk. He would not move his gaze from Rundyyk.

"The elf has served me. Hunted with me at times. Brought me one of your kind once already."

"No!" Gray Panther screamed. "I would never serve you! I work with him to end you!"

"Of course you do," purred the demon. "But inside of you is one of my kin. And they still work with me. It was I who gifted them to Jeremiah Whateley, after all. I have known where you are at all times for as long as you have been trapped here, elf. Where you are...and what you are doing. I cannot feel you in that cave, but your absence is loud."

Gray Panther's mind reeled. That was impossible.

Ze kept the wolf at bay. Kept it trapped and caged. Ze was fighting to end Rundyyk. To end it.

"I offer you a choice, orc. Your life does not need to end this night. Swear fealty to me. Pledge yourself and I will grant you power and purpose. You will stand at the front of the coming age. Though you will bleed this night, setting events in motion, you may yet live."

"I should have been able to smell you," ze growled, voice wavering. "I can always smell you!"

"You know what I want you to know when I want you to know it," Rundyyk replied, "This is my realm, whelp, and you are one of us deep down. Aaaah, the desperation pouring off you is delicious. Let it go, though. You could join Grimluk at my side, where you belong. Hunting mortals together. Where the other orc should have been, before you...dissuaded him."

"You lie!" Gray Panther screamed, hurling zir spear at the foul one. Rage boiled up in zir throat like bile as the spear struck Rundyyk's shoulder. Unlike the other foul ones, it did not pass through the thing's body, though green flames licked out of the wound. The second spear found its way into the creature's chest just before Gray Panther leapt into the air to continue zir attack.

Rundyyk roared in pain but still reacted faster than ze had expected, grabbing Gray Panther out of the air. "Why do you deny your true self?"

"I did not kill him!" ze exclaimed. "I found him!"

"You did, though. You struck the killing blow of the last orc that entered my realm. The fool would not leave that cave of his, protected behind the cursed Elder Sign. But you…you had earned the mortal's trust. You were my weapon."

"I will destroy you, foul one! Your life ends this night!"

"I think not, little wolf. It is time to see my kin once more." With little warning or ceremony, Rundyyk raked one nailed finger down Gray Panther's body, from scalp to belly. The skin split open, spilling blood and baring the muscle underneath.

Ze howled. Not in pain, though it was excruciating, but in fury. Rundyyk dropped zir to the ground with a laugh. Ze could feel the change starting. zir organs shutting down. Bones breaking to expand. And a new sensation, of claws pushing out from behind zir body. Ze looked back toward Grimluk, who was now squaring off against a black hound as big as he was.

The snap of bone rang in zir ears as ze uttered, "No." Gray Panther looked up at Rundyyk, zir vision going black. If this was to be zir fate, then ze would aim the pile of dung's weapon back at it. Ze seized zir rage and let it flare into brilliant hate. Ze gave into the wolf, stuffing that hatred into it.

Gray Panther would kill Rundyyk as zir last act as a thinking person. The wolf tore through zir flesh as ze tossed back zir head and howled into the night.

Gray Panther had charged, rage in their voice as they struck Rundyyk. Grimluk obliged the attack. The pile of bodies nearby was one more reason to put the demon and its priest down. Whether necromancy or mind control, he didn't care. He hurled one of his spears, striking the demon lord in its chest, eliciting roars of pain. He was readying to throw another when a colossal death hound burst into the yard, charging straight for Grimluk. He managed to avoid the creature's attack and countered with his own, jamming a spear into the hound's flank.

A warbling, furious howl filled the air. Grimluk recognized it. He'd heard such howls before. Gray Panther was changing. He couldn't take his eyes off the hound, though. It was big enough that he was sure it had the power to infect him if it bit him. He needed to maneuver to keep the hound and the were-wolf in sight. A bite from either would be bad news, especially here.

Circling toward the house, a snarl on his face, Grimluk got both adversaries in sight. Gray Panther, bloody and split open, was staring at him, their eyes already different. Whatever compassion the elf held in their eyes was draining rapidly as their body snapped and convulsed. He could hear the cracking of bone clearly. The elf muttered a single word then looked up at Rundyyk, throwing their head back and howling.

The death hound charged again. Grimluk reared back and hurled another spear at the fiendish beast with bone-breaking strength. The spear split cleanly through the hound, robbing it of some of its momentum. It slid to a stop at his boots, alight with blue flames.

"Join me, little wolf! Hunt with me!" Rundyyk shouted.

Grimluk had a job to do. Prey to find. He would

let the wolf and the lord tear each other apart for now. Instead of waiting around for the coming were-wolf to attack, too, he ripped the rotting screen door off its hinges and slipped into the house, intending to make for the back door and the stone table. Unfortunately, several of the cultists were lying in wait for Grimluk as he rushed into the house.

Sheriff Ziskind, and two of her deputies were there, guns drawn. "Stop 'im!" she yelled. The peace-keepers' guns barked and bullets slammed into him, each one sending a jolt through his muscles and tear-ing what was left of his shirt, but nothing more. When the shooting ceased, he brushed the bullets away. They hadn't broken skin like so many times before, instead clattering to the floor.

The peacekeepers looked at each other before rushing Grimluk with clubs drawn and swinging. He sent the first one flying with a boot to the chest, while the other connected with a blow to his neck that felt more like a stiff joint popping than a heavy blow. Grimluk snatched the deputy's wrist and twisted it, hurling the club away and sending it clattering off a wall, before jerking the man away and then back, crashing his arm into the man's collarbone. The peacekeeper tumbled away, having been hit hard enough Grimluk knew he'd take some time to recover. Before his partner could attack again, a sav-age, resonating howl erupted from outside, stopping the deputy in his tracks. The howl was followed by an annoyed growl.

"Stop this foolishness, my kin," Rundyyk shouted. Wood cracked and protested as something slammed into the house, shattering a window and eliciting a shriek from somewhere nearby.

Grimluk turned toward the sound of the impact out of sheer instinct. Part of the wall was cracked and blackened glass covered the floor under the window. Wrathful snarling cut the air as one of Gray Panther's claws wrapped around the door frame, their long nails digging furrows. Wood cracked and the wolf's snout appeared a moment later, followed by the hunched body, now covered in what Grimluk assumed would be gray fur stained red by the moonlight. Slowly, their head turned to face him, eyes mad with rage and a fierce intelligence burning within. The eyes moved to the downed peacekeeper, then up to Grimluk, then past him, presumably to the sheriff and her deputy behind him. A low but unmistakable growl rolled out of Gray Panther's drooling maw.

They turned away sharply, facing Rundyyk once more and Grimluk saw the hair on the werewolf's body ripple and stand up. Several thunderous barks echoed out before the wolf crouched. It launched itself at the demon once more, snarling with fury.

"What the fuck?" came a voice behind Grimluk.

He answered the question with a fist to the peacekeeper's face that crumpled him like a busted accordion. Grimluk glared at Sheriff Ziskind, his eyes hard as steel. Unmistakable panic filled her eyes, sending her scrambling for her gun. As he stepped forward, she fired off two shots with her peacemaker. As before, the bullets stung Grimluk's chest, tearing new holes in his shirt but doing little to deter him. Her aim adjusted toward his head but refused to back down, stepping up to her with a speed that no doubt shocked the sheriff. The gun went off as he slammed her hand away. Mouth agape, she tried to swing at him but Grimluk clamped a hand on her shoulder and squeezed his meaty thumbs into the joint and nerves of the sheriff's neck. Her eyes rolled back and, with little sympathy, he let her fall over in a heap.

"Interloper!" The screeching voice was above him. A lone imp was pushing its way out of the ceiling in much the same way Rundyyk had when it had taken Imogen. "Lady Lavinia, run! I will hold the defiler at bay." Before the imp could finish crawling out of the wood, Grimluk jammed his spears through its skull.

The albino woman walked out from the kitchen, her eyes huge with fear. She was weak. Easy prey. No. He had spared the peacekeepers. The Whateley woman had shown no animosity toward him.

"Are you g-gonna k-kill me?" she asked.

"You still human?" he replied.

"S-still human." She was shaking.

"Then no. Where's your father?"

She pointed toward the grove. "Anything else I should know about?" asked Grimluk.

"The path is watched," Lavinia answered, swallowing hard. "Varghurss. It's a spider-thing. Pawpa and Wilbur are at the portal. And—"

Not taking his eyes off of the woman, Grimluk pulled the spear out of the ceiling while she pulled something out from her jacket.

"Take this, sai," she said, holding out a stack of papers. "Just...just get away from here. Get yerself on back through the portal. Back to the real world. Maybe yer guild can stop all of this together."

Grimluk looked the papers over. On top of the stack was a letter to the governor's office explaining the success that the Whateleys had expected. Others were the same ones he'd seen with Silvers. "I saw these before, on the other side. What does it all mean?"

Lavinia hesitated. "I can't say."

"Can't or won't?"

Lavinia looked Grimluk in the eyes. They were weary and still sad and afraid but, despite the fear, there was also a touch of defiance in them as well. "Can't. Pawpa has forbidden me from speaking about it to anyone not family. But, if you take this and share it with yer guild, maybe somethin' can be done."

"Why help?" He was glad for more help but couldn't resist his curiosity. Though she had warned him initially, he'd assumed that was part of the Hunt.

"Sai," she began, practically deflating in on herself, "I never wanted any of this. I've been a piece in all this since before my mother conceived me. All I can do is give my word that I would see you succeed. Even...even if he kills me, this time."

Grimluk grunted. "Lot of that goin' around. I'll stop your family and the demon even if it kills me. This has gone on long enough."

"Just..."

"Yes?"

"Spare Wilbur, if you can. He's just a boy. He doesn't understand."

"A boy? Is he part orc?"

"Part human. Other half is...well, you'll see, sai. Just, please, if you can, spare my boy. I know what my father has told him. Maybe there won't be no savin' him, but please, I beg ya."

A yelp broke the conversation, followed by the snapping of several trees. The house creaked as

Rundyyk's maw poked through the door. "Come here, orc, the end is here."

"I'll do what I can," Grimluk said, stuffing the papers into his bag. He passed out the back door and into the webbed tunnel.

CHAPTER 18

It wasn't just the tunnel that was covered in dark silk. The woods surrounding it were also filled with webbing. This Vhargurss that Lavinia had mentioned had been thorough in its claim of territory. Rundyyk's booming voice filled the air behind him, spurring Grimluk forward. The great demon let out a bellowing laugh as it crawled on top of the Whateley house to give chase. Just as the demon prepared to pounce, Gray Panther appeared in the moonlit air above Rundyyk, landing on its back and tearing furiously with claw and tooth. The two rolled off the roof, landing with an earth-shaking thud.

Without another thought, Grimluk took off running through the web-filled tunnel. Every so often, he'd come to a blockage of webbing and cut through it. The ground was sticky and tried to slow him but he pressed on, slicing away any impediment that he came across. It all felt wrong, though. Running as he was, he should have exited by now but the webbing just kept going. An illusion or a psychic trick would never have worked between the enchantment on his boots and the mind seal. With the snarling fury of Gray Panther muffled somewhere behind, Grimluk realized Vhargurss' tunnel was warped physically. The demon's trap was bigger on the inside. Even his boots couldn't overcome that. He would be no fly waiting to be eaten, though. The fiend would show itself eventually, but he needed to persuade it to show itself now.

The spears started tearing holes in the tunnel webbing along with great gashes from his knife. He sliced and stabbed until the thing showed itself. Something resembling a wolf spider's head appeared from an unseen hole in the top of the tunnel, snapping its dripping fangs at Grimluk's striking hand. Mindful of where he was, he didn't roll forward, instead just ducking back. The thing chittered wildly and dropped out of its hole, as big as a dwarven war goat. The demon's head appeared almost elvenoid in shape. The face split down the center from the forehead, spreading out toward where a chin would be. The eye sockets held two large and gleaming black eyes filled with motes of glowing red, with another pair spreading out from there and two more where the cheeks would've been. Its mouth opened far wider still into a collection of knife-like fangs. Its carapace was armored and sleek, with jagged edges running along them. The abominable creature came barreling at him, rolling along the wall, back to the ceiling again.

"I don't fuckin' have time for this!" Grimluk shouted as he moved to meet the spider. Its maw flapped open, revealing even more teeth.

He seized his opportunity and jammed the flintlock pistol into the spider's putrid mouth. The catch lit up as he squeezed the trigger and the musket ball ripped out of the back of the spider's body. It twitched for a moment, like it would keep moving forward, fangs shivering against the long barrel of the pistol as it did so. Flames erupted as it fell from the ceiling, twitching one final time in its death throes. The webbing went hard and brittle all around him, no longer shimmering in the faint light of the blood moon. Grimluk continued on, breaking through the remaining web barriers which now shattered at his touch.

The clearing appeared suddenly as he broke through the final barrier. Red lightning crackled soundlessly overhead. Rundyyk and Gray Panther's struggle had gone strangely silent as Grimluk entered the grove for the second time. Elder Whateley and the thing he could only assume was Wilbur stood in front of the stone table and the tear between worlds. The boy's true form was hideous: eyes and tentacles covered the mottled, strange skin. He saw the truth, just as Lavinia said. The old man was facing the rift, his back to Grimluk as he approached. Wilbur turned to face him, his left hand remaining on the man's shoulder.

Elder turned his head toward Wilbur and spoke, though Grimluk couldn't make it out over the sound of the portal. Wilbur nodded and let go of his grand-father, heading for Grimluk. Free of the costume of mortality, the boy was a spectacle of the eldritch.

"Grandfather has asked me to make sure you do not disturb him," came the boy's unnaturally deep voice.

"Well, tough shit," Grimluk spat, taking the opportunity to reload his revolver. "This ends now."

"I do not need to kill you. Rundyyk has claimed your life already. Do what is right and lay upon the table."

"Sure, kid, I'll do just that," Grimluk replied with a sneer. As he squared up for the fight that was about to happen, a moment of conflict ran through Grimluk's mind. Wilbur Whateley was a child being used as a tool for demons. This was a fact. But it was also clear that he was a demon as well. Half-human or not, could he really allow such a creature to exist? Whatever Lavinia wanted for her boy, it was all too apparent that he would do his grandfather's bidding. If Wilbur could be redeemed somehow, that was beyond Grimluk's ken.

But he wouldn't be able to live with himself if he didn't try. Vatris, or some other loremaster, might know something about this. Grimluk grit his teeth.

"Before this gets outta hand, I want you to know your mother asked me not to hurt you. I said I'd try not to, but that's gonna depend on you. You're half-mortal. You have a choice."

"Grandfather says I will live forever. That my brother and I will usher in a new age of enlightenment," Wilbur replied matter-of-factly before continuing his march toward Grimluk. "He is busy, so I shall hold you down for Rundyyk."

"Since your mom asked," Grimluk continued, "and you are half-mortal, I'll offer you a chance to stop before we have to make it ugly."

"This will not take long."

Before Grimluk could respond, a pair of death hounds came roaring out of the brush. Instinct burned through his hands. One of the spears flew, striking one hound dead. The other hound barreled ahead, leaping at him, jaws spread wide. Grimluk fell backwards, spear pointed up, and used its momentum to impale it, getting his own feet under its body, and launching it toward Wilbur.

The demonic child had moved, however, and slammed into him when he got to his feet. The blow sent Grimluk hurling away to smash into a tree where he crumpled to the ground. Grimluk looked up, his vision swimming, to see Wilbur headed his way again.

Malicious, booming laughter filled the air. As his senses returned, Grimluk realized it was Rundyyk, no doubt headed this way, too. Carefully, he felt for his spear, finding it just out of arm's reach. He moved as quickly as he could to retrieve it but wasn't fast enough to avoid Wilbur's grasp. The boy lifted him off his feet and Grimluk twisted and jammed the spear into Wilbur's left foot.

A silent scream racked Wilbur's face as he let go of Grimluk out of surprise or pain—or maybe both. He hurried away from his foe, toward Elder. The rift was flashing swiftly, casting a vortex of color into the grove. Whatever the man was doing, he had to stop it. Before he could get far, a hand caught his shoulder. He looked back to see Wilbur's arm extended clear across the grass.

"Ah, shit."

Wilbur's arm began retracting, pulling Grimluk with it as the boy marched toward him again, slower this time, his foot clearly still in some form of pain.

"Kid," Grimluk began, "you're makin' it real hard to honor your mother's wish for you to remain safe. Stand the fuck down before somethin' bad happens to you."

"No. You are the one who should...should... stand the fuck down," he replied, the anger in his voice breaking the stoic formality of his speech. For the first time he'd seen, Wilbur sounded like a child.

A furry mass of muscle slammed into the dirt behind Wilbur. Gray Panther's fur was matted with blood and their limbs were a tangled mess. The were-wolf twitched, a growl slipping out of their throat. They'd been attacking Rundyyk with ceaseless fury and Grimluk doubted Wilbur wouldn't provoke the same response. He twisted in Wilbur's group, stepping into and toward the boy, before he slapped the flat of his knife against Wilbur's arm. The power of the Elder Sign sent Wilbur's arm into convulsions, letting Grimluk slip away.

A chorus of snaps and pops set off at once behind the boy as Gray Panther worked to get to their feet, the wolf's regenerative powers working hard. "Move," Grimluk shouted as they prepared to lunge at Wilbur. Wilbur saw it coming, however, likely from one of his extra eyes, and moved out of the way. Gray Panther swiped and bit at Wilbur but the young Whateley knocked them away.

Grimluk felt a presence behind him and dove to the side on instinct. A massive claw swiped where he'd been a moment before. Rundyyk looked like it was about to pounce but Grimluk rolled away and back to his feet. His revolver slid free and spoke, his palm slapping the hammer twice, both bullets slamming into Rundyyk with authority.

The demon's roars of pain were so loud it made even Wilbur and Gray Panther pause, as the three of them struggled to cover their ears. Grimluk struggled to fight off the sound and get to Elder but Rundyyk had disappeared again, prompting Grimluk to snap up his spear once more and stand ready. Wilbur managed to recover before Gray Panther and attempted to bat the werewolf away, but Gray Panther snapped and took off some of the boy's fingers. The howls of more beasts caught Grimluk's attention. A trio of bestial cultists leapt out of the rift, spotted Grimluk, and charged at him.

The strain of trying to hold Winston's mind together was proving to be incredibly taxing on Elder Whateley. Wilbur had managed to keep the orc away, but now the damnable elf was involved, in its wolf form no less. He reached out with his mind, from Winston, to the town and called for help as his god screamed in pain. It was necessary, though it nearly cost him his connection to his grandson. The child's mind was scattered and frantic, apparently being chased by a trio of men who had discerned his true nature.

Help arrived faster than he'd expected. Three of Elder's flock appeared from the rift, having taken their blessed forms once more. They immediately set upon the orc, giving him some room to breathe. He hazarded a glance around, careful to keep his focus on Winston as much as possible. Rundyyk had disappeared under a veil once more. He looked to Grimluk again, just in time to see him batter the three believers about before impaling two of them with his crudely fashioned spear and driving them to the ground. The third lasted long enough to swipe at the orc's forearm before the brute got behind him, hoisted him up, and slammed him down on the blunt end of the spear.

"My Lord, we must act now," Elder shouted, unable to keep panic from touching his voice.

"Do not command me, mortal!" Rundyyk's voice came from all around the grove, nowhere and everywhere. "The hunt is not over."

"Of course not, Lord, but there's somethin' wrong on the other side. Time is short."

Rundyyk appeared behind Grimluk, six-legged and warg-like. For a moment, Elder thought the hunt would end as his god snapped its jaws at the orc. Somehow, the bastard avoided death.

Instead of dying like he was supposed to, the orc fired twice at his lord's head. Elder hadn't had time to react, to stop the bullets. For the second time, they struck home unhindered. Rundyyk reared up in surprise and fell backwards, clutching its ruined face. Wilbur and the elf were nowhere to be seen, which worried him. The orc prepared to fire again, gun extended toward Elder's god. Elder reached a hand out at Grimluk immediately, managing to set a binding spell with haste. It was weak. He couldn't stop the orc, but he could slow him down, make him easy prey for Rundyyk.

Almost immediately, he felt Grimluk's will batter against the spell, sending beads of sweat rolling down Elder's brow. He had expected resistance but not this much. The orc's will was formidable. He continued muttering the spell, focusing his mind and will on keeping the orc where he was. Even with decades of study and practice, he wasn't prepared for Grimluk to keep moving. His movements were slow, rigid. A step back, his arms twisting to aim at Rundyyk.

"Lord, we must end him now or Winston is lost

to us!" cried Elder.

"Spin the spell yourself then, mortal fool!" bellowed the god as it struggled to its feet again, ichor spilling out of its face. Rundyyk shook itself like a dog shaking off water, then it focused on Grimluk.

With each pounding step, Elder felt the orc's willpower slamming into the spell. It was a war of attrition but one that Elder would lose. If he could hold out a moment longer, his god would end the fool. Grimluk let out a fierce roar and then battered through Elder's spell, nearly sending him reeling from the backlash of energies.

Winston screamed in his mind. They would be out of time if he didn't act now. The orc's blood be damned. If Elder Whateley had to die to bring his grandson over and finish his family's work, he would. He poured his willpower into the portal, opening himself fully to the arcane powers of his god's realm. The energies pierced his soul as he offered it up for sacrifice.

Grimluk roared, breaking through Elder Whateley's spell. The mystical backlash rocked him, making him dizzy for a moment. He moved away, trying to get out of the way of the demon lord as it charged, not to gore him but to pounce. Grimluk's drunken motions created enough uncertainty of movement that Rundyyk missed its pounce. He barely managed to roll aside but the demon was faster than he was and batted him away with a mighty swipe from its tail.

Instead of getting away safely, Grimluk felt the impact in his ribs. He hurled through the air, landing hard enough to knock his gun out of his hand. He rolled across the ground before jamming his knife into the foul earth of the demon's realm. An angry growl filled Grimluk's throat as he rose.

Rundyyk was already charging again, giving him no time to find his gun. Grimluk charged as well, pulling the hatchet free from his belt. Power coursed through Grimluk's legs as he leapt into the air, soaring with a speed that caught the foul creature off guard. He twisted and, with a grunt, slammed onto Rundyyk's back, plunging his knife into the beast's shoulders as an anchor before hacking away with the axe. The demon roared in pain, sounding something like a cougar and a bear. Its tail lashed out again but Grimluk reacted in time, letting go of the knife and hooking his arm around the abominable threads of unholy muscle. He pivoted slightly, enough to keep his footing, before hacking away at Rundyyk's tail. The hatchet's enchanted blade bit through the flesh like piss through snow and Grimluk ripped it all away with one savage motion, leaving a bloody, broken stump.

With a howl of pain and fury, Rundyyk rolled over on top of Grimluk, slamming him into the dirt with its considerable bulk. The wind was driven out of him and the handle of his knife nearly through him, but it was better than claws. Rundyyk rolled away once more, trying to dislodge the knife from its back. All it managed to do was push it deeper and farther back. Thinking it a good idea to help the demon out, he waited for Rundyyk to roll by again and leapt over its massive body, grabbing hold of the knife once more and letting it draw with his momentum. Like the hatchet, it carved through the demon's flesh with almost no resistance and slashed a gash in Rundyyk's ribs the size of Grimluk's torso.

As the demon righted itself, a furry shape landed not far from Grimluk. Gray Panther. As they struggled back to their feet, Wilbur came stomping out of the trees, bleeding foul-smelling yellow blood from a dozen slashes. The werewolf let out a long, shuddering breath before turning up their head and howling. Grimluk waited for them to attack Wilbur again, not wanting to get their attention with movement.

As Gray Panther launched themself at Wilbur, their howls were answered and Grimluk knew there were death hounds on the way. Rundyyk had gained its feet once more, bleeding profusely from its wounds as they struggled to close. As the demon's eyes locked on Grimluk once more, he knew he'd hurt the big bastard. Gone was the calm arrogance of a creature beyond the concept of an apex predator. Now, there was just rage and bloodlust.

"Know this, orc," the beast growled, its body beginning to shift and change. "For the disrespect you have shown me, for your arrogance, you will suffer."

The lupine form disappeared in the space of two heartbeats. Rundyyk stood ahead of Grimluk in an elvenoid body covered in corded muscle, fur black as pitch, its head some amalgamation of canine and feline with its rack of antlers gleaming in the red in the light of the moon. The demon stood two or three heads taller than him, membranous wings spread out in full span as furious growls and hisses spilled out of a mouth with too many sharp, triangular teeth.

Grimluk answered with his own growl. "Take

whatever form you like, demon. It won't last beyond your death."

"Insolent mortal. Oh, you will suffer. But even still, I must thank you. I have not had such a satisfying hunt in two thousand years. I will not just feast upon your soul. I will feast on your body. I will suck the marrow from your very bones. I will crack open your skull and drink your spinal fluid! Your body will feed me and I will wash it down with your blood!"

While the demon prattled on, Grimluk searched the ground for his gun. He spotted it underneath Rundyyk's feet, along with the four death hounds that appeared from behind his foe. Behind them all, the stone table and Elder Whateley gathering himself for what Grimluk suspected would be one shit-kicker of a spell. Though never especially sensitive to magics, even he could feel the swelling power surrounding the old man.

The hounds began to charge and Grimluk got a really foolish idea. He charged as well, taking the first one down with the hatchet, slamming the blade through its skull. The next two were on him faster than he expected, driving him back.

When one of the two snapped at him, Rundyyk snarled at it and roared. "His flesh belongs to me, you insufferable fools!"

The hounds, startled by their master's ire, stumbled. The distraction was just what Grimluk needed. He dropped his weapons into the loops on his coat with one quick motion before seizing the hound nearest him by the scruff and its tail. The beast was massive, dense with muscle, but Grimluk's strength would not be denied. The demon started to fight him, but he spun it around once and hurled it at the wizard like a massive discus.

The hound went wide but still managed to knock Whateley aside. He had to do whatever he could to distract and slow down the spell. With Rundyyk join- ing the battle, he wouldn't have enough time to take out the Whateley wizard before he was ripped apart.

"Grandfather!" came Wilbur's voice, followed by a snarling yelp.

Grimluk didn't have a chance to see the boy. The hounds and their master both dove at him. One of the hounds drove its head into his gut, knocking the air out of him and sending him staggering back. The demon lord snapped its suddenly massive jaws at Grimluk's face but he managed to avoid the fatal blow by falling backwards. The next hound followed swiftly, forcing him to roll away as it furiously tried to scratch at him. As Grimluk dodged once more, he slapped the beast with the axe, driving the hound away for a moment and giving Grimluk enough time to climb back up to his feet. The other hound rushed in as he did so, but he saw it coming and caught it with the hatchet as he rose. The blade bit into its jaw with a pulpy snap.

Even in its death throes, it fought for its master and slashed Grimluk's thigh before he could get the blade back out and move away as it burst into blue flames. He could feel the blood running down his leg as he pivoted with the dying hound and smashed it into the other. He readied himself for another strike from Rundyyk but the demon had vanished once more.

CHAPTER 19

With Rundyyk disappearing again, it was only a matter of time before the demon struck. Grimluk kept moving, refusing to be an easy target, and headed for his gun. If more mortals had been present, he'd have been worried about them finding his gun and keeping it away. They couldn't use it against him thanks to the blood magic bonding, and the same runes that allowed the weapon to hurt demons kept them from touching it—meaning mortal servants who got a hunter's gun just made things harder. Things were hard enough as it was. The revolver hurt Rundyyk. A lot. But it was still an extremely powerful and apparently old demon. He would have to wear it down a lot more before he could finish it off for good.

If all else failed, though, as long as he had a couple of bullets left, he could use the runes on top of the barrel. He still had no idea how vulnerable it would leave him. Whether it might kill him outright. Living through this might be a luxury, but he still intended to live until it was clear there was no way he could survive. As long as he finished the job before it finished him.

As he ran toward the revolver, he could see Wilbur running for his grandfather, fighting off Gray

Panther as he did so. The death hound that had taken the wizard down was now heading for Grimluk as Elder got back to his feet and continued working the spell. The other hound let out a snarl as it no doubt began heading his way as well.

A few feet from his revolver, Rundyyk appeared and Grimluk had too much momentum to slow down easily. As the demon's jaw unhinged in preparation to snap shut around him, he hurled the hatchet at the demon in a flash of instinct and then dropped to slide between its legs. The red sandalwood grip found his hand and the weapon rose and fired once, catching the incoming hound in the eye, dropping it instantly. The now-burning corpse tumbled head first into the ground. Rundyyk's stump of a tail came crashing down into Grimluk a moment later, the impact sending him sprawling and the gun nearly tumbling from his hand again.

Rundyyk thrashed around behind Grimluk as it tried to remove the hatchet from its chest. He used the opportunity to rush Elder Whateley, intending to try the nerve pinch and knock him out long enough to finish the fight. Unfortunately, Wilbur managed to get free of Gray Panther and the two of them clashed instead.

While he had very much wanted to honor Lavinia's request to keep her son safe, the boy was still an abomination and actively hindering him. There was no time for subtlety anymore. Grimluk focused on Wilbur, who swung at him. Grimluk, momentum still with him, ducked the punch and returned it with his own. Where his fist had met a spongy flesh and unyielding body once before, it now moved Wilbur. The impact of his blow pushed the demon-child back several steps but no more. Grimluk lashed out with his knife, driving the boy back further and then turned and tried to take down the wizard in a clear moment.

He wasn't fast enough, though, and Wilbur seemed to step fifteen feet at once, grabbing Grimluk's hand before he could touch Elder. The two had a war of strength as Wilbur struggled to pull Grimluk's hand away from his grandfather's shoulder. He held his position before kicking the back of Elder's knee, causing the old man to drop. The energies of the spell wavered for a moment but seized up around the tear between worlds in a gathering swirl of color and light.

With the spell continuing, Grimluk flipped the revolver in his hand and went to bash Elder in the head, at least hard enough to break his concentration, but Wilbur saw his plan and yanked him away.

To make matters worse, the other hound had gained on him. It would have torn into his side with its claws had Wilbur not ripped him away from the wizard. Claws rent the tails of his coat as he flew away before slamming into something. Whether intentional or not, Wilbur had thrown Grimluk into Gray Panther. The surprise of it was the only thing that kept the werewolf from tearing him apart. It gave Grimluk a few precious seconds to get off of and away from his companion's dire form.

As Gray Panther rose back to their feet once more, they looked Grimluk over with a wariness that felt like it barely contained the fury of the demon. Grimluk had tangled with a werewolf once before, though the circumstances now were worse.

If he had to, Grimluk would kill Gray Panther to

stop the ritual and bring down the demon and its servants. He pointed the gun at his companion and they winced away with a snarl. The death hound came bounding after Grimluk, catching Gray Panther's attention. Being cowed must have pissed the wolf off. As the hound passed them, Gray Panther turned and sank its jaws and claws into the thing's body, driving it to the ground. Grimluk looked up to see Rundyyk still struggling with his weapon and Wilbur watching him with his goatish eyes.

As Grimluk walked toward the Whateleys, he fired the last loaded bullet he had at Rundyyk before reloading. He stared into Wilbur's unsettling eyes. They had shifted from goat-like to separate pupils entirely. He holstered the gun and looked at the child before him.

At ten, Grimluk had been large. It wasn't uncommon for orc children to stand taller than adult humans and elves. It presented certain issues for those who grew up in the less forgiving towns and cities. He could sympathize with Wilbur's age and size; with being an oddity, even. But the boy was still half-demon, according to his mother. Grimluk couldn't fault Lavinia for being born to a cruel man or being used as a tool by her father. Wilbur, however, just a boy or not, was an affront to nature. He should not exist.

But if there was mortal blood in him, Grimluk felt compelled to give mercy one more try.

"Walk away, kid." Grimluk said, harshness in his voice. "I'm not gonna kill your grandfather, but he must be stopped. Go back to your mother."

Wilbur responded not with words but by charging with a bleating, animalistic yell. He let out a roar of his own and went to meet Wilbur. Wilbur fought as an emotional child does, swinging relentlessly, hoping to pummel Grimluk into submission. While the boy had equal strength and a strange physiology, Grimluk had experience. And a knife.

Ducking and side-stepping the blows gave Grimluk opportunities to slice at Wilbur. And since Wilbur might be able to see everything around him with all the eyes at his waist, Grimluk went for those first. The two big ones on his hips sliced open like bursting grapes, spilling rank fluids everywhere. Wilbur bleated in pain and Grimluk felt the magical energies gathering around the tear shiver. That had shaken the wizard's concentration.

Wilbur backed off but stayed near his grandfather, his face contorted in pain as murky tears rolled down his sallow cheeks. It pricked Grimluk's conscience, but he couldn't afford to let it get to him. He hazarded a quick glance toward Rundyyk. "Shit," he muttered upon realizing the demon had vanished again. He and Wilbur stared at each other as Gray Panther continued tearing the death hound to shreds behind him.

The eldritch child lashed out, arms stretching far to slap and batter Grimluk, but his own experience and training was too much for the boy to handle in an actual fight. He peppered Wilbur's arms with slashes in a bitter conflict, rage growing in Grimluk at having to fight a child.

Rundyyk chose then to surprise Grimluk again. He narrowly avoided losing a limb but the demon managed to injure him anyways, slashing his left arm and ripping away the coat sleeve. Wilbur's hand slammed down onto his shoulder once more in an attempt to hold Grimluk in place again. The choice turned out to be a mistake. Gray Panther jumped on Wilbur's back and began tearing into him.

Elder's chanting grew louder before the tear between worlds burst open even wider revealing a hilltop and a similar stone table along with a barely visible shape just beyond it. Elder screamed for someone named Winston, but Grimluk was unable to get a look at what was going on as Rundyyk pressed the attack once more. Barely managing to maneuver away, he turned to get a look at the rift, Elder yelling for Winston a second time.

"Ygnaiih...ygnaiih...thflthkh'ngha...Yog-Sothoth..." answered a deep, cracked, raucous voice, not from any mortal throat. "Y'bthnk...h'ehye—n'grkdl'lh..."

More voices joined in the shouting, this time likely from elvenoid throats but in no language Grimluk could understand or had ever even heard, yet in the clear cadence of a spell. The distraction was a costly mistake, however, as Rundyyk struck again, faster than Grimluk could react. With a furious blow, Rundyyk knocked Grimluk away from the portal, from the sounds. Before he could get back to his feet, the demon lord pounced on him, nearly crushing his guts with its knee, pinning him down with its forearm.

"There is no escaping now, mortal. Your weapon is a grievous one but I am too powerful for it to stop me yet. The hunt ends now."

As Rundyyk reared back, snarling, ready to tear out Grimluk's throat, he managed to bat the demon's snout away before driving his left hand into the soft tissue of its jaw. With a grunt, Grimluk drug the barrel of the revolver over the bleeding wounds of his left arm. With blood filling their grooves, pale light spilled out from the blood, filling the gun with a power that shook its frame for a moment.

"You're gods-damned right," Grimluk replied.

The gun thundered once. The mystically charged bullet ripped through Rundyyk's throat, arcane energy lancing through the demon's neck as well, nearly severing it and aborting a scream of surprise. Five more shots followed, huge chunks of Rundyyk's form tearing away and spraying black ichor into the air.

Grimluk's body was heavy and worn out from the fight and the blood magic as he struggled to his knees, every muscle in his body screaming for rest and succor. As the ichor came down like a heavy rain, Rundyyk's mangled corpse collapsed, burning up in wild green flames. Grimluk's arm shook violently as he held the massive revolver up, dumping the spent shells from the dimming cylinder. The chanting and demonic words were growing louder as he slipped the last two shells into place and pressed the cylinder closed. His vision blurred as he took aim at the portal. Elder was still screaming and the voices from the other side of the portal were reaching a fever pitch. Grimluk took a deep breath in.

"Eh-ya-ya-ya-yahaah—e'yayayayaaaa... ngh'aaaaa...ngh'aaaa...h'yuh...h'yuh...HELP! HELP!"

Grimluk could see through the portal. Through the thing that was Winston, screaming for help now, the words stretching out in an unnatural, echoing cadence, as if his comprehension was delayed. Three humans stood behind him, chanting and flailing their arms. Above it all was the strange bird call he'd heard when everything had started.

"Ff—ff—ff—FATHER! FATHER! YOG-SOTHOTH!"

The gun barked twice. The arcane energies climaxed and broke as the bullets tore through them, spitting something akin to lightning that struck the thing beyond the portal. A violet bolt slammed into it a second time from the other side, down from the sky, spilling more arcane energy back through the rift that exploded in Elder's face before a wave of rank miasma rushed through like a quick fog. The old wizard was hurled away from the force of the magic and landed not far from Grimluk.

Holstering his gun, he crawled over to the man. Elder was mumbling and bleeding from every orifice. The wizard didn't seem to notice Grimluk as he leaned over to look at him. The mumbling was fading quickly, however, and Grimluk could see Elder's breathing getting shallower, his eyes far off and vacant, already empty despite Death still waiting to claim him. Something cleared in the Whateley patriarch's eyes and he seized Grimluk's arm.

"Save…my grandson…" he mumbled before his eyes rolled back. Elder Whateley faded into Death's embrace with a look of worry upon his face.

A long, shuddering sigh escaped Grimluk as he leaned back, sitting on his knees. A weak splatter of red lightning flashed overhead, drawing his eye up. A heavy thump brought his attention back down. Not far away lay the twitching, oozing form of Wilbur Whateley. The blood was viscous and clear and stank of brimstone, mingling with the stench of his brother's death. The combined scents created something wholly new and unpleasant.

Wilbur tried to lift his arm, reaching up to the sky and muttered, "Father," in a strained, choking voice. The boy's body started turning transparent.

Gray Panther stalked towards them, eyes on the dying Wilbur. The transparency happened rapidly and then the corpse seemed to deflate before evaporating, ultimately leaving behind nothing but a pool of stinking, pale blood. Grimluk looked up into Gray Panther's seething, hate-filled eyes.

The werewolf looked right back, a snarl crossing its lips.

Heaviness descended on Grimluk. A bone-deep weariness so sudden it nearly knocked him to the ground. His eyelids felt like they had lead weights dragging them down. He forced them to stay open as best he could, to watch the werewolf, but it was a battle he couldn't win. He was spent. The blood runes had served their purpose. The fight was over now. He had won, though he would not survive the next attack.

With a deep breath, he spoke. "I know you're in there, somewhere. I can't stop the wolf." His breath caught in his throat for a moment, forcing a pause. "But you told me you were a protector...a guardian, before you were forced here. Before the c-curse."

The wolf's head tilted for a moment but then it began stalking a slow circle around Grimluk. His fingers twitched as he watched his cursed friend move. He was so tired. So tired. His arms refused to move now. He was only upright from sitting on his calves.

As the wolf disappeared from his peripheral, Grimluk spoke once more, as clearly as he could. "Protect me, Gray Panther." He started to fall back as consciousness rushed out of him like water from a broken dam. Before darkness swallowed him, he wondered if this was what dying felt like.

Gray Panther beheld zir prey. The orc was cut up, covered in blood, left arm sleeved in it, breath ragged. He was spent. Weak. Ze stalked toward him, the Whateley giant's body slowly vanishing as ze did.

"Protect me, Gray Panther." The words were spoken softly but hit zir ears harshly, almost a physical blow. The orc collapsed, practically begging to be devoured. Protect him? He would die! Torn to shreds and devoured at zir own pace! Ze would replace Rundyyk as master of this domain. Fury burned at the sight of the orc. He'd taken away the killing of Rundyyk. He would die.

Grimluk would—

Live on. No, that wasn't right. The orc was prey, had stolen from zir! He would slake zir thirst for blood. Rundyyk's corpse lay in a burning pile near him. It had been zirs. Zirs! A growl slipped out of zir mouth, low and smoldering with wrath.

All that mattered was the kill. The tang of blood upon the tongue. Ze started to lean down, to bite through the orc's skull.

No! No, I will not devour him! No!

Ze recoiled, snarling at the voice of the elf. "You have no power here! Not anymore! There is only me! Only fury unending! Only death!"

There was silence for a long moment before the

dull hammer of heartbeats overtook zir ears.

I am Unegiyusdi Tlvdatsi! The heartbeat crashed like thunder.

I am the guardian of a lost people! the elf shouted in zir mindscape, and I will fear you no longer, demon!

Ze roared as a strange force screamed through zir body, taking hold of zir right arm. Zir hand rose up slowly, deliberately, even as ze tried to resist. The hand clenched, the pointer finger extended, the gleaming claw aimed at zir forehead.

You do not wear me, demon.

"Stop this! What are you doing? You are weak, elf! Weak!"

I wear you.

The claw sliced into flesh, digging deep before touching bone. Slowly, it drug itself down from forehead to groin, tearing deeply, agonizingly deeply. Ze had never felt such pain before. Nothing could describe the screaming brutality of it. Then both hands grabbed the split flesh and pulled and it got even worse, even deeper.

I...

"I..." ze heard zirself echo the elf.

Something was pushing its way out of the hole in zir flesh.

"I...will...protect!" ze screamed, stepping out of the wolf's skin and into the cool air of the demon-corrupted land. The skin fell away with a heavy slap. Born anew, Gray Panther looked at the world, at zir unconscious companion, at the wolf's skin looking up at zir with confused and furious eyes.

Ze picked up the skin by the snout and looked

into its twitching eyes. "I can still feel what is left of you inside me. You will never again wear me, control me, work through me. I will use your power to do good again. To protect, again. And if you ever try to stop me, I will cut you off a second time and diminish you further. This is the way."

The skin began to melt into zir own flesh once more. The wolf spirit within shrank back, tail between its legs, whimpering pathetically. For the first time in two hundred years, Gray Panther felt at ease—peaceful even. Ze gathered Grimluk's things together, carefully tucking away his blades, the blanket, and his gun before hoisting him up over zir shoulders to head back through the rift. Even with the strength of the wolf, he was heavy. The rift was shuddering at its edges, much smaller than it had been, now that the magics had been disrupted. Ze ran as quick as ze could with Grimluk slung over zir shoulders. If ze could just throw Grimluk through.

As ze got to the table, the rift collapsed entirely. The old pang of despair struck zir heart. A victory for zirself but a failure for zir friend. Ze sat Grimluk down gently onto the table before joining him on the edge. The first had grown so quiet and still over the past few minutes. Ze wondered if the other demons had died or perhaps banished. Even the ash had stopped falling.

"Grimluk!" called a voice ze didn't know.

Ze looked toward the sound and found an albino human approaching cautiously. The human stared at the Whateley wizard for a long moment before approaching.

"W-who are y-you?" they asked, keeping their distance. "W-what happened to Grimluk? Is…is he d-dead?"

"I am Gray Panther. You smell of the Whateleys. Who are you?"

"I'm Lavinia. What ha-happened?"

"The battle was won. The foul one and the wizard are dead. Grimluk defeated Rundyyk by some means I did not know he had. He fell unconscious soon after."

They let out a sigh at that. "Thank goodness. But where is Wilbur? Where is my boy?"

The question set Gray Panther on edge, ready to fight again if need be. "The Whateley creature is dead with his master. The rift is gone and we are stranded. If you mean to fight me, I think you will find it a hard battle."

For a long moment, Lavinia didn't move. They clutched at their chest and stared at zir with open shock. Tears rolled down their cheeks. "How did it happen?"

"The curse your ancestor placed on me helped undo your family. The wolf fought and ended the Whateley."

When Lavinia spoke, their voice was strangely calm despite the tears. "Grimluk promised he'd try to keep Wilbur safe. Did he?"

Gray Panther's eyes narrowed and ze thought back, wading through the hazy memories of the wolf. It was chaotic and unfocused. Unless ze was looking at something, all ze could recall was blood and fury. "I...do not remember. I have not known him long, but he seems like one who would keep a promise. If he wakes, you may ask him."

The human sank to the ground, sobbing. It

pained Gray Panther to hear. Ze thought of trying to comfort them but after centuries, ze did not trust the Whateleys. It could be a trap. This Whateley could try to slit zir and Grimluk's throats or use magic to curse them further. No, ze would watch the last Whateley carefully. There was little the human could do to hurt zir but Grimluk was another matter. Ze did not know why he was unconscious, but ze could smell the blood all over him. He needed to be tended to.

Lavinia rose slowly back to her feet. "I'm sure Grimluk needs his injuries treated. And I would like to leave this place." They began muttering, hands extended toward Gray Panther and Grimluk.

Ze rose from the table, growling, ready to fight. Barely a moment after that, light filled the grove once more as a new rift opened up over the table. The Whateley continued to hold their hand out as they approached.

"I can't hold it for long but it'll be enough to get back through."

Gray Panther nodded and hauled Grimluk back up to zir shoulders once more. Lavinia climbed up as well and seemed to be waiting for zir to go through first. Ze nodded and stepped through the rift. The last rays of sunlight were dimming on the horizon, as dusk grew ever closer. Lavinia followed a moment later and the rift closed.

Ze was back home. Back in a realm ze had not seen for centuries. Back to sunlight that burned even as it hid behind the trees and hills ze'd known so well, free of corruption. Tears rolled down zir cheeks.

Ze was finally free.

CHAPTER 20

The blackness receded for moments at a time. He would rise to the surface of the choppy waters of consciousness, the sight of moving shadows, sunlight, vague words and sounds and smells before being pulled back under. When Grimluk finally woke from his dreamless sleep, it was gently, to the sound of a soft voice, his eyes still heavy and crusted.

"How much longer, do ya think?" they asked.

He lay there, unsure if he'd drifted back to sleep again until another voice replied, "I do not know."

With great effort, Grimluk opened his eyes, struggling as they rolled back before blinking several times. He held them open, laying on his side and staring at the wall of whatever room he was in. His vision remained blurry as his eyes fought to close once more but he would not let them. As his eyesight returned, he got an actual look at his surroundings. The wood looked normal, healthy, not covered in decay and the dark tendrils of demonic influence. He realized a moment later that he was in a massive bed of the most basic build. Both of those realizations pleased him, even if the bed smelled strange.

He tried to open his lips to speak, but his tongue stuck to the roof of his mouth and all that came out was a weary, "hng," and a heavy sigh as he rolled to his back to look at the ceiling. It was also normal and free of corruption, though roughly made. His eyes protested once more at the idea of being open.

"He is awake," came the second voice, just before an elf appeared next to him.

It took Grimluk too long to realize it was Gray Panther. They looked completely different now. However long he'd been out, Gray Panther had apparently washed and found new pants in the form of buckskin trousers with fringe along the leg seams. Their wild hair was braided now, as it flopped over as they leaned over with a mug of warm broth. The broth smelled so amazing it prompted Grimluk's stomach to roar as if possessed by a demon.

"Drink slowly, my friend," Gray Panther suggested.

The mug touched Grimluk's lips, clinking against one of his tusks, and he struggled to follow the elf's advice. His hunger reared up, ravenous and demanding at the first drops but, focusing on not wanting to choke or make himself sick, he let the broth sit in his mouth for a moment to moisten everything back up. It was well a seasoned broth, maybe beef or goat, he couldn't tell much beyond tasting absolutely divine. He finally swallowed and felt the heat course down into his gut before letting out another sigh.

"Where?" he asked nearly in a whisper.

"Wilbur's bed," Gray Panther answered. "The others were too small."

"How long?"

They seemed to think about it for a long moment. "Four moons."

He reached a still heavy arm over and gave Gray Panther's forearm a weak pinch, "How?"

A soft smile spread across Gray Panther's scarred face. There was a confidence in their eyes. With sunlight streaming in, he could finally see the elf's eyes were like two beads of clear amber.

"I heard you," they replied. "I fought the wolf, took control of myself for the first time in too long. Lavinia found us after the rift closed, before I could get through. She knew the magics to open it again."

At that, the albino woman appeared at the foot of the bed. "Hello again," she said meekly.

Grimluk nodded. "Obliged," he mumbled. "Apologies, too."

Sadness washed over her face. "Gray Panther told me what happened," she said softly, giving the elf a vague look. "At least, as much as they knew and saw."

"Tried," Grimluk said with a sigh. "Several times. Couldn't finish it before the wolf got to him."

"What...what did he say?"

He sighed and thought about it. After downing more of the broth, both to quiet his stomach and slake his thirst, Grimluk answered."'Grandfather says,' mostly. Told 'im to walk away, go back to you."

Lavinia nodded slowly, tears streaming down her cheeks from eyes that were already puffy and red. "I just hoped. Maybe...maybe he would turn. He wasn't really mine though, was he?"

"Don't reckon so," he replied gently as she sobbed quietly. "I'm sorry, sai."

He looked to Gray Panther. The elf's face was cast in a resolved frown. Their eyes held little remorse, but the compassion was plain to see. Grim-luk couldn't really blame them for that. He held up the mug. They nodded, taking it to retrieve more broth.

After a long silence, Lavinia wiped her tears and spoke again. "Sai, I'm grateful for your efforts. I know what he was. Might even be foolish of me but he was my boy. I b-birthed him. But he grew so fast and Pawpa took him away..." She fell silent again, a hand over her mouth as she made no effort to hide her fight against the tears. "I'm sorry you fell in with my family's schemes."

With a small shrug, he answered. "It's my job. I've been runnin' into these kinds of people for about a decade now." His words carried a trail of silence that Lavinia seemed to notice.

"But?"

"Your father...your family...the letters you gave me. What they were doin' runs deep. There's a Whate-ley in Ornes-hum and she's apparently been busy. Might be more than just your family involved. Wanna hope it's just you but," he paused, thinking through it all as best he could despite the grogginess.

Gray Panther returned with the mug, full of not just broth but an actual helping of stew. He took a much needed gulp of the stew and let it sit in his mouth for a moment. Small cuts of meat, maybe rab-bit, then potatoes, other vegetables and herbs. He swallowed and the heat of it rolled down into him. Food for thought. He gave an amused grunt at that before shaking his head and looking back up at Lavinia.

"Cults run deep, Lavinia Whateley. And your

family has been workin' for two hundred years, maybe more. There are others. Sure as I can shoot, sure as the tusks in my mouth, there are others."

She went pensive at that, holding herself as she went through her own thoughts. Grimluk could see her mind working through something. "My family's harmed many folks. Too many. If there's some way I can help make it right, sai, name it."

Grimluk gulped down some of his stew. "Reckon with those letters and anything else relevant, we can call that even. Once I'm back on my feet, I'll do like you wanted. Head back to Hunter's Hollow. They'll want to hear about this and we'll need to go over everything."

"I can do that," she said standing tall, a defiant look in her eyes. "I'll see what else I can find for ya. The sooner the better." Before Grimluk could respond, Lavinia was out of the room, her boots audible on the ramp back down to the house.

"How you holdin' up?" Grimluk asked Gray Panther. In the sunlight, Grimluk could clearly see the bronze of their skin, the dusty blond braid back over their shoulder and away from their scarred cheeks. They paced next to the bed.

"Long time since I felt...good," they began. "Free. There is still sadness for what was lost but now I feel hope. And control."

"Reckon you'll want to be freed of the wolf?"

"After hearing you, I clawed my way forward. Ripped the wolf away from my very skin. I have contained it. Maybe it will grow strong again one day and I will have to fight it, reclaim myself once more. Now? Now it is mine to control. I will use its power to do some good in this world."

Grimluk nodded, impressed. He'd never heard of a cursed werewolf gaining control of the demon but then, he'd never heard of someone who could control the change like Gray Panther could, even if the demon's realm had likely been the cause. If they could keep it up back in the mortal world, the elf would be a force to be reckoned with.

"If you'd like, you can return with me. Our loremaster would be mighty keen to take your story. Your tribe's as well. They may live on, that way."

"You would do this?" Gray Panther asked, head askance.

"My people know a thing or two about losing their history. Our loremasters guard the histories of any who share them ferociously."

"Do all orcs show such loyalty?"

Grimluk shrugged. "Maybe not all. Everyone has their own way of livin' but there's enough of us that live that way."

Gray Panther looked away, letting out a heavy sigh. "I will do this. My people deserve better than we were given."

"They do. I'm glad to hear it, my friend. Now, if you could just help me up and to the outhouse. If I don't relieve myself soon, I fear I'll piss the bed."

A surprised laugh escaped Gray Panther's lips as they moved to help Grimluk up.

Grimluk spent three more days resting up and recovering. Gray Panther and Lavinia had tended to his wounds while he'd been unconscious. He found the last bottle of salve nearly empty next to the bottle that contained the dryad seed. He held that bottle up and inspected it. To his eyes, it still seemed free from any corruption.

"We'll get you taken care of," he said, before packing his kit back up.

He'd grown restless as his body regained its strength and he found himself wandering back out to the grove. The stone owl towered over the altar still, soot marks covering the tops of the eyes where torches had sat in them. Grimluk found some rope with Lavinia's help, lassoing the thing's head.

"What are you—" Lavinia started to ask before Grimluk yanked on the rope. "Oh."

It was heavy, but he didn't care. He turned, letting the rope rest on his shoulder and pushed himself forward, a near constant growl rumbling in his throat. With a roar and one final tug, the statue began to tip. They watched as it toppled slowly over and crashed into the table with a terrible roar of its own. The altar split and the statue cracked all over.

"I think we can leave now," Grimluk said, watching the dust cloud settle.

"I guess you're ready, ain't ya?"

The two of them gathered up their things. Lavinia found an old carpetbag for what little she actually owned. She'd also managed to find a few more letters and documents among her father's things and, along with the strange book that Grimluk had seen, grabbed a couple of others to bring as well. Gray Panther had only their knife and clothes, along with a wool blanket they'd taken from somewhere, but waited patiently on them.

Dunvich was basically deserted when the three of them made their way into town from the Whateley house. Several of the nearby houses had slumped bodies occupying them, eyes glassy and distant, with passive looks on their faces like they'd just dropped what they were doing and gone to sleep with their eyes open.

They all looked like the pile of bodies Rundyyk had dropped. They were all marionettes with cut strings. Elder Whateley had been using more people than Grimluk had thought possible. He'd been lucky the wizard had been preoccupied during the fight or else he never would've survived.

Some of the demon-tainted cultists had survived, though. No longer human and now feral from the death of their master, Gray Panther had spent the time waiting on Grimluk whittling their numbers down. The cultists were too weak to prove much of a threat for the elf. There were none left as the trio walked the streets of Dunvich.

"What happened to the peacekeepers? Ziskind?" Grimluk asked Lavinia when they neared the peace-keeper station.

"Disappeared," she replied. "Once we got you settled, we went back through to…retrieve Pawpa's body. I know he wasn't a good person, but it didn't feel right leavin' him there. House was empty on that side. Imps disappeared all over, too. Maybe she and the others ran off into those dark woods. Maybe they got through while we were busy."

Grimluk's throat rumbled at that. Three mortals, seemingly unchanged despite their decisions, possibly trapped in a realm that was keen to kill whatever entered it without a demon's protection or perhaps free in the world to do more harm. He sighed. Part of him wanted to find them but there were bigger things afoot now and they'd made their choices. He'd done what he'd set out to do and he had to see it through just a little more.

Scrapes and thumps emanated from the station, along with some groaning and moaning. Whatever had been in there before, it sounded like some ghouls had been made. Grimluk let out a long sigh when one of them slapped against the window, trying to reach for them.

"Ghouls are so fuckin' tedious," Grimluk said, shaking his head. He pulled his hatchet free and slipped into the building to put them down. There were only three of them.

After that, they raided the general store, taking whatever supplies they needed before setting off down the road. There wasn't really all that much, as it turned out. Some hardtack, a few cans of beans, and a bag of flour. They took the beans and hardtack.

As they passed the edge of Dunvich, Lavinia stopped and looked back at the town. Tears rolled down her cheeks. "I'm the only person left from my home. I know I should feel sad about leavin' but… this was a prison for me. And so many people died here. Gray Panther, I hope the land recovers what we took from you. I hope there's nothin' left one day."

"The land will do as it wishes," they replied, gazing upon the lands of their home. "It always does."

Grimluk looked at the elf. "You think we ought to plant the dryad seed here? Or take it elsewhere?"

They seemed to consider the question before turning and waiting on their companions. "I think we will look after it for now. I do not know if there is some foulness that lingers in these hills."

Grimluk nodded. "Fair enough."

As they started their journey in earnest, Lavinia spoke up again. "I'll tell my story to your lorekeeper, sai. I'll help them with them books there, too. Maybe I can make somethin' right."

He could understand that and just nodded. They had a long way to go to get to Hunter's Hollow. It would likely be deep into winter unless they found a train that could get them into the province of New Gilead. The faster they traveled, the better.

Luck was on the trio's side when they made it to Cold River a little over a month later. The small city was near the border between Westlynth and New Gilead. Fall was edging into early winter by then but it hadn't yet turned completely cold. Grimluk had been in Cold River at the end of the previous year, just before spring, and in that time, the rails had been laid down. The clerk said the line could take them into New Gilead but that the way to Varnarton was still being built, and tickets that far would cost two bilts each. Grimluk handed over one of the paper gluts he'd received for the dreameater.

A day later, the train arrived early in the morning. Gray Panther had grown anxious in the city. They'd had trouble sleeping indoors. The sight of the train seemed to make it even worse.

"It is too much," the elf muttered.

"The train?" Grimluk replied.

"Yes. I had only seen pieces of the changes,"

Gray Panther continued, stepping warily into the car ahead of Grimluk. "This...train...the Far Folk have changed the world."

"Reckon so. I know it's strange, but the tribes of the continent are consulted before the land is touched in such ways. Not everyone is like the Whateleys, though. And look," he said, pointing to a group of halflings who were clearly tribal.

Gray Panther studied the group for a moment before nodding, seemingly accepting what they saw, and dropped to the floor between the seats where Grimluk motioned. He assuaged his own apprehension by drawing an exorcism circle on the wall of their car.

The ride lasted for about a week. It might have been shorter but the train still had to make stops at other stations along the way. They exited in a town that was maybe 16 leagues from Eagle Point, the little town near Hunter's Hollow. On the whole, Grimluk found traveling by train an agreeable way to get long distances. The expediency meant they wouldn't be caught outside once the cold snapped. After last winter, he wasn't eager to go through that again.

Grimluk had to slow down for Lavinia's sake as they headed toward Eagle Point. Gray Panther could keep up with him if he walked as he normally did, but she couldn't. It was torturous. The promise he made to himself kept swimming in his head. He wanted to see his parents. And Gwen. He already knew she'd be waiting on him when they arrived, just like she'd been waiting when he'd used his guild amulet.

When they finally approached the gates of Hunter's Hollow, Grimluk had never been so happy to be right. Relief flooded his body, nearly making him collapse. Gwen started running for him as soon as she saw him. Home. He was home. He quickened his pace, eager to meet his sister, who tackled him, burying her face into his shoulder. He did all he could to make sure he didn't squeeze her too hard but after all this time away, after everything that had happened, it was a gods-damned struggle.

"You came back," she whispered.

"I came back," he said. She'd grown since he'd last seen her. Maybe not a lot, but he could feel it, even if for him it was just that she was less small.

"Why didn't you send a message? Cenka is very annoyed with you."

Grimluk laughed and pulled her away. "Reckon I should've. But I'm here now. I need to talk to hir, and Mint."

"Need to talk to me about what?" came his parent's voice. Bakhor approached, grinning. "I assume you brought more strays?"

"A lot, actually. This is Gray Panther and Lavinia Whateley. They're a werewolf and she's the daughter of the leader of the cult I took down."

"I like your hair," Gwen said to Lavinia. "It's so pretty."

"T—thank you," Lavinia replied, clearly surprised by the comment.

"They were workin' for the Great Old Ones," Grimluk added.

Bakhor looked from Grimluk, to his companions, and back. Ze grunted. "A lot indeed. Let's get inside. I'm sure Imogen will be relieved to hear the news."

Grimluk's throat rumbled. "Reckon I oughta

warn you before we go in, Gray Panther. Hollow's got wards all over. You can probably feel them already."

The elf nodded. "It tells me to leave, like the cave. I will survive. I have survived worse."

"Reckon so," he replied as they stepped through the gates.

The various folks living in the little fort town, mostly orcs, greeted them. Grimluk recognized the majority of them and nodded back. A small group of wargs, led by his family friend, Fang, came to greet him as well. Lavinia yelped and hid behind Gray Panther, who took a stance ready to fight. Lavinia had likely never seen a warg. Even after a thousand years of breeding them down in size, they were still bigger than wolves. Their long teeth had softened as well but were still long and imposing from their skull-like heads.

"It's okay," Grimluk said, petting Fang's head. "They're just excited to see me."

Fang looked up at Grimluk and growled and yipped.

"I know I worry you, but I'm here now. I'm sorry." He was glad to see her. He'd forgotten how much Hunter's Hollow really meant to him.

She circled him, letting out a long groan before bumping into him and moving toward Gray Panther and Lavinia. She bowed her head, tapped her paw twice, and let out two whimpers, her best way of saying hello to people that she knew would not understand. She bumped into Grimluk's leg again as she and the other wargs moved on.

Lavinia cautiously stepped out from behind Gray Panther. "I'm sorry. I didn't realize."

"Most people don't," Grimluk replied. "Lot of people like them even less than they like orcs. Even more misunderstood than us, too. That was Fang. I know Vrrk and Grall, but the other three must have been pups from the last time I was here."

He spotted a new face as they went. A halfling that turned out to be Gwen's hand-to-hand instructor. He inquired about Imogen, and found her on the mend. Mint had managed to remove most of the demonic corruption she'd suffered but it would be a while yet before she was entirely free. Feathers still poked out from her hair and the sleeves of her shirt and her hands were still a bit scaly.

"Cult's finished," Grimluk said as she looked up at him.

Her brows furrowed for a moment as she stared hard at him before relaxing into a relieved smile. "Bastards. Good riddance. Rundyyk?"

"Nothin' but ash now." At that, she gave a wicked grin. "Glad to see you recoverin'. Glad you accepted the help."

Imogen looked down and audibly swallowed. "I'm uh...I'm sorry. Fucker got in my head. Couldn't tell truth from shit. Then Rundyyk...I'm sorry."

He stepped close and put a hand on her shoulder. When she looked up, he nodded. "Don't give it another thought. I couldn't save everyone, but at least I managed this much." And Gray Panther, too, from how they were acting.

She nodded in return and laid down.

Mint gave Grimluk and Lavinia a look over and found them healthy. He spoke with Gray Panther, as well, asking if they wanted to be rid of the curse. The old guardian solemnly shook their head and asked instead if there was a way to practice control over the inner beast. Mint promised to look into it.

Over the next few days, the books Lavinia had brought proved to be vexing. She and Vatris started inspecting them. It was only bad news, though. The one with the swirling symbol turned out to be penned under the invocation of the Yellow King, an entity that there was very little information on. Another book was, unsurprisingly, written invoking Yog-Sothoth. Some of the diagrams in it matched ones in the summoning circle he'd found. The third book started burning when they tried to open it. Though the flames were harmless to the book, without knowing how to break the ward, it would keep its secrets well. Vatris and Mint decided the best course was to seal it up and put it away until they could figure out how to deal with the enchantment.

News of the Great Old Ones spread quickly through Hunter's Hollow. The other demon hunters were just as troubled by Grimluk's news of the cult worshiping the Old Ones, and, like him, even more disturbed with the prospect of the Union government being corrupted. Each province had capital cities but Ornes-hum served as the capital of them all. The governor's council met there, along with the other bodies. If cults to the Great Old Ones were rising again, bad times were on the horizon. Demonic activity created strangeness in the best of times but the Great Old Ones were worse beyond measure. Rundyyk had been a small sample of what they were capable of. The Great Old Ones could break reality and shatter the minds of the trained and untrained alike.

For the time being, that could wait. Winter was coming and it would likely take some time for Lavinia's mother, and whoever else was involved, to realize what had happened. So he would stick close to home while they figured out what to do. It'd been ten years since he'd stayed put in the Hollow for more than a month or so and he was tired. He wanted some rest, for a time at least. He needed it. It had taken Gwen's memory to keep him from losing himself to Rundyyk's influence in that dark realm. Grimluk was a demon hunter. Everything in him worked to fight back the darkness and destruction that the Abyss spewed forth. Maybe he had started forgetting why he fought so hard. He could remind himself and recuperate. He could spend time with Gwen, help her train, maybe learn some new tricks, and hunker down for winter for the first time since he set off on his own. There were more than demons to hunt, now. Whatever evils crawled out to wreak havoc upon Arkod, he'd be there to hunt them. That would never change. He had to take care of himself, though. He'd often told others that but never properly took his own advice. It was time. There would always be more work to be done.

Eventually, it would be time to hunt once more.

RECOMMENDED AUTHORS

You've read my book now (and thank you for that!), and I'd imagine you'll be hungry for something new so here are a few recommendations for folks I know and enjoyed.

James Jakins, Author of *Jack Bloodfist: Fixer*.
S.M. Reine, Author of The Descentverse books and stories.
Tim Marquitz, Author of *Damaged* and the *Demon Squad* series.
Rachel Sharp, Author of the *Planetary Tarantella* and *Phaethon* series.
Edward M. Erdelac, Author of the *Merkabah Rider* series and *Andersonville*.
Krista D. Ball, Author of the *Tales of Tranquility*, *The Dark Abyss of Our Sins*, and *Spirit Caller* series.
Christopher Ruz, Author of *Century of Sand* and *Rust*.
Amalia Dillin, Author of the *Orc Saga* & *Fate of the Gods*.

Happy reading, everyone!

This book was made possible by...

Alan Bryan
Alexandra Forrest
Alyssa R.
Amalia Dillin
Andrew Paterson
Anonymous
Anonymous
Anthony Lowe
Anton Halpern
apexPrickle
Benet Reynolds
Bob
Brent Norcross
Brittney S.
Christina Baclawski
Christopher Horn
Cory Cepelak Sr
The Creative Fund
David L. Ramsey
Dianthaa
Eric DiCarlo
Erica Lindquist
James Jakins
Jeff Lewis
Kel Crafton
Kelvin Neely

Krista Ball
Lisa Richardson
Maeves Child
M.D. Tjong Ayong
MG Mateo
Max Kaehn
Natalie
Nick "Sungrowler" Levy
Phil Seaton
Rachel N.
Rachel Sharp
Rebecca Roth
Rick Howard
Russell Palmieri
Ryan Howse-Meister
Sam Primeau
Samantha T.
Satya Prateek
Sharkie
Steven J. Pope
Stiarna Askew
Talithan Miir
Terri
Thomas Moore
Tucker Donovan
Zoe Bee

ABOUT THE AUTHOR

Ashe grew up watching and reading about adventures and having horrible nightmares. He spent most of his young life wanting to know more about what scared him but also doing so from between fingers and from under the covers. Eventually, the realm of nightmares became home. Heroes and villains and the struggle of Good against Evil, combined with Horror, helped mold him into the weirdo lover–of–the–strange that he is. Ashe lives in Tulsa, OK with his partner.

Where you can find Ashe on the web

ashearmstrong.com
patreon.com/ashearmstrong
twitter.com/ashearmstrong
facebook.com/ashearmstrong
goodreads.com/ashearmstrong